I0788234

The Other Side of Apart

EMILY COX
&
NICOLE ALLEN

MONSTER IVY
PUBLISHING

DEDICATION

To whatever comes next.

CHAPTER 1

Red and blue lights swirl with morning fog, making a purple haze like the sky is bruised. I grip the handlebars and glance over my shoulder at the cop car speeding up behind us.

No way this is happening. I clench my jaw and focus on the road, hoping the lights and speed are for someone else, but the siren blares a warning. Only three hours out of San Francisco, and it's already over. Cop's gonna recognize us. Or maybe the motorcycle. Both. Not to mention we have a tampon box full of diamonds stolen from a criminal burning a hole in Mei's bag. If the cop goes through our stuff, it's over.

I swear and veer to the shoulder, slowing to a stop.

Mei's arms tighten around me from behind. "Why are we getting pulled over?"

I swallow and shake my head to disrupt the hot surge of fear, mentally scrambling for what I'm gonna say to the cop to get us out of this. If I say the wrong thing, I could be in handcuffs, headed back home to answer to Dad. Mei could have a one-way ticket to Taiwan, or worse, back to her parents. Nick. No way am I gonna let that happen.

"You weren't speeding, though." Mei's words scatter as the fear we've been running from for the past three hours catches up.

I shake my head again and glance at the cop car behind us, talking to Mei over my shoulder. "Not sure what's happening. Just…keep your helmet on." Our helmets are the only shield we have if Dad sent out an alert with pictures of us and the bike.

The cruiser door shuts behind us and gravel crunches, but I stare straight ahead. My eyes move up the road, over sun-bleached asphalt and along double yellow lines that stretch around the bend we would've been way past by now. But Dad's found us, and I'm seconds away from losing Mei all over again. Panic curls my fingers around the handlebars and floods my legs, hardening like lead in my feet.

"Hi there," the officer says as she approaches on our right. "Mind taking off your helmet for me?"

Curse words explode in my head like fireworks. I fumble with my chin strap, then peel off the helmet, exposed and vulnerable. Mei keeps hers on, and the officer doesn't say anything, her eyes laser-focused on me. She's seen my picture —she's doing mental facial recognition. Scanning all the details. But at least she's not looking at Mei's black-and-blue face. That would get her asking questions I can't and won't answer.

"Was I speeding?" I ask, my voice ragged and shaky. The wind whips it away and blows my hair across my eyes.

"Everything's fine," the officer says, "Just a courtesy stop to let you know your bag's blocking your license plate." She waves her hand to Mei's duffel strapped to the back of the bike.

"Oh. Yeah, sorry." I twist on the seat, then hesitate, but Mei's already tugging the bag free. Now the officer will see the temporary license plate. She'll log it into her database, and Dad will know exactly where we are. I gotta get us out of California.

The officer laughs, and my eyes snap to her, searching for any hint of a way out of this. Steep hills and forest on the right, cliffs and angry ocean on the left.

"I promise I'm not going to arrest you or anything. But I do need your driver's license and registration."

Fear splinters any remaining hope of escape as I pry my fingers off the handlebars again and reach for my back pocket in slow motion. "I have no idea where the registration is…" The words are metal shards scraping up my throat, but I hand her my license.

"New bike?"

I nod. "Graduation present."

"Nice." She smiles. "I'll pull up your registration." She takes my license, then turns to Mei, and my heart slams against my chest. Mei's helmet shields most of her bruises but not the purple splotches. Bruised cheekbone. Finger marks on her neck.

"Where are you two headed?"

Her question is directed to Mei, who immediately responds. "Checking out the coast before we head east. Graduation trip. Finally!" Her voice is light and calm. Smooth. Like this isn't her first time looking a cop in the face and pretending everything's all good.

"Congratulations." She smiles, glances at my license, Mei's face, then up the coast to the wall of dark clouds stacking over the ocean and spreading toward us. "You need to be careful. Storm's coming."

Of course there is. Probably a hurricane. Dad probably arranged it.

"There are a couple of roadside motels ten or fifteen miles up the highway, and if I were you, I'd pull in. You don't want to be riding when it hits." She taps my license against her thigh. "Sit tight. I'll run this, then get you on your way."

She heads back to her car and its flashing lights, and I close my eyes. I'd rather ride straight into that storm than be on the side of this highway waiting for whatever's coming.

"That was close," Mei whispers over my shoulder, and when all I do is nod to my lap, she leans against my back. "You okay?"

I pause and nod again. "Yeah, just...it's not over yet. If my dad found the message I left, we're done."

Her body stiffens against my back. "What message?"

I look at the waves losing the battle as they slam against jagged rocks and thrash like my insides. Mei and I haven't exactly had time to discuss everything that happened between me finding her at Guo's, and what went down with Dad. "He basically put me on house arrest, but I left a note saying I was out."

"House arrest?"

"He has pictures of us together. From Nick's phone." I pause as a semi-truck rumbles past, sending a gust that makes me dig my toes into my shoes to keep us upright.

"What?"

"Yeah..." I look at the ocean again, since it's just as frantic as I am right now. "He knows about us. And that you're involved with Nick." How involved is still the question.

"Marcus, I'm not—"

I shake my head and sort through responses, but the cruiser door shuts again, and I close my eyes. My heart pounds up my throat as the officer approaches.

"Good to go," she says, handing me my license.

Relief gusts through me and I let out a shaky breath. Forcing a smile, I shove my license back into my wallet. The cop's eyes sweep Mei's face again. Even with her helmet on, it doesn't hide everything, so I rush a "thank you," put on my helmet, and start the engine.

The officer pulls a card out of her shirt pocket and holds it out to Mei. "If you need anything, call this number." Mei takes it and the officer walks back to her car. She thinks I did that to Mei's face. If only she knew those bruises are why we're running.

I rev the engine and pull back onto the highway. Mei's arms tighten around me. I focus on breathing through anger and confusion and all the hurt that's settling inside me now that we've been still for twenty minutes too long. Jaw clenched, I check the rearview mirror every other second.

With each mile marker we pass, my head clears a little like the wind is taking pieces of my freak-out and scattering them behind us. Mei's arms are wrapped around me, and I relax into her. She's here. We're together. I haven't lost her, and I'll do anything to make sure that doesn't happen. I'm gonna make this new life perfect for her so she never has a reason to leave.

Thunder rumbles through my thoughts and lightning slashes at the sky as the clouds break open and dump everything they've been collecting on us. I shoot forward on the seat and slow way, way down.

Mei huddles against me, yelling above the storm, "We should pull over."

But we're not far enough away. I want to keep going until we hit Seattle. Until all the stuff left unsaid between us blows away or dissolves in the rain. Until my thoughts are jostled into place by this bumpy road. But if I don't stop, I'll lose control of this bike, and I'm so tired of not being in control.

Rain runs off my helmet and down my face and neck as I search for somewhere to wait out the storm. When my eyes land on a rickety lifeguard hut down the beach, I veer off the highway and race across wet sand. Mei holds on tighter, and we roar to a stop beside the hut.

I push the motorcycle under the deck, pull off my helmet, and hang it on the handlebar. Grabbing our bags with one hand, I take Mei's hand with the other and we sprint up the ramp. I crank the rusted knob and shove against the door. When it scrapes open, we dart inside and flinch when it slams shut behind us, throwing us into stale, murky darkness. The smell of rotting wood and rusty metal hangs in the air, and I hope nothing's alive in here.

Crusty towels slump in one corner next to a couple of cracked plastic chairs. On the floor, toppled beer cans rock from the breeze squeezing through the wooden slats. It smells like old pee and seaweed, but I drop our bags onto the floor anyway, like they're anchors to this reality I don't want, but am too tired, wet, and windblown to think beyond.

Why did we think any part of this would work? We still have ten hours of driving, but don't have that long before Dad finds out I've left and sends someone after us. Or Nick. He might be in jail, but that doesn't stop his guys from coming after us.

Mei fumbles with her helmet beside me, her hands trembling, body shivering. I reach out, unbuckle the helmet, and carefully slide it off. Her face is outlined by a sliver of light coming through the broken blinds over the window. "You okay?" I ask, my voice raspy, and she nods, meeting my eyes. My fingers twitch to pull her close, but her whole body is shaking, her teeth chattering, so I snap into motion, yank open the zipper on my bag, rummage through it. A section of the aluminum roof flaps against the rafters as I hold a dry hoodie toward her.

She takes it from me and holds it to her chest. I shake my head. "This is insane. What are we doing here?"

"At least it's not a hurricane in here." Her voice lilts at the end as if she's trying to smooth it out—make everything alright. But it's not alright. Maybe it never will be.

"Yeah, but you're freezing. And exhausted. And we're… here." I'm stuck in a tangled mass of things I should say and things I shouldn't, and I can't sort through it all right now. Perfection is impossible when everything has been blowing up in our faces for the last twelve hours.

She searches my expression. "Marcus, you don't have to be here. I can—"

"You look exhausted. And you're soaked." My eyes trip across her face, then across the floor, over the cracked counter, the craggy rafters. "We're not going anywhere anytime soon, so I'll make a spot for you to rest after you change." And avoid conversations that take us back to unresolved issues I don't know how to deal with right now.

I reach for a life raft drooping over a weathered wooden beam above us, and it falls to the sandy floor. Fumbling along the side, I twist a nozzle and the raft hisses to life, filling the space between us.

"I'll just wait outside." I turn and reach for the doorknob, but pause when she says my name.

"It's pouring out there."

"It's okay. Can't get any more soaked than I already am." Honestly, I'm more afraid of the emotions that caught up to me on our ride slipping out than I am of the rain.

"Marcus?" Mei's voice is small, and I turn to face her, one foot out the door. "Thank you."

A dry laugh rushes up my throat. "For bringing you to this hellhole?"

"No. For making me feel safe. This place is gross, yeah, but it's the safest I've felt in weeks."

I glance at the floor, swallow, then nod before stepping onto the narrow deck, hugging the wall under the overhanging roof. I lean my head back, close my eyes. My brain buzzes, my body vibrates and twitches, knowing it should be on the road, putting more distance between us and San Francisco. Wondering how long it will take Dad to find us and hoping Guo's brother won't give up on us if we don't arrive tonight. Wondering how to help Mei and what we should and shouldn't talk about, but knowing it all—everything left unresolved when we hit the road—will have to come out, eventually.

When I shiver, I peel off my soaked shirt, fling it over the rickety railing, count to thirty, then sixty, then ninety before stepping back through the door, hoping Mei's dressed. But when my eyes adjust to the murky room, she's lying on the raft in my hoodie, her legs pulled inside it. Asleep.

Warm.

Safe.

I watch her, grateful she's here and feels safe enough to crash. One of us needs to, but it's not gonna be me with my head this full. Even if I haven't slept in...two days? Don't know. I don't know so many things. Like what's hiding in Mei's head after what happened to her. What ifs and whys race through my mind so quickly I can't keep up. They turn to fear and unexpected anger, and they're crowding me out of this space.

I slip off my soggy shoes, reach for the knob and hurry out of the hut toward space and fresh air. I sprint down the ramp, burning off energy and emotions—anger about Dad's lies, guilt over leaving the way I did. Fear from the pictures of Mei and me on Nick's phone. Leftover anxiety from driving the motorcycle at top speed to outrun our old lives. Confusion about why I found Mei broken at Guo's and why she left me for that. Self-loathing for being at prom with another girl while Mei was getting beaten. Worse.

I break into a run, rain slashing at my face and blurring my vision until I'm at the water's edge. All the brewing emotions stretch inside me, blending light with dark, calm with frantic, assault and surrender. I jumped back into Meiland headfirst when I found her at Guo's, but slammed against new, impenetrable layers. And now? I'm trying to find my footing and balance, but maybe I'm trying too hard. Maybe I reacted too quickly when I found her at Guo's and my emotions drove us here, not my logic. Maybe I'm desperately holding onto something that was never solid in the first place. Maybe I'm not supposed to be here and was never meant to have Mei.

CHAPTER 2

My eyelids slide open when thunder rattles the hut. Sitting up, I blink in the dark, but there's no Marcus. I don't remember falling asleep and am unsure how long I've been out. Scooting off the raft, I scramble to my feet, reaching for the wall when I lose my balance. Last I remember, he went outside so I could change. Surely he's not still sitting on the tiny deck. But maybe he had second thoughts about coming with me and left. I wouldn't blame him.

On my way to the door, I stumble over his shoes and take a shaky, relieved breath. He's still here. I open the door and scan the deck, ramp, then the horizon before spotting him far down the beach where he stands knee deep in reckless waves. He's shirtless, his skin red and glossy from the cold rain, hands clasped on top of his head as he watches the chaos of the ocean.

Despite being dry and warm, I rush down the ramp, across the beach toward him, rain pelting my face and bare legs. His back is tense, the muscles holding in whatever he's wrestling, and I pause, not sure if I should keep running toward him or give him space. Maybe he needs it. Maybe he's second guessing leaving everything behind for me.

My fear about his thoughts pushes my voice up and out, and I call his name over the wind. His head snaps over his shoulder, his hair plastered to his forehead, rain dripping from his eyelashes.

"You don't have to come with me." I shake my head. "I can—"

He turns toward me. "Don't do this, Mei."

I swallow, wrap my arms around myself, already soaked again. "Don't do what?"

"Try to get rid of me."

I shake my head. "That's not what—"

"I'm here because I choose to be here. I wanna be here. With you," he calls over the crashing waves.

"I'm just saying, you don't have to walk away from your life because of me. You're not obligated to do any of this."

"Obligation? That's the first word that came to mind?" He looks away, his jaw pulses.

"You think you have to protect me," I call, "but you don't. It's not your job."

"Oh. Right." He nods, his stare holding me in place. "I'll just have to be okay with whatever Nick did to you. Because he's practically your family and all that. Yeah—sorry. Sometimes I just forget how great he is when I'm looking at all the black and blue love he left on your face."

I sort through responses, but he goes on.

"Why did you leave?" He squints through the rain. "We could've worked through anything. I know I was frustrated and said things I shouldn't have that day at the clubhouse, but we could've figured it out. Then you wouldn't have gone back to Nick, and we wouldn't be here right now."

"I didn't go back to him, Marcus. After your grandma walked in on us, I was afraid I'd ruined everything for you. I was so embarrassed. So I ran home. I was planning on calling you, but Nick was waiting at my house. And he knew about you. He threatened to hurt you if I ever talked to you again or if I didn't go to L.A. with him." I blink back tears. "I told Baba I didn't want to go, but that wasn't an option. I knew deep down something bad was going to happen, but I was trapped."

He watches me through the mist caught in the tension. "Why didn't you tell me?" His voice is raspy. "Because if I'd known what was happening, I would've done anything to get you away from him. And it has nothing to do with obligation, Mei. I called and texted after you ran, but you never responded, and I thought that meant you wanted out. That you were done with us."

Pain pulses through me, hot and sharp. "I wanted to call you. But what was the point? I knew I couldn't have you, so why drag you into my life any more than I already had? Why torture myself with things I couldn't have? You would've gotten hurt."

He throws his hands in the air. "Getting jumped would've felt massively better than wondering if maybe someday you'd talk to me again. And the worst part is, if I hadn't come looking for you after prom and found you at Guo's, you would've disappeared, and I never—"

He breaks off when my hand clutches my chest, a command to keep breathing after hearing the word "prom". Because of course he went to prom. Of course he continued living his life. Why should I be so shocked? Hurt? I did this to myself by running, and my feet ache to take me away from images of Marcus with another girl.

He swears under his breath. "I got asked, Mei. I said yes."

He lays the words right between us, watches my face and the tears rolling down it. "Maybe I thought I was ready to move on like I thought you had. Maybe I liked that someone was running toward me instead of away from me. Or maybe I wanted to hurt you like you hurt me. I don't know. But whatever I thought, Nick was hurting you while I was making up conversations with you in my head to make myself feel better that you were gone. It's so messed up."

The air between us swells, his face shiny with rain, and I search for responses, but he throws a question across the sand toward me and my brain skids to a stop. "What did you do with your feelings for me?" The waves roar and surge, but he keeps his eyes on me, his body rigid. "Was any of it real, or did I just imagine it all because that's how I wanted you to feel?" He swears into the mixed-up sky, wipes his hands down his face before looking back at me. "Just give me something—anything! I didn't think I'd be anywhere near you again, and now that I am, I can't hold in what I've wanted to say for weeks because keeping it inside hurts too much. I've been trying all day, and I just can't. I have to know where I stand with you." A surge of waves slams into him from behind and he wobbles, sidestepping to stay standing. He jumps onto a large rock, wipes rain and salt spray out of his eyes. "You messed me up day one, Mei," he yells as the clouds bump against each other and send down more rain. "When you left, I tried not to be messed up. Didn't work. And even though my dad's a total liar, he was right about girls, but I wanna be messed up by you. It's a billion times better than being messed up without you." His voice trembles. "I'm so crazy happy that you're safe and right here in front of me and that we're out of San Francisco together. More than anything, I wanna erase all the pain Nick left on you, but I can't. I can't take it away or change it and I'm not sure what you need me to do now. Or be. I just don't know how you feel. And I need to know."

My heartbeat competes with the wind and waves. The rain slows, and I step closer to the frantic water, hand on my chest. "You want to know where my feelings went?" I say, honesty pouring out of me, scattering the storm. "They're all right here, because I shoved them so deep inside, no one could ever find them or take them from me. They're mine and I'll keep them forever even if I shouldn't."

"Why shouldn't you?" His voice is weary, cautious.

"Because I'm a disaster. Your life was so good before you met me."

"No." He hops off the rock and wades through the water toward me, stopping a few feet away. "Nothing mattered after you left because all I wanted was you, and I still do. I want you to keep messing me up. I want you in my life, and I don't care about Nick or where we come from or what we should or shouldn't do." Rain trickles down his face from his wet hair as he moves closer. "So what do you want? What do you feel, the good and bad? Don't shut me out again—I wanna know it all."

I shake my head to the sand. "I feel too much."

He's in front of me, his warmth an inch away. "Tell me. Please," he whispers, and I hear him despite the chaos around us. "What do you want?"

I look up, waves tugging at my ankles, but I resist them, held up by the intensity building around us, "I want you. That's it. All of my feelings just mean that, nothing else."

"Do you want whatever comes next with me, too? Because I don't know what it is."

"Yes." I grit my teeth to stop their chattering, blink at the sand, then back up at him. "I want everything with you."

Wind whips between Marcus and me, blowing apart the

tension and uncertainty. The frustration in his eyes drifts across their surface like clouds and disappears, leaving only blue.

"Then it's you and me, Mei. I knew it the night I met you. Whatever happens next, we leave everything that happened behind us. Two days ago, I thought it was all over, so I'm not giving anything a chance to hurt you or ruin us again." Rain quivers on his lashes, slides down his nose.

My body trembles from the cold rain soaking through his hoodie. My bare legs and feet are numb, but my insides stretch toward Marcus's warm light. He's standing in the turbulent ocean under an angry sky, in front of me. A place I never dared to dream he'd be again. I thought I'd only have memories before Nick's darkness smothered them and whatever was left of me. But we're here somehow, the sand insistent that we stay right here regardless of the storm or misunderstandings or freshly reopened wounds. The wounds will heal, and Marcus's eyes tell me we will, too. I grab onto his belief.

He blinks away the crying sky that seems lighter now that the storm between us has calmed. His hand slides around the back of my neck, and his nose brushes mine. His lips are so close, unspoken words hover between us.

"What are you thinking right now?" he asks, still holding me tightly.

My hands smooth up his bare chest, over his shoulders and down his arms, gripping his forearms. I dig my numb toes into the sand to keep me steady. "I was just thinking ... we've been in some crazy situations together, but this might be the most insane. And coldest." There's no way I'm admitting my real thoughts out loud, because being this close to him is making them run wild.

"You sure that's it?" he smirks, easing closer.

I open my mouth to respond, but lightning slits the sky and thunder crashes. I shriek and run toward the hut. "Hurry!" I yell over my shoulder as Marcus sprints out of the water behind me. "The last thing we need is to be struck by lightning!" A wild, shaky laugh bursts out of me, and when he reaches me, his fingers slip through mine. We sprint through curtains of rain to the hut where he pulls me up the ramp and shoves open the door with his shoulder.

We bust through into damp, drafty darkness, and the wind slams it closed behind us, shutting out the storm. We stand in the middle of the hut, catching our breath before he pulls me to his chest, wrapping his arms around me while we shiver against each other, creating a puddle beneath us. His fingers thread into my wet hair, his palm cradling the back of my head as I tremble in the cold and heat colliding between us.

His hand slowly smooths over my back, pressing me to him as we stand in the dark, motionless, silent. He lowers his forehead to mine, our noses touching. "Hey," he whispers.

"Hi." I meet his eyes, glossy in the dim light.

He inhales, deep and slow, then presses his lips to my forehead. "I said a lot of things out there, but in case you missed it when I said it before, I need to tell you again. One very important thing. Like…the very most important thing I could ever tell you."

"That you've been recruited to go to Mars to practice intergalactic horticulture."

"So close," he whispers, sending goose bumps over my body.

"That prom was a total disaster without me."

"Definitely. But irrelevant."

"That you're really a Twizzlers guy?"

"No, never, and I love you," he breathes, taking my face between his hands.

I clutch his wrists and close my eyes, his honesty painting bright colors all over my heart against this gray, weathered backdrop. "I love you, too," I whisper against his lips, not for the first time since we met but definitely for the first time in this second chance. "For three months and twelve days, actually. No end in sight."

He groans. "I wanna kiss you so bad right now."

"I need you to kiss me so bad right now."

His lips crash against mine, salty and cold, but opening to the heat steaming from him, wrapping me in it.

I clutch his back, urging him closer so this day doesn't have another chance to take him from me.

"I missed you," he breathes when we surface, but he dives back in before I can respond. Heat flares inside me as the kiss mimics the intensity of the storm just outside the slats—fierce, rolling, electric, surging. "I never wanna spend another second away from you. Like…" He kisses me deep and lingering, like he's gathering all the pieces of me. "I wanna be…" His mouth moves to my eyes, my forehead. "So close to you…" His lips urge mine until I'm practically climbing him. "No space between us ever again.," he whispers before turning me and pressing me against the door. But his weight squeezes out a memory of Nick I hurled into the back of my mind, hoping it would evaporate. I mentally kick it down as it rises, but it pounds at me like a jackhammer, sending chunks of memory flying through my head: Nick's weight on me, darkness, my frantic pulse roaring in my ears, rough hands. My fists clench to squeeze the images out but my body jolts, then stiffens, and Marcus jerks back, his hands flying up at his sides.

"I'm sorry. Mei, I didn't—" Thunder cracks, and the room

flashes white. He curses, taking another step away from me. "I didn't think. I'm so sorry."

A chill rolls over me, drifting from the distance between us.

"I'm so sorry, Mei," he repeats, raking his hand through his wet hair, talking to the ceiling. "I shouldn't have...this whole thing. It's all wrong—timing, weather, this place." His words and body are distant, even inside this tiny hut, and my tears drip, mixing with the rain sliding down my face. "Besides, we're soaked, you're freezing. Everything's salty and covered in tetanus." His attempt to lift the moment gets whipped away by the wind howling through the cracks. "And you're hurt. And I didn't think about that. In the moment."

I squeeze my eyes shut, angry at myself for letting Nick slip between us. "You didn't do anything wrong. I'm just... yes—cold. My teeth are chattering. We're soaked." None of it is a lie, but I need a minute to gather myself. I need to figure out what just happened in my head and body. I don't want to relive any of it, especially not with Marcus watching. If he knows the whole story, he'll keep his distance. He'll be afraid of me forever.

He's pulling on a dry shirt, shaking out his wet hair, talking to everything in the room but me. "Doesn't look like the storm's letting up anytime soon. Since you've soaked my favorite hoodie, here's my second favorite." He holds it out and I take it from him. "I'm gonna step out to change out of these shorts so you can change too. Then...I guess we'll just... get some sleep, yeah?" He grabs a pair of sweats from the pile of his clothes on the raft and heads toward the door, avoiding my eyes. "I mean, we've got a perfectly good raft and at least if it floods while we sleep, we'll float."

He steps outside and I quickly change into the dry hoodie

and drape the wet one over a stool. A few seconds later, Marcus cracks the door to ask if it's safe to come in, then steps back inside, tossing his wet shorts on the counter before easing onto the raft, stretching out on his back. His feet hang over the edge and I crawl onto the raft and settle in beside him, staring at the ceiling through the haze of discomfort and gloom, wondering how to rewind time and erase my panicked reaction to his closeness. He's not Nick. He would never hurt me.

"You okay?" he asks softly, his hands splayed on his chest. "Your bruises look painful."

"I'm okay. Really."

He nods, and itchy silence settles in the space between us before he talks again. "I wish I could wipe them off. Erase all your bad memories."

Frustration burns through me. I hate that I let Nick in when we were so close to being back to normal.

"Do you wanna talk about it? About what happened? With Nick?" His voice eases toward me in the gray light.

I want to tell him. He deserves to know that my reaction had nothing to do with him. I wish I could open my head and show him everything, so I don't have to say the words out loud. I want to open my chest so he can see how big my feelings for him are. But then he might see the leftover darkness lurking there. It could change the way he looks at me, and if I'm being honest, I'm not sure how he'll react. We're both better if everything stays locked inside me until it eventually goes away.

I shake my head, staring at the ceiling. "Can we just push pause on this conversation? For now?"

"Yeah. Yeah—definitely." He clears his throat. Wind rattles the hut and rain slashes at the windows, sending ripples through the tension until Marcus slides his left hand toward me, his fingers gathering mine and weaving through them.

I close my eyes, focusing on the heat between our palms, the relief easing through me from this one touch. My mind unwinds, but the wind shoving through the cracks in the hut gets in my head, flinging the events of the last twenty-four hours against my skull until I roll into Marcus, burying my face into his arm like I can hide there.

He shifts and winds his arm around me, pulling me against him until we sink into the middle of the raft. I breathe in fabric softener on his shirt as I battle the thoughts, trying to pull me far from Marcus. But when his voice rumbles through them, I cling to his words:

"I love you, Mei."

CHAPTER 3

Ten minutes until whatever comes next.

Mei yells over my shoulder for me to take the next exit, so I change lanes and exit the highway toward Guo's brother's house. Seattle's lights shimmer on the water, bouncing the light into the sky where it gets stuck in the fog and hangs there. Kind of like my hope that Guo's brother will actually answer the door at 1 AM. We've been driving in rain, fog, and wind since we left the hut ten hours ago. Like nature is doing Dad's dirty work.

Mei gives me more of the directions Guo wrote on the Post-it after I burst through the shop door and announced I was going to Seattle with Mei. Guo had somehow already known I'd go with her, but Mei was surprised. Not sure why; there was no other choice for me. Even if things are a little different now. A little more frantic, more uncertain. Soaking and cold and tense, like a pebble in the road could easily roll us. I lost control at the hut—emotionally and physically. Told her things I shouldn't have. Did things I shouldn't have. The bruises all over her neck reminded me that I'd promised I wouldn't touch her and that she has wounds I can't see. I have to be completely opposite of Nick in every way. I almost messed that up, and it's not gonna happen again. It's gonna kill me having her this close, all to myself, but I want her to know she's safe from me and my hormones as well as Nick and deportation. We're gonna start over. Make this our thing, our way. And I hope she'll talk about what happened so we can leave that behind, too. I want to make sure she's really okay. But I don't know how to bring it up without bringing up the hard stuff that comes with it. Dad told me about how wrecked people are after stuff like this—how many years of therapy they go through. But I'm not a therapist, so I'll just protect her from anything bad from now on.

I weave the bike through neighborhoods strung along the edge of the city, the houses settling down for the night. Warm light spills onto the glossy streets, slipping beneath our tires. I just wanna get to Guo's brother's house and shut the door against anything and everything that might have followed us from home. But I also don't because I don't know what to expect. Nothing has turned out the way it should have so far, and I'm too tired to hope it'll be any different when we get there. And when we do, how long are we going to stay? A week? Two? A month? Forever? Will Stanford respond to the email I sent before we tossed our phones in a dumpster on our way out of San Francisco? Will they forgive me for turning down a full-ride scholarship and offer it again? I gotta get a new phone so I can check my email.

Mei rests her chin on my shoulder, calling out more directions. "Turn right at the next stop sign. Third house on the right."

I want her to keep the contact between us, so I nod and accelerate, gripping the handlebars as I swerve around a speed bump. My hands are cramping after ten hours of driving. For the first few hours, I was on edge, but I'm pretty comfortable with the getaway vehicle now.

Mei points to a house on our right. "I think that's it," she yells.

A tiny dog sits on a porch swing. The front window curtains are wide open at 1 AM, like the house is watching for us. I pull into the driveway and cut the engine, putting my foot down, but we both just sit in the silence, our legs molded to the seat.

I stare at the house in front of us. We made it. Step one of together. No clue what step two is.

A garage door shudders open a few houses down and an electric car hums past us. I glance at the front door, flexing my toes in my soggy Adidas.

"I'm scared to knock." Mei's voice curls over my shoulder and into my ear and I hesitate, then nod. Fear's the only thing I can expect right now—its claws have pretty much grown into me.

I shove the kickstand down with my heel and slip the key into my pocket. I'm gonna have to park the bike somewhere out of sight once we get our stuff inside.

Mei unwinds her arms, and I wait for her to slide off the seat before following.

"He might think it's weird if we just hang out in his driveway." I pull off my helmet.

Mei hangs it from the handlebars. "Marcus…are you—"

"We're finally here. Knocking on the door is the easy part." I want to hold her in this in-between place—between what's happened and what's about to.

I shake my arms which are buzzing from the vibration of the road, and I rub the tension out of my neck. Taking a deep breath and letting it out slowly, I turn toward the door.

Mei grabs my hand, and it's so comforting and familiar.

My palm is extra sensitive against hers, my mind rewinding to our time in the hut as we walk past a fountain circled by dwarf trees pruned into globes, a couple bronze statues. A faded rubber duck floating in a pot filled with rainwater. Definitely the right house. That's something Guo would do. I wish for the thousandth time she was here.

The gray door reflects our shadows, and they're as smudged as I feel, but I raise my free hand and knock.

———

"And here…," Jerry says, sweeping open the door to the red cottage huddled under the trees in his backyard, "is your new place. For however long you need it." He grins at us and nods. "My sister said it needed to feel like home, so I hope you like lanterns and silk pillows because that's what Wen picked out."

I scan the room, my bag strap cutting into my tense shoulders. Home? No Ansel Adams on the wall or giant flat screen TV or Dad's stack of books on the end tables. No Dad.

Perfect.

And far from San Francisco.

Even better.

Just me and Mei.

"Wow. This is perfect. Thank you." I say to Jerry, who's standing by the door in his robe and slippers, his beaming smile just like Guo's. "And bunk beds!" I turn toward the built-ins in the corner—puffy, orange comforters piled with red, white, and blue silk pillows. Dad would hate them. Unless Kenna wanted them.

I flick the thought away and smile at Jerry. "I always wanted bunk beds but never had anyone to share a room with. Until now." Now, when I actually want to share my bed, there are two and a bruised, battered, freaked out Mei. I gotta keep distance between us; otherwise, the moment she gets close, my hormones will threaten to break the promise I made myself to give her space

"The bathroom's just in there." Jerry points to a door I'll have to walk through sideways unless I want to get stuck. "Small for some of us." He snickers to himself, just like Guo does when she makes fun of me in her most loving way. "But it will be safe here. My sister was insistent, and I never want to make her mad."

I laugh. Mei says thank you, her voice soft and breezy like she just floated back into the room from somewhere else. "We really appreciate this, and we'll make it up to you any way we can."

Jerry nods and steps toward the open door. "It's been a long day for you, so I will leave you to settle in. We can talk about hours at the restaurant and warehouse after you've had some rest."

Help at the restaurant. Warehouse. In exchange for rent. I've never had a job or rent. I've barely been out of California. How did I get here?

Jerry blinks at me, then Mei, and back again. I jerk my head in confirmation. "Yeah. Perfect. We're so grateful. We'll help any way we can."

He smiles, and Mei shakes his hand before he slips out of the cottage. She shuts the door, locks it, and turns around, back against it. Smiling, she bites her lower lip. "This is much nicer than the hut of despair."

I tense because she's driving me crazy looking at me like that. My mind is swirling with the memory of all of her pressed up against me at the hut. Then how she tensed. She said it was because she was cold, but I know there's more to it.

Her gaze moves down my body, then makes a U turn and moves back up, and I swallow my thoughts which land in my stomach with a thud. The jolt helps me remember what she went through right before we left.

I dig my toes into my shoes to stop my legs from stepping toward her, pulling her onto the bed to finish what we started in the hut. Instead, I turn to face the bunks, my whole body on fire. "I call top!"

CHAPTER 4

One Month Later

Mei,

I just want to humbly say thank you for dinner last night. Marcus let me taste some of his, even though you put me on a diet because my midsection is getting out of control. But now that I've tasted your pineapple curry, no one else's will do, and that's just great—I'll save all that money I was spending on DoorDash. So my budget and my belly thank you.

Yours, Buddha

hang my towel on its hook and stand in front of the bathroom mirror, debating with myself. Marcus has been hands-off for a month now, and I want to show him I'm not the fragile girl from the hut. I want to show him I trust him. Because I do. He's not Nick, and I want to prove to him that I don't see him like that. I need to prove it to myself, too. So maybe I should walk out naked and see if that changes anything. If it says, "I don't want to be just your roommate."

Maybe Tension will run out the door. He's been our loud, obnoxious, third roommate long enough and made himself way too comfortable but…leaving my towel behind could get rid of him. Maybe. Or maybe not. How would I know? Two months ago, we couldn't keep our hands off each other, but we were in a very different place back then, literally and figuratively. Emotionally. All the way back then, we couldn't stand space between us, and now that's pretty much all we've got, even when space is hard to come by.

I close my eyes. I really need to talk to Marcus about more than the funny things that happen at work or what we want to do on our day off. I need to know what's behind his emotional wall that came up the moment we got to Seattle and has surrounded him like a fortress ever since. I need to know if he's feeling trapped like I am.

The steam in the bathroom is too thick and crowds me out, but I haven't decided what to do, so I opt for the security of clothes. When I open the bathroom door, a trapped cloud of steam follows me out.

Marcus is still in his bed—on the top bunk—reading a book with the cover torn off, his feet hanging off the end.

I talk as I pull my wet hair into a ponytail. "I'm off around seven tonight, and Jerry said he can drive me home, so you don't have to come pick me up."

The bed creaks, and Marcus props his head on his elbow and looks over the edge, filling the small space between his mattress and the ceiling. "What if I wanna pick you up?" His smile reaches down to me, and I curl my toes into the rug, trying not to stare because I don't want him to read what's in my eyes.

He's a constant reminder of what I'm not sure I have, and a temptation for what I want so badly I can't think straight. When he wakes up and hangs over the edge of his bed to say good morning, I want to run my fingers through his messy hair, but I don't dare. At night, we talk in our separate bunks about nothing meaningful until way too late, and I stare at the wood slats holding him so far above me. Wonder what he'd do if I climbed the ladder to him. I think of ways to tell him to stop tossing and turning and trying to scrunch himself into his space because there's room for him in mine. And when he's in the shower, just behind a flimsy door, I have to distract my hands so they don't turn the knob.

The distance between us is filled with sticky confusion. He has his motorcycle. No one's gonna find us. We don't have to sneak around anymore. He told me he wants to be here with me. He's mentioned more times than I can count how much it messed him up when we were apart, but his words don't match his actions, and I'm not sure what to believe now.

"It's okay," I respond when I feel his gaze lingering on my back like it always does, and freeze, letting them warm me like sunshine. I grab my jacket and head to the door. "Jerry's headed home anyway. See you later."

———

The restaurant is buzzing tonight, the hum of chatter and shrieks of laughter mixing together and pulling all my noisy thoughts into them. If I wasn't constantly moving tonight, nostalgia would surely have me wishing for a time before everything that's happened in the last month. Like the first time I met Marcus and fell instantly in love with him.

I clear another table and head to the kitchen, setting the dishes in the sink area. It's not that Marcus hasn't done anything Marcus-y all month. He has. A couple weeks ago, I found notes from "Buddha," some sweet and some funny. Like the one he made into a tiny sailor's hat and propped on Buddha's head that said: *Your roommate's hot, Mei. Can I get his number?* Or the one I found taped to Buddha's hand that was left inside my pillowcase. Didn't see that one until I laid down and it jabbed my ear: *Do you find it weird that I watch you sleep at night? I try not to, but I physically can't close my eyes. Sorry, not sorry.*

Since the day we arrived in Seattle, he's been the perfect guy. He always lets me shower first. He's made me dinner at least twenty times, even though he can only make elaborate turkey sandwiches, complicated omelets, and gumbo.

But he still hasn't touched me except for the occasional foot touch under the table or random hand hold.

I roll my eyes, turning the corner to the break room and hanging my apron on a hook. Washing my hands, I glance at the clock. I wonder what Marcus is doing at the warehouse. I wonder what he's thinking. Wonder about his prom memories and if there's another girl squeezing between us—one who was running toward him instead of running away like I did. I wonder if he touched her. He never told me who he went with.

Pressing my lips together, I stop the thought before it spirals. I'm being ridiculous. Things would be different if I hadn't panicked in the hut. If I hadn't gone to L.A. If I hadn't run from his apartment in the first place. None of this is his fault. He's here, even after everything. Still, I wonder if it's regret that makes his body tense when he accidentally brushes against me. If anger is what keeps his jaw clenched and his eyes skittish, like I might catch and trap them. Does he feel trapped?

I yank my phone from my satchel and take a seat at the table. Turning it on, I see a text from Marcus.

Marcus: Hey

He sent this twenty-three minutes ago, probably when he was on his break at the warehouse. I type:

Mei: Hey back.

Marcus: There you are!

Mei: Here I am.

Marcus: How's work?

Mei: Slightly fishy. Yours?

Marcus: Good. Warehouse-y. Lots of cardboard.

I stare at the phone, wondering what I should text back when three dots appear, and I wait for whatever Marcus is texting to come through.

Marcus: So… I feel like things have been weird. They've been weird right?

Not the word I'd use but yes. Weird.

Mei: Maybe it's because you went from boyfriend to "bunk mate."

I hit send before I can stop myself and grip my phone. I shouldn't have sent it. It's not his fault. All of this is mine, and I don't want to take it out on him.

I glance at my phone. The other end is silent. I said too much. I start to text *Sorry*, but his response slides onto the screen.

> Marcus: I don't know what you want me to be. And I don't want to hurt or scare you.

> Mei: How would you do that?

> Marcus: You froze up on me in the hut. I could tell it wasn't from the temperature. It freaked me out. Never wanna do anything that makes you think of Nick or think I'm like him. I want you for all the right reasons. And some that might be wrong, but I don't know the right way to handle any of it.

> Mei: Bruises heal. I'm not fragile, so stop treating me like I might break. This weird, "pretend we're roommates" thing hurts worse than any bruise. I thought about walking out of the bathroom today naked just to see what you'd do. Anything to find out if you're still interested in me. Are you?

I put my hand on my chest, all the boiling emotions inside me erupting and burning through me until I want to run from myself.

Three dots appear on the screen.

A text.

> Marcus: Tell Jerry I'm picking you up from work tonight.

CHAPTER 5

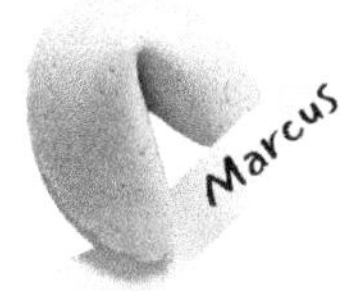

My grip tightens on the motorcycle handlebars because I kind of hate coming to this Chinatown. It reminds me of the other Chinatown. My Chinatown. And when I think of that Chinatown, it reminds me I can't go back—can't go home because it's not home anymore. Right now, it's kind of like Mei and I don't have a home. The cottage is fine, but it doesn't feel comfortable like home should. Maybe that's because we're not comfortable. Haven't been in weeks. Not since the hut where I said too much about some things and not enough about others, then lost my mind when I felt her against me. Made it all physical, even though I promised myself I'd give her space and prove I want her for all the right reasons. I slipped up, let my hormones drive, and they slammed into a brick wall in the form of a stiff, traumatized Mei who wouldn't talk about it. She still hasn't. I clench my jaw. I will never do anything that makes her stiffen like that again, like my touch reminded her of Nick.

He left marks on Mei that go deeper than bruises. I'm not

sure she'll ever fully heal from what happened, and I wanna give her the space she needs. But after reading her text, maybe I gave her too much space. I don't know. Don't know what's going through her head since we haven't really talked about much of anything important, using words or eyes. I'm terrified I've changed things permanently by not asking questions that need to be asked. I asked questions and said things once, and next thing I knew, I didn't see her for two weeks. Never thought I'd see her again, and now we're here together, yeah, but we're still such a mess.

I'm still dying to take the next big step with her, but also kinda not. Going there has been the end of relationships for too many people I know, and at this point, I'll do anything—or not do anything—to keep Mei with me. I wish I could ask Dad exactly what he did wrong with my mom so I could avoid all of it. But that's not gonna happen. What I need to do is be honest with her, even if she runs from me. I did a decent job with honesty at the hut until testosterone took over. I thought things would just naturally go back to normal, but I think we left normal in San Francisco. In the space we created between us the night we fought, and Meemaw walked in, and Mei ran. Meemaw's not here, but that doesn't mean Mei won't run if things stay uncomfortable.

My hands haven't stopped shaking, and my appetite found a great hiding place after I read her text earlier today.

I veer the motorcycle into the alley behind the restaurant and park at the back entrance. Jerry and Wen told me I could come in this way since Mei and I are family. It's been comforting, having them in the house just up the path from the cottage. Even if Wen asks me every day when Mei and I are getting married, like she's the Seattle version of Guo. She's old school and doesn't like the idea of us living together. Dad would hate it even more, even if nothing's happening. I always give Wen a made-up date because the truth is, I'd marry Mei today if I knew what tomorrow was gonna look like. Just don't have anything to offer right now, and I'm not sure what she wants. Most likely something way better than what she's currently getting: a scared, confused, clueless guy who doesn't know how to be in charge of his own life, let alone hers or ours or whatever this is. I once thought I could be enough for her, back when everything had logical next steps and real life was theoretical. Now…I'm not so sure.

Letting out a breath, I pop my knuckles, open the back door, and step into the restaurant's storage room. I weave around shelves filled with weird-smelling boxes and spices and push aside the drape to the break room.

The three times I've been here, it's always been empty, but tonight, a girl's standing in front of a big whiteboard. She looks over when I come in, and I lift my hand in a half-wave.

"Hey. Just waiting for Mei." I throw my thumb over my shoulder toward the back entrance. "Jerry told me it was okay."

She holds a dry erase marker, clicking the cap on and off, and turns toward me, her eyes sweeping my face before doing a quick full-body scan. "Definitely okay," she says in perfect English. "Please tell me you're her adopted brother."

I laugh and jiggle the motorcycle key in my hand. "Uh… that would be…bad. And illegal."

She smiles. "So, driver?"

"Boyfriend." I nod. "Definitely boyfriend." Seems like I should be way more than that by now, though.

"Ah, the infamous Marcus we've all heard so much about." The girl tilts her head. "If you're ever not her boyfriend, let me know."

"Oh. Yeah… ummm…looks like there won't be an

opening anytime soon. Hopefully never. She's kinda my favorite thing."

"How did she land that spot?"

"By being Mei."

"She's that good?" The girl tilts her head to the other side.

"There's not even a word."

"Wow. Lucky her and all that." She stares at me a little too long for comfort before moving away. "I'll go tell her you're here, Lover Boy."

"Perfect. Thanks."

She leaves the room, and I ease into a plastic chair, grateful to be done with that conversation and her visual x-ray.

The break room smells like grease with a dash of shrimp, and I lean my elbows on my knees, putting my head in my hands. I rehearse what I'm gonna say to Mei. Wonder what her face will look like when she sees me. Lately, her eyes have been completely locked down, and when I catch them and try to read the thoughts in them, they're skittish and won't land. I just need her to know how much I want this, but how much I don't know how to do it. And that I'm so scared of losing her, I've paralyzed myself. I haven't touched her like I want to since we got to Seattle, and it takes way too long to go to sleep every night because all I wanna do is climb in bed with her. I usually let myself think about that until the fear creeps in and sends all the what-ifs sprinting around my head.

A door sweeps open at the end of the hall, and I sit up just as Mei rounds the corner into the break room and stops. "Oh. You came." She looks tired. Or sad?

I stand. "Yeah. And I grabbed takeout on my way. Thought maybe we could go talk. If you want to."

She watches me, pressing her lips together, her fingers

fidgeting with the belt loop on her black uniform pants. "Give me five minutes?"

I nod, watching her for any signs of the old us. They showed up on the beach during the storm, then in the hut, but the adrenaline and hormones drowned everything we couldn't say. "Yeah." I nod again. "I'll just go wait outside."

She disappears down the hallway. Now that we've acknowledged the tension and weirdness, it's barging into every second, and I don't know how we're gonna beat it.

I head for the back door. Mei and I have to figure this out tonight. I'll tell her everything I've been holding back. It's gotta come out before it breaks us again.

———

I pull up to the waterfront park, shut off the motorcycle engine, and take off my helmet. Mei's already off the bike, facing the water as she unbuckles her own helmet. When she pulls it off, I glance at her out of the corner of my eye, still not sure how to start this conversation. I wish she could just see it all in my eyes. We'd be done and back to normal.

I pop the seat and pull out the Thai food I picked up along with the sheet I took off my bed. If all goes as I hope it does, I won't need it or the top bunk anymore.

Mei hangs her helmet on the handlebar, and I catch her eye, hold out my hand. She looks at it and takes it, biting her lip. But she still won't look at me, and my stomach drops. Maybe she doesn't wanna talk. Maybe she'll say something I really don't wanna hear. Maybe she's done waiting for me to figure myself out. Maybe I've kept my feelings too close, and she can't feel anything from my direction. Or she's got a completely different direction in mind. Or maybe—

"Where do you want to go?" Her voice is light and timid

like she's barely holding onto it as she scans the area for a place to sit.

"Back to normal."

She looks up at me.

"I don't care where we go tonight, I just want things between us to go back to normal," I say. "So if you know where that is and how to get there, let's go there."

"Marcus." She closes her eyes, shaking her head. "I'm sorry for what I said in my texts. I just don't know—"

"No. I'm glad you said it. All of it. It needed to be said, and I was too afraid."

"Of what?" She waits like she'll pull the words from me if I don't offer them willingly.

"To say anything."

"What do you want to say?"

I glance around, the moment squeezing me. "Can I say it over there?" I point to a grassy spot looking out over the water.

"Sure." She nods. Too fast. "Yeah."

I hold onto her hand so tight, like I don't even want air to come between our palms and risk it sweeping away any of my pathetic courage. I need all of it.

We spread the sheet out on the grass, and she sits down. I set the bag of food down, kick off my shoes, and ease down beside her, leaving enough space for another person. I lean back on my elbows, stretching my legs in front of me, and fill the space with honesty.

"What you said in your text…about me not wanting you…it's exactly opposite of that." I squint into the setting sun. "I want you so bad, I'm paralyzed by it. I don't know my next move, so I'm just not making any. Last time I touched you, your reaction was nothing I ever expected and…the time before that—after Meemaw—things didn't end well. I lost you. I'm not risking that again."

She's quiet for a minute, and I let the words soak in like we're both sunbaked deserts and the words are rain, trying to find a place to sink in. I flex my feet, curling my toes. Wait.

"What happened, Marcus?" The setting sun lights the right side of her face, making her glow.

"What do you mean?"

"After the hut. I know I made it weird and I'm sorry, but ever since then, you've just…pushed me out and kept me out."

I inhale through my nose, like the reasons inside me just need a little more fresh air to coax them out. I don't know why this hurts so much to let her into this space. "You were afraid of me. I felt it. And then you just shut down, and I didn't know what to do because we never talked about why. And we still haven't."

She stares at the sheet, her finger rubbing the seam of her pants. "It's…overwhelming, and I don't want to talk about it. I don't want to give it air to breathe. But I wasn't scared of you. I've never been scared of you."

"It felt like you were."

"I didn't mean for it to feel like that. I didn't mean for any of it to happen at all." Her eyes meet mine. "And now, it's just…we've wanted nothing but to be alone, no one barging in or tearing us apart or telling us we can't. We've had alone-time for a month, but we're acting like roommates, and I'm confused. We laugh and share things, but it only goes so far, and then there's this invisible wall between us, and I've been slamming against it ever since we got to Seattle. I don't want you to be scared of me or how I might react, and I don't want to be your roommate, but maybe that's what you want."

I shake my head. "No, Mei. That's not at all what I want.

Not even close. I just…I need to know what you're thinking, but I don't know how to bring it up without bringing up bad memories. So yeah—it's been super weird, and it's not your fault, it's mine."

She rolls her eyes. "Cliché."

"I know. I know—it totally is, but it's…I don't know how to…"

"What?" She throws her hands in the air. "Why can't you say things to me anymore? When did you become so careful about what you say? What are you afraid of?"

"I told you. I'm afraid of hurting you or scaring you. I have no clue what's going on inside your head, so then I try to guess, and I get stuck in my head and don't wanna ask, and I'm going in circles." I run my fingers through my hair, gripping it between my fingers. "You've been abused. Used? I don't know. You've never told me exactly what happened, and I know you don't wanna talk about it but it's not just gonna go away if we ignore it."

She looks down at her lap, the minutes stretching on the breeze before she speaks again. "If it hadn't been for Su Ling or Nick being drunk, I wouldn't be here right now." She closes her eyes, breathing deeply through her nose. "He tried to rape me. In a hotel room. I fought him, but he was strong and would have succeeded." Another pause. "But Su Ling found us and smashed a vase over his head. We both ran." She closes her eyes. "Nick told me he always gets what he wants, but that night he didn't."

My fists clench, my throat goes dry, and I want to track Nick down and make sure he never has the option of getting what he wants, but Mei's eyes pull me back from the edge. *"I'm here, and Nick's not, and that's all that matters to me."*

It's the first time her eyes have talked to me since the day in my apartment.

She smiles. "And now it's your turn to tell me the truth."

"About what?"

"About what you're really feeling."

I sit up, elbows on my bent knees, my fingers wrestling in front of me. It's too stupid to say now that she told me what happened to her. I scan the horizon. "I hate what he did to you. But so glad you fought. That you're here, and that you told me. I know it was hard for you, so thank you." I watch a speed boat swerve through the waves. "But I'm still afraid."

"Of…?"

"Losing you."

She squints at me. "Losing me as a friend? Because that's what I am right now, and I guess if that's what you want, then—"

"No. I definitely want way more than that. But I still don't know what you want or don't want or what's okay and what's not. But I want to know. I need to because I want… everything. All the things I've imagined doing with you since I met you. Since I first kissed you or saw you in your bra." I swallow the itchy, squirming honesty crawling up my throat, like it's scared of the light but can't go back to the dark. "I want way more than just your body, but I'm afraid of taking the next step and you thinking that's all I'm after. I'd be lying if I said I haven't dreamed every single day about being with you." I glance at her, then look away. "I have so many feelings for you, and I don't know how to show you how strong they are without making things physical, and I promised myself I'd prove I love you for all the right reasons. That I'd never make you uncomfortable or leave you feeling used.

"But that day at my apartment…before Meemaw walked in…everything seemed so confusing. Like all my feelings got shoved aside by hormones, and I was afraid of myself. I've heard the stories from all my friends and guys on the team about how things end after they do it with their girlfriends, and I just…I don't want that. I don't want that to be us, and I never want to feel you stiffen when I touch you again.

"But I can't lose you. Can't even think about it. It's a dark hole I was in before, and now I won't go anywhere near it. I made a choice back then, when I thought we were over, that if I ever got another chance with you, I wouldn't mess it up. I promised myself I wouldn't have sex until I was fully, one hundred percent committed so you'd know you can trust me forever."

Mei's eyes dive into mine. "Like, committed how…?"

"Like married committed."

A slow smile spreads across Mei's face. "Then what are we waiting for?" When my eyebrows jump, she laughs to the sky. "Kidding. Kind of."

I give her a shaky smile because more words are piling up, falling out of me. "I know we're young, so I'm not saying we need to get married right now. I just know once we go there, there's no going back for me. I'll give you all of me. But that doesn't mean you'll want all of it. And I'm not willing to risk losing you." I hold her gaze, trying to pull her into my feelings so she can understand what I'm not saying very well. "I'd rather spend my whole life just holding your hand if it means you'll stay with me."

She slowly turns her whole body toward me on the sheet. "Marcus," she whispers, and her voice wraps around my name, holding it between us like solid ground we can meet on. "I wouldn't be okay holding your hand forever because it's not enough for me. I want all of you, too. Including all of this fear and worry and feelings, no matter how big or heavy. Because at least I know this all means something to you."

I stare at her, looking for any possible scenario in her eyes. Am I stupid to think we're different than every couple I've ever known who didn't make it through their toughest times? That we'll last when none of them did? Maybe they never felt like this. "What if you decide you don't want this? What if you leave?"

"Why would I ever leave you?"

"People leave, Mei. They just do, and sometimes we don't get to know why, and that's what scares me. Because if I knew, I'd do everything perfectly. But I don't think I can, even if that's what you deserve."

Her eyes glisten, and a tear slides along her nose, quivering on her upper lip before dropping to the sheet between us. "There's no such thing as perfect. I figured that out a long time ago, and I like our messiness. Messy is kind of our thing."

I laugh to my lap. "Uhh, yeah. We're pretty good at it." I clench and unclench my jaw a few times, thinking. "So…" I pick at a thread on the sheet, watching it curl between my fingers. "What should we do about all this imperfection?" When I look up, our eyes collide, hover, linger.

Her fingers rake through the end of her ponytail draped over her shoulder. "Maybe we should just stay together forever and see how imperfect we can be."

"That sounds like the first perfect thing we've said in weeks."

She smiles to the sheet, rubbing a spot on her pant leg. "Now what? Is this our official restart? Leave the past in the past and move forward together as hopefully more than roommates?"

I smile over her head, collecting all the bright spots with my eyes—boat lights, the Ferris wheel on the pier. Streetlamps, emerging stars. Mei. "Guess you'll have to stick around to find out."

CHAPTER 6

Marcus doesn't let go of my hand as he unlocks our front door, but he hesitates, the key dangling from the lock. "Never done the whole doorstep goodnight kiss thing." He smiles down at me. "Since neither of us had an actual doorstep, I'm kinda dying to try it now that we do."

His eyes move to my lips. I press them together like they're going to leap off my face and attack his if he doesn't get on with it, then grin up at him. "I mean…I had a fire escape, which is basically the same thing. So many missed opportunities."

"Which I *deeply* regret," he murmurs, leaning down until his lips brush my ear. "Not gonna miss this one." His hands slide around my waist to my lower back, gathering me to him. My arms wrap around his neck, settling into the place they've created and still fit perfectly into after all their time away from him.

His mouth moves against mine, hesitantly, like he's

waiting for my response, and when I press against him, relief and anticipation mix in a desperate sigh.

His hands slide over my hips, his fingers pressing into them as he sidesteps us to the door and bumps it open with his shoulder. "Jerry and Wen can't watch us in here," he breathes against my mouth, pulling me inside and shutting the door with his foot.

He backs me against it in our dark cottage, his lips pulling sounds from me as his hands glide up my sides until he's cradling the back of my head, fingers threading through my hair.

Relief rushes through me, a familiar crackling heat that sweeps away the past and hurt and misunderstanding. Our bodies curl around each other, but I'm still not close enough to him. He whispers "I love you, Mei" in my ear, and the words pool in my stomach before flooding my legs, swirling through my body as his mouth skims down my neck. All the time that has piled up between us melts in our heat, his body pinning me in a corner of the world only big enough for the two of us. I deepen the kiss, my hands on the back of his neck, curling in his hair.

He swears, guiding me backward toward the couch, holding me close as my back meets the cushions, his body hovering over mine.

All the thoughts he's held inside rush from him in heated whispers, his mouth leaving his feelings in warm patches all over my skin. I pull him down, his weight pressing me deeper into the moment, deeper into the heat and relief winding around us. Our mouths and hands desperately release all they've been holding back until his smooth, warm hands slip under my shirt trailing fire.

I gasp, my fingertips digging into his back, my legs wrapping around his hips to close the space between us, but he curses and stills, drops his head to my shoulder, chest heaving. His heartbeat pounds through me as I clutch at him to keep him in the moment with me, but he growls, frustrated as he talks into my neck. "I gotta cool down or clothes are coming off."

"Which would be bad because…?" I breathe into his shoulder, my hands in his hair.

His mouth takes control of mine again, my head swirling, body weightless even with his weight on me.

"Remind me why I wanted to wait," he rasps against my lips, both of us breathless. He drops his head to the center of my chest, then groans and shifts to the side, settling between me and the back of the couch.

One hand moves to my neck, the other to my hip and he rolls me to face him, then leans his forehead against mine, our heartbeats bouncing off each other. "Whyyyy…" he sighs, his lips brushing my temple.

I bring one hand to his neck, curling his hair between my fingers, holding him in the steamy inch between us. "Because you have something to prove, apparently." I smile up at him and catch his lips with mine for a soft, lingering kiss.

He pulls me closer until our stomachs are pressed together. "And also…" I whisper between long, deep kisses that drag my soul up to him, "you said you wanted to marry me first."

His eyes are glossy in the dark, and I kiss his jaw, smiling when his body wraps around mine again. His fingers play with the waistband of my jeans, sending goosebumps across my back and around my stomach.

I draw a heart on his chest with my fingertip, my body slowly sinking into the couch as my hormones sigh, dejected but happy for any Marcus time. "But until then, I'm okay being here, just like this. With my favorite roommate."

His teeth catch my lower lip, his arm wrapping around me, squeezing me until a laugh bursts from me. "I'll be your roommate," he says, sliding down so we're face to face. "Your roommate with some pretty great benefits. With limits. For now."

"I'll take any of your benefits," I say, kissing him, our bodies sinking into each other again, and when we surface a few seconds or minutes or hours later, he smiles, beaming light into the darkness blanketing us.

"Good news is…we don't have curfews. No parents, no interruptions." He kisses me until my legs tingle. "We could make out all night."

"Clothes on?"

"Necessary," he says, his lips making detours under my jaw, up to my ear. "And I'm just glad neither of us had a doorstep before now. We would've been in so much trouble."

One Week Later

Sunlight peeks through the crack in the curtains, like it's afraid to disturb us but has to get the day going. A golden pool spreads across the wood floor and onto my face, brushing me with warmth, but not nearly as warm as Marcus's bare chest against my back or my legs tangled in his.

Everything around me feels light and perfectly placed. Abundant and full, no matter how sparse our cottage is, like Marcus fills all the space around me, even when we're apart. Like he's filled all the craggy places where Nick used to lurk and dissolved all the dark memories.

I smile as Marcus's arm tightens around me, pulling me

closer in a tug-of-war with the morning—the same as every morning this week when I've had to get up for work earlier than he has. After our hour-long make out session a week ago, we'd stayed tangled together on the couch in the dark, listening to the trees rustling against our roof. When I'd kissed his ear and gotten up to get ready for bed, since I had an early shift the next day, Marcus watched me, his eyes glossy from where he lay on the couch in the dark. After I'd slipped into my bed, he'd gotten up and walked into the bathroom, then come out and crawled over me in bed, whispering good night as he'd kissed my neck and pulled me back against his chest.

I'm so grateful we talked that night. I'm so, so thankful we were honest with each other. I wish he knew how his fears make me feel even safer with him. I know he would never do anything to make me uncomfortable, and I want to do the same for him.

I stretch and attempt to slip out of the covers without waking him, even though I want to stay like this all day. He groans in protest, and I smile, bending down to kiss him.

"My chest's so cold now," he mumbles.

"Maybe you should put on a shirt," I suggest with a smirk.

"Maybe you should take yours off..." He smiles a slow, lazy smile.

"You taking back your stupid rule?"

He squeezes his eyes shut, shakes his head, and looks at me again, grinning. "No matter how much I want to."

"Your loss," I laugh before walking into the bathroom.

———

"Oh good! Just in time," Jill says when I push through the door to the kitchen, the restaurant's cordless phone in her hand. I just finished with my last table of the night, and after being here for ten hours, I'm so ready to get home to Marcus, lock the door, and pretend nothing outside it exists.

Home. Marcus. Our place. Our life. The new us, the do-over. Not only was I the only Marcus winner in the universe the first time, but somehow, I'm also the winner for a second time.

"In time for what?" I ask Jill, jerking back to reality. I untie my apron and hang it on its hook.

She holds the phone out. "For you." She shrugs. "Not Marcus. I would've kept talking to him if it was."

I stare at the phone while a familiar unease stirs in my stomach from where it's been dormant for almost a month. If it's not Marcus, then who? Jerry and Wen are the only other people I talk to, and they're up in the office. Guo Mama gets updates from Jerry. No one else knows where we are.

Unease hardens into fear as a very unwelcome thought stomps through my head: What if it's Nick? What if Nick found us? Or did he find Marcus and is calling to threaten and hurt me in the one way he knows he can?

But Marcus has been at work all day—hidden in a warehouse on the outskirts of Seattle. How would Nick find him there? Also…Nick's in jail. But what about Xander? Chaz?

My stomach coils around every name, and Jill must see the discomfort on my face because she tilts her head and frowns. "Want me to take a message?"

I nod. "Ask who it is," I whisper, and Jill studies me before holding the phone to her ear again.

"Can I ask who's calling?" She keeps her eyes on my face. Pauses. "Oh. Yeah. Okay. Hold on." Jill pushes mute and holds the phone out to me again. "Guo Mama?"

I leap toward Jill and snatch the phone out of her hands. I've only talked to Guo Mama once since arriving in Seattle, and that was a quick call from Jerry's phone to tell her we arrived safely.

"Hello?" I blurt into the phone, before waving a shaky hand and mouthing "thank you" to Jill as she leaves. If it were Marcus on the other end, she would have lingered and eavesdropped. "Hold on." I walk into the break room and shut the door behind me, pressing my back against it. "Hello!"

"Xiao Mei." The calm in her voice warms the distance between us and relief ripples through me. I will call you another time to catch up, but right now, someone needs to talk to you."

The phone rustles, and I frown, flipping through possibilities. But before my thoughts go too far, a familiar voice says my name on the other end, and my brain grinds to a stop.

"Mama?"

"I am so happy to hear your voice."

My throat dries, and the words shrivel and blow away in the gust of shock and confusion. I thought she was gone— deported by now. With Baba. I have so many questions but all I get out is, "Hi."

"Are you well?"

Tears sting my eyes, and I wait for my mind to recover, squeezing out a single syllable. "Yes."

"Good." A pause. "Good."

I clear my throat. "How are you?"

"Your father is in custody, and it is only a matter of time before we are deported. Together or separately, I don't know, but I don't care. I've been staying with Guo Mama. You're safe, and that's what I care about most."

My mind snags on her sentence, examining it for truth.

"To answer your question, I haven't been this good in a very long time."

My legs surrender to the shock, and I drop into a chair, my hand at my mouth. Custody? Was Baba doing the same thing Nick was doing…? If so, I'm the one who called the police. I'm the one who sent him to jail.

"I'm so sorry, Mama," I whisper, my voice cracked and crumbling. "It's my fault he's in—"

She shushes me. "No. It is his. All of this is his fault. You've done nothing wrong."

Silence stretches between us. The picture in the folder she gave me the last time I saw her rises from where it's been buried under more recent worries. The Facebook profile of a guy I've never met and a note in Mama's handwriting: *"He doesn't know about you. But you should know about him."*

I search for where to start on the long list of questions I've been collecting since getting Peter Mitchell's picture. "What you said before I left." My heart drums, urging me to keep going. "Is it true? Is Baba really not my father?"

The silence on the other end is like gravity, pulling me into it, and I press the phone closer to my ear like that will make her answer faster.

"He's not," Mama whispers. "I'm sorry—I wish I had more time to explain, and someday I will, I promise, but that is not the reason for my call." She takes a deep breath. "Nick's been released. They didn't have enough evidence to hold him, and he's been asking questions. He doesn't know where you are, but you must be careful. You can't come back here, or he will find you and Marcus. It's not safe here."

My eyes burn, and I circle my hand around my throat like I can suffocate the scorching memory of Nick's hands around it. How did the police not have enough evidence? There was a hotel full of it. I led them to Su Ling and the other missing women. If trafficking, kidnapping, and attempted rape isn't enough to hold him, what is?

But I didn't show the police the evidence he left on me. Only Su Ling saw. And Marcus. Guo Mama. My tip was anonymous.

And then there are the pictures on Nick's phone—the ones of me and Marcus. The evidence that sent us both running.

"He should be locked up for the rest of his life. I don't understand."

"When the police found him, he was hurt. He told them you attacked him. We are all sure no one believes him, but they have no other evidence to hold Nick, only others. So now the restaurant is closed, and things are uncertain. Especially since Su Ling worked for us before she disappeared. It doesn't look good." She trails off, her voice thick when she talks again. "I didn't realize the extent of what he was doing, and he threatened me when I asked questions. If I had known, I never would have let you go to L.A. I'm so sorry I didn't stop it. I wish I never married that man."

Old, stale anger crackles in my stomach. I'm sorry she didn't, too, because now Nick has turned everything upside down and inside out.

"I just needed to know you are okay before I go back to Taiwan. And also…"

My breathing is trying to outrun her words.

"I needed you to know I love you, and I'm so proud of you. You are so brave. Guo Mama will keep me updated about you and Marcus. Look after each other. I will see you again."

After she rushes a goodbye and ends the call, I keep the phone at my ear, frozen in the news and in the space between past and present and the fear that holds my two realities together.

I hate Nick more than ever. I hate that he's part of my story. I hate that he's been released. I hate that he lied to the police and blamed me and that he thinks he has the right to ask questions about me. I hate that he will never go away and especially hate that Su Ling and I didn't kill him when we had the chance. But most of all, I hate that I have to tell Marcus any of this. Things have been so good this week. We started over and kind of forgot about anything from before. I haven't had any flashbacks or panic attacks. We've fallen asleep curled together every night. We've made out like we used to, laughing and driving each other to the edge, teasing and torturing ourselves but loving every minute of it because there's no rush. There's no time limit. There's no desperation to hold onto each other because someone could rip us apart. The threat of Nick was gone until this moment, and we were so light. But now, I have to drop this heaviness on Marcus once again. It could crush us this time.

"Mei Li?" Jill's voice calls from the other side of the break room door. "Someone just came in and sat at table seven. I'm two tables over already, and I know you're off, but I could really use your help. I promise not to lust after your boyfriend anymore if you do this for me."

I squeeze my eyes shut for a few seconds then open the door. "I've got it." I grab a tablet from the counter and make my way to table seven, signing in as I walk. I don't look up until I'm in front of the table. In front of a guy with messy dark blond hair and blue eyes that cut through the dim restaurant as they meet mine with a smile that shatters this tiny spot on the planet with its light.

I collect myself, the surprise of seeing Marcus sweeping away my earlier news. Everything is okay. We're safe. Somewhere Nick can't find us. We're together. "Hi. Welcome to

China Isle. My name's Mei Li, and I'll be taking care of you tonight."

"I bet you will." Marcus smirks and sits back in his chair. He crosses his arms over his chest, wiggles his eyebrows. "I fully plan on letting you take care of me tonight."

I bite my bottom lip to keep a straight face. "Can I start you off with something to drink?"

"A nice, tall glass of Mei-Z would be perfect."

"Sir, I'll ask you to leave if you can't behave yourself."

"This *is* behaving myself."

I clench my jaw to keep from smiling, eager to keep up the banter so I don't have to think about how to tell Marcus about Nick. "Are you ready to order?"

"Definitely. Easy. It's my favorite thing at this restaurant. Like, I honestly can't get enough of it. Crave it all day every day."

"Ah. Sweet and sour pork. Great choice." I tap a few buttons on the tablet, my focus decidedly on Marcus in my peripheral vision.

"I don't think she'd appreciate being called that. And she's wayyy better than sweet and sour pork, and I consider myself a connoisseur." He smirks. "Besides…tonight, I'm looking for something a little…spicier, maybe?"

I lean closer, my lips on his ear. "Pantry's empty…"

"Ooh." He turns his head toward me, our noses touching. "The pantry would be the perfect place for me to tell you my news. And then celebrate it."

His words stomp through me, kicking up dust from the news I got earlier, but I breathe in through my nose and slide into the chair across from him. He's practically buzzing, his knee bouncing, fingers fidgeting with his watchband. I lean toward him. "Do you really have news?"

He smiles and nods. "Yeah. Big news."

"You're pregnant."

"I thought I'd just eaten something funky but…yeah. And you're the father, Mei. I didn't know how else to tell you, so I'm just saying it."

"But I'm not ready to be a father."

"I'm fifty-eight weeks, so too bad because I'm about to give birth to some seriously big news." He leans back in the chair, puts his hands over his stomach, spreads his legs and pretends to push.

I laugh again, then stop. "Wait—in all seriousness, why aren't you at work? Don't you work swing tonight? Did you get fired? Don't give birth to that news, please."

"Nooo, but I might after this because I got the news and couldn't wait until 1 AM to tell you. So I left."

"What is it?" I ask, his excitement nudging my curiosity and hope.

He leans forward, his chair legs landing back on the floor. "I got in. Back in, actually."

I frown, searching his face for clues. "Back in where?"

His smile spreads, his eyes lighting up. "Stanford. I got back into Stanford, Mei. Just got an email. And I got my scholarship back. They still want me. Next week, for pre-season."

Marcus's excitement rolls toward me, lifting me out of my chair, and I lean over the table until our faces are inches apart. "Are you serious?!"

"So serious, Mei. Like unbelievably, dead serious." He presses his forehead against mine and takes my face in his hands. "Life could not get any better than it is right now—we're together again and now Stanford."

Stanford.

Realization settles after the explosion of news, and I feel the blood rush from my face. Stanford is close to San Francisco. Too close. Mama's news murmurs through my mind, and my stomach drops away from it, pulling my smile down with it until Marcus frowns at me.

"You okay?"

"Yes!" I blurt, plastering a smile back on my face and sitting back in my chair. I have to pull it together. He can't know. "Just really surprised. This is…sudden, but so exciting!"

"Crazy, yeah? I can't believe it either. Our whole life is about to change. Again. But for the better. We're outta here next week!"

Out of here, headed closer to San Francisco.

"That's…so soon." I say, breathless.

"No more waiting, no more wondering. Just us, starting over in a new place we can call home for a while."

I push down the growing panic spreading like acid through me because I'm going to lie to Marcus. I can't tell him about Nick, and ruin this moment or any future moments. I've taken him from one life already, and I won't do it a second time. He wants Stanford, and I want us, so I'll keep what I know to myself and pray to any and all gods who will listen that Nick never finds us.

CHAPTER 7

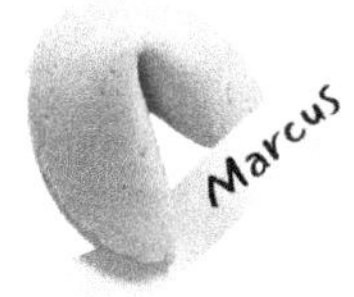

Marcus,

Answers to your 3 questions.

Yes, yes, yes. And once more in case you're confused: yes.

Just below my belly button...mm-hmm. Yep. I'm sure of it.

Maybe, maybe not. You'll have to wait and see.

I love you,

Mei

My autopilot feature is back in action. Thought it broke when we left San Francisco, but as I scan boxes, moving them, stacking them, my head's nowhere near this warehouse. It's already at Stanford. Already on the soccer field. Settling into a new place with Mei in the best of all possible worlds. Wish I could call Dad and tell him. but then again…no, I don't. Our worlds are now two very different places.

I bend and lift a heavy box to burn off the hurt and anger that always slips in when I think about Dad. I toss the box into the passing trailer, not even breaking a sweat. This job has kept me in shape, but that's about it. I definitely won't miss it when I walk away from it next week. Except I'll miss the paycheck. The agreement was that Mei and I would work for Jerry for free rent and a small stipend, but he's paid me every week and paid me well. I've saved a bunch of money. It's not enough, but it'll help us get settled at Stanford. Just not sure where yet, even though we'll be there next week.

I've said a lot of panicked but grateful prayers this week, and my mild panic is the only thing keeping me from wishing we were leaving today. Also, after talking to my coworker on lunch break, I wanna take Mei somewhere cool before we head to Stanford.

He told me the perfect place for a mini vacation. A mini vacation…or a honeymoon. If this is gonna be my new life, I want it with Mei, and thanks to Wen and all her prompting, marriage has crossed my mind about a hundred times, making a few permanent tracks through my head.

My cell phone chirps, and I set down my scanner, pull the phone out of my pocket, and glance at the number. My thumb immediately slides over the button. "Hello?".

"Hi, Marcus? This is Sherina returning your call about on-campus housing."

"Oh—yeah, hey. Thanks for calling me back. Just curious about the process to get into your couples housing. I have a full-ride soccer scholarship, but my girlfriend's coming with me so we need an apartment, and I was wondering if my scholarship could help us get campus housing."

"I'm happy to go over all your options if you have a minute."

I glance around, looking for my manager's orange hair, which is usually pretty easy to spot in a world of cardboard and metal, but he's nowhere, and I gotta take this call, so…if he fires me, he fires me.

I walk down the wide aisle between towering stacks of boxes and forklifts whizzing past me and head outside where there's less beeping. This conversation could mean a place for Mei and me to live. Together. Motorcycle, Stanford, Mei. Happiest Marcus ever.

I ask Sherina a thousand questions, she gives me two thousand answers, and when I hang up, I set my phone on the cement picnic table I've been sitting on, my butt numb because I didn't move so I could catch every detail. But holy freak.

An ant strolls across the cement table, navigating around all the holes that are probably more like craters to him. I wonder what he's after and hope he gets it, because I just got everything I wanted, plus some. If I marry Mei, we can apply for grants for her to go to culinary school. My scholarship will pay most of the rent. If I marry Mei, she stays with me forever, starting right now. If I marry Mei, our life begins officially, and no one can end it. It's ours. Nick can do nothing about it, even if he wasn't in jail. Mei and I can put everything that's happened in the last six months behind us. If Dad thought me dating Mei was crazy, he'll give birth to a donkey when he hears I married her. If I ever talk to him again, which is doubtful.

I blink away from the ant and back into my world where the craters I was navigating this morning have disappeared. I squint into the hazy sun. Marry Mei? Yeah. Definitely. Right now, though? Like…this week?

I scan the gray metal buildings. They're stuck in one place, rust creeping onto them. Doing the same thing they did yesterday and who knows how many days before that.

Not gonna be me. I'm marrying Mei. We're doing this life thing together.

So if I'm gonna marry her, I need to propose. And it has to be like…soon. Tomorrow, actually. We have to be married before Stanford. Six days. It'll take that long for us to get there if I take Mei to San Juan Island. Three days there, two days driving…one day left.

My heart picks up speed and takes a crash course through my head. Every corner I turn has a flashing "MARRY HER" sign, and there are no brakes on any of these thoughts—just full throttle toward Mei.

I snatch my phone and jog back inside the warehouse, looking for orange hair, which I spot bobbing above row 38. "Darrell!" I yell, and he whirls around, his orange safety vest reflecting the florescent lights.

"Yeah?"

"So…change of plans. Today's gonna be my last day."

I don't remember driving home because my thoughts were nowhere on this motorcycle, nowhere close to Seattle, but I bump into the driveway, cut the engine, and grab my back-pack before racing to the cottage. I toss my warehouse name badge in the garbage bin as I pass. Good riddance to swing shifts and the required twice a month graveyard. If I stay up all night from now on, it'll be because Mei's keeping me up.

The idea pumps adrenaline through my veins and swims through my head. I smile to myself and unlock the door, tossing my backpack on the table and looking around the cottage for proposal inspiration. Silence pounds against my ears, and the next six days stretch in front of me like a timeline. Propose tomorrow. Get married day after. Honeymoon on San Juan Island. Life could not get any better. I mean, okay…maybe there are a few things I'm dying to add, but then I'll really have it all. If Guo can marry us like she hinted at doing before we left San Francisco.

I flop on the couch and scoot forward, elbows on my knees. Phone clutched to my ear, I wait for her to answer. Come on, come on…

"Wei?"

"Guo?"

A gasp, a shriek. "Marcus Miller, is that you, boy?"

"Guo! I miss you!"

"Oh, you. Not as much as I miss you and Mei Li. It's too boring around here. Nothing but tourists and fried rice. Bah."

I laugh. "You should come to Seattle, then. Like…day after tomorrow, maybe? Wednesday?"

"Why should I come so quickly, Marcus Miller…?"

I collapse back against the couch, running my fingers through my hair as I smile at the ceiling. "I got back into Stanford so…I'm gonna ask Mei to marry me tomorrow. And I want you to marry us. You mentioned once you could do it for us if we ever needed it…"

I flinch when she shrieks rapid-fire Chinese in my ear. Then I laugh and swear. "Wow. That was a reaction."

"I AM SO HAPPY, MARCUS MILLER! You just know exactly how to make all the women in your life so happy."

"I got your excitement loud and clear. And it might be the last thing I ever hear." My heart squirms a little, pushing tears too close to the surface. I've missed Guo's energy and shady guidance in my life. "Think you can do it? I only want the Love Hunter to marry us, no one else. I'll even give you full credit, even though I had serious doubts."

"Yes! Marry her, please! It is all I will ever ask for. Yes, yes, yes. You and Mei Li were meant to be together. I knew it long before you ever met."

"How's that?"

"There was an invisible red thread tied from your ankle to hers. It got very tangled with all the different paths you took around each other, but it's straight now, and it will never break. You are meant to be. I see it, you feel it. I'm right. The end."

"I definitely feel it, Guo. Wish I'd listened to you a lot sooner so I could have had Mei in my life for longer, but now…she'll be in it forever."

"Oh you. It melts my heart to hear you speak about her. I told you that you would love her deeply, and I hear it in your voice. It has happened. You love her more than even yourself, and I will be in Seattle on Wednesday to make it permanent."

CHAPTER 8

Marcus: Jobless + no Mei = Slowest day in my personal history. Can you get off early? Pull the fire alarm? Fake an injury? Just something that will get you home faster?? Anywayyyyy…continuing our game of Go Fish…

Mei: If you win, I'll do something minimally criminal and come home early.

Marcus: DO YOU HAVE A GREEN SHARK?

Mei: ………go fish.

Marcus: *#!@#

Jerry's vintage truck rounds the corner into the neighborhood, and I smile. Finally. I've been at the restaurant since 11AM and was ready to come home to Marcus before I even left him to go to work. Since he quit his job at the warehouse yesterday, I've schemed ways of going home early all day, but Jerry needed help with inventory. It took a long time, and he kept checking the clock, then asking me to cross check everything. I can't be annoyed with him after everything he's done for us and it's a good thing he had me double check my numbers; my head was home with Marcus, laughing so hard at something he said that I had to run to the bathroom or pee my pants. Dancing around the kitchen in our pajamas and seeing who could slide the farthest across the wood floor in socks. I win every time, and I bet he practiced while I was gone.

We pull into Jerry's drive, but the house is dark. No porch lights, no yellow glow in any of the windows, and I frown. "It's so dark. Wen never goes to bed this early," I say, gathering my satchel and jacket.

Jerry waves his hand. "Oh, she's probably tired tonight since she stayed up way too late listening to one of her true crime podcasts last night." He glances at the gate that leads to the cottage, then the dashboard clock. "I'm sure Marcus will be very glad to have you home, so go put him out of his misery." He looks at the gate again, and I almost expect Marcus to be standing there, but he's not.

"Have a good night, Jerry, and thanks for the ride. I hope Wen doesn't have nightmares from all those podcasts." I shake my head. "There's no way I could listen to those. I like to pretend crime doesn't exist."

"Me too." He throws me a sympathetic smile, and I wonder how much Guo Mama has told him about my past. They've never said a word about it, and for that, I'm grateful. He and Wen have been like parents to Marcus and me, and my heart has grown roots here in the tiny cottage in their backyard, knowing they're steps away. "We're going to miss you. Thanks for watching out for us."

"Thanks for your help at the restaurant, Mei Li. I think

you'll like the bonus you'll get with your final paycheck. I wish it could be a bribe to make you stay but I'm happy for you kids."

"Please don't, Jerry. You've already left money on our counter every week, and that was never part of the deal."

"I can't help it. I like you two. It's my only way to say it."

I wipe away tears that slip out. "Jerry, that's just so—"

"Now, now. We aren't talking like this yet. I don't like it." He checks a text on his phone and nods toward the gate. "Besides, I'm sure Marcus is waiting so we can talk later, Mei Li."

I say goodnight and slip out of the truck, walking toward the gate, but pause when the motion sensor light that usually flicks on doesn't. Hurrying through the gate and down the path, I squint in the darkness, but as I round the corner of the house, something crunches under my right foot. I freeze, imagining my shoe landing on one of the giant garden snails that also shares our path. When I dare lift my shoe, a crushed fortune cookie lays in shards on the brick. I brush crumbs off the bricks, so ants won't invade, then pick up the pieces and toss them in the garbage bin on my way to the cottage. But I stop when there's another fortune cookie in the middle of the bricks. And another one a few steps later, a whole trail of them stretching straight to the cottage door.

Frowning through a smile, I pick up each one on my way to the door. When I open it, my eyes follow the trail of fortune cookies spiraling around the room toward the table. But the only sign of Marcus is the lit candle with a book next to it. He's been reading by candlelight lately—something he said his dad does.

"Marcus?" I call, shutting the door behind me. I drop my bag and the pile of cookies on the table right next to Buddha. He's wearing a tiny paper party hat, and there's a heart drawn with metallic silver Sharpie on his belly: a note taped to it that says OPEN ME.

My stomach leaps at Marcus's handwriting. I peel the note off Buddha and carefully unfold it: *"Mei Li Miller has a nice "ring" to it, don't you think?"*

My hand flies to my mouth. I read the note again. Mei Li Miller. Mei Li Miller. Ring. RING?! What ring? Where? I look around, but it's just Buddha on the table. Mei Li Miller?!

The bathroom door swings open, and I spin around as Marcus drops to both knees in front of me and takes my hand.

"Marcus…what are you doing?" My hand goes to my throat, unsure whether to cover my eyes to hide the tears threatening to spill or cover my mouth to prevent the squeal-sob that might come out. "What does this mean?" I hold up the note. "What are you saying…?"

He smiles, its light beaming up and spreading around me. "I'm saying…" He reaches into his pocket, pulls out a fortune cookie, and holds it up to me. His eyes never leave my face as I open it and slide out the paper where Marcus has handwritten: *YOU WILL MARRY MARCUS MILLER AND LIVE HAPPILY EVER AFTER?*

I stare at the paper. Read it again.

"What are you saying?" My voice climbs, chased by hope, surprise, and a surge of emotion. "Are you saying now, or soon, or in two years, or…?"

"I'm saying marry me. Tomorrow." He grins. "I'm down on not just one but both knees, begging you to say something like, 'Of course I'll marry you because I'm so madly in love with you, I'd be homeless with you for the rest of my life, or live on only turkey sandwiches, or ride a motorcycle to China if it means I get to marry you'." His eyes spread neon blue around me. "Or you could just say yes if that's easier."

"Yes!" I blurt, nodding, crying, laughing. "YES! And all those other things but mostly just so many yeses. YES! Yes, yes, yes!"

Marcus hangs his head before looking up at me again. "This could've gotten super weird if you'd said no."

I throw myself at him, knocking him backward on the floor with a grunt and squealing into his neck. I kiss him until I'm breathless.

"I love you, Mei," he breathes. "Mei Li Miller…"

I squeal again, grabbing his face with both hands, and take complete control of his mouth.

He rolls me onto my back, kneeling over me, and slips a sharpie from his pocket. The smile lines around his mouth are deep and full of pride, and he takes my left hand and draws a circle around my ring finger.

CHAPTER 9

Mei: I can see you through the blinds, but you can't see me. You clean up nice, Marcus Miller. Can we be married yet?!

My head snaps up when the back gate swings open, and I shoot to my feet, standing in front of the evidence like I can hide the Just Married streamers I made out of an old t-shirt and a Sharpie. But Johnny strides through the gate, a smirk on his face. "Never thought I'd miss that gorgeous face as much as I have." He stops and throws his arms out. "Bring it in, loser. Bring it in, bring it in."

When my brain catches up to what's happening, I jog across the yard and pull him to me for the first time in our friendship. We pat each other hard on the back, and a lump swells in my throat, so I slap him harder. "What are you doing here?"

"Got recruited."

"Did you save some love for me, Marcus Miller?"

I pull away from Johnny and watch Guo teeter through the gate, smiling so big I can see all her teeth. I scoop her into my arms and lift her off her feet, my eyes stinging.

"When Guo told us what was about to go down," Johnny says beside us, "she said she could use a couple of witnesses, and there was no way I was gonna miss this. I just want you to know, I dropped a fairly hot second date so we could leave for the airport at six AM to get here in time. Six AM, Miller." He gets in my face. "If that doesn't prove my love for you, there's nothing that will. Hope Mei Li knows she comes in a solid second place to me."

Johnny and I laugh, and I grab him and bring him in for another hug. "I have missed you, brother."

Someone squeals, and we break the hug as Lin pushes through the gate, wheeling a carry-on suitcase behind her.

"I cannot believe this is for real! I feel like I'm in some kind of rom-com right now." Lin's excitement is at an eleven and she might explode if it amps any higher.

I turn to Guo. "You really can make everything happen."

She pats my face. "I am so happy about this. I wanted to tell everyone but...you know. I honor your privacy and safety."

I wrap my arms around her again and want to pick her up and hold her on my shoulders like she just won the championship game for us, but Lin steps up.

"I don't recall you asking my permission to marry my best friend, but if you let me in on the hugging action, I'll give it to you." Lin holds out her arms.

I laugh and lean down to give her a full two-armed hug.

"I'm just going to say this once and never again, even if I think it, and I definitely will: I am wildly jealous of Mei Li. Also...you smell...wow. And muscles and face and legs and...okay." She steps back, waves her hands. "Done. I'm so done. You're all Mei Li's. I just remembered. Taken. Solidly taken. Permission granted. I can live vicariously. I'm really good at it by now."

She beams at me, and I smile, rubbing the back of my neck and hoping Mei will come out soon. Like, right now.

"Where's the lucky lady, anyway? She's going to *freak* when she sees me, and I'm just so ready for it."

"Inside." I point toward Jerry and Wen's house, and Lin takes off running, her suitcase bouncing behind her. It takes under two seconds for squealing to erupt from the open sliding glass door.

"This is for you and Xiao Mei," Guo says, holding out an envelope. "So tuck it somewhere very safe. And this," she says, holding up a piece of paper from some weird online ministry service, "is proof I can make you and Mei Li very official. Also, I have a slightly forged marriage license, but no matter. It will work. Desperate times."

Guo checks her watch. "We were later than planned, and it's time we got this party started." She laughs at her own slang. "You go finish getting ready. When it's time, Lin will walk Mei Li down the aisle." She waves her hand toward the brick path between Jerry and Wen's house and our cottage. "Let's do this, Marcus Miller." She pats my chest, chuckling, and shuffles toward the house. "I will go say hi to my brother, I guess."

Johnny slings his arm around my shoulder. This whole scene turns into a still shot I'll never forget: gray sky, green ruffled trees arching over us like a canopy, Guo bright purple, Lin red and orange, and when Mei comes out of the house, she'll set this place, and me, on fire.

I take the card Guo gave me and put it in the seat of the motorcycle as Johnny inspects my streamers.

"Not bad, man. Looks like you've figured out life on your

own. I'm impressed." He points at my shirt. "You're even wearing a real shirt. Looking good, Miller, as usual, but you're missing one thing, brother."

He digs around in the backpack he set on the ground when he came in and pulls out a tie. The one I used to wear on game days.

I take it from him. "How?"

"You think you're the only sneaky one?" He dusts off his shirt. "You're not."

Staring at it, I laugh and wonder how he managed to get into The Clubhouse. I resist the urge to check if it smells like my closet.

Johnny snatches it from me and wraps it around my neck, tying and adjusting it. "Let's get you married, Miller."

We walk toward the circle of trees, just enough room for all of us to gather, and he nudges me with his elbow. "You nervous, man? This is seriously crazy."

I run my fingers through my hair, and Johnny swats my hand away, fixes it. "Not nervous to marry Mei, just…want it to be perfect, and this is so far from it."

Johnny looks around. "Seems pretty downright perfect, if you ask me. I get it's not the usual way. But different isn't a bad thing. And you…?" He smiles, squinting at me. "You're different. In a good way. Like you've gone and grown up on me. Like you're a real man now. Welcome. It's a great place to be. I've been here in Man-land for a while. Got everything ready for you." He sniffs dramatically, then busts up laughing, and I flick his ear. "I mean…"—he gestures at the motorcycle "I assume you're in the gentleman's club by now since you got that and are all shacked up with your girl…"

"We waited," I say, glancing over my shoulder to check for Mei. "Saw your disasters and didn't want any of it for us."

"Wow. Alright, then. Alright, okay. Good for you, man.

Just proves my theory that when Marcus Miller says he's gonna do something—or not do something—just stay out of his way, 'cause it's gonna happen just like that." He pats my face and smiles.

The lump in my throat stretches, and I pull Johnny into the third hug in twenty minutes. "Thanks for being here. For being in my life through all the craziness." I let go of him and swallow hard. There's one more thing I gotta ask because it's eating at me. "You seen him?"

Johnny nods, knowing exactly who I'm asking about. "Yeah. Been by to see him a few times. He'll be okay."

"Will you check on him every now and then? Just text me and let me know he's okay? I can't talk to him for so many reasons, but just wanna know."

Johnny squeezes my shoulder. "Easy. You got it."

"I owe you."

"Uhh, yeah, you do. But we can figure all that out later, 'cause right now, you're getting married." Our focus shifts to the path where Guo shuffles toward us. I rush over and take her arm in mine to help her the rest of the way.

She pats my arm and chuckles. "I mentioned I am a love hunter, right? I forgot to mention I am a very good one. Probably the best."

Before I can respond, my eyes catch the shimmer of Mei and Lin skipping toward us through the tree tunnel. Lin is humming an off-key wedding song, and Mei is laughing, the sound ringing all around us. She's wearing a traditional white Chinese dress like the ones in Guo's shop, the golden embroidery reflecting through the tree limbs. But her smile lights the whole backyard, and mine stretches toward it, my hand over my heart as I blink against tears and light and another perfect still shot.

Lin and Mei slow, ducking under branches, and Mei hugs

Lin, who goes and stands beside Johnny, Jerry, and Wen on the grass. Mei approaches me, biting her lip, and I lean down to kiss her, but Guo slaps my chest before our lips connect.

"Oh, no you don't," she scolds while Lin and Johnny laugh. "Plenty of time for that later. For now, you wait and listen to me because I am just so happy and love being so right." Everyone laughs again, Guo included. "I saw this coming, you know. Many months ago, I asked you to ask Magic 8 a question, and here we are. Magic 8 and I make a good team. But Guo always knows." She beams, and I squeeze Mei's hand as she leans into my side.

"Now, I would like you to face each other." She motions at us, and I turn to Mei, holding her hands and staring into her eyes. *"Hey. I love you. 365 forever."*

She smiles up at me. *"I love you more than whatever's more than 365 forever."*

"We're really doing this."

Her eyes sparkle. *"It's exactly what I want to be doing. Perfect."*

Guo says a few things in Chinese, and I send another silent message to Mei. *"You're it, Me."* But she doesn't get to respond before Guo interrupts our private conversation, and I smile and say "I do" out loud. *"I so, so do,"* I add just to Mei.

She says "I do" when it's her turn, not taking her eyes from mine, and Guo asks us to exchange rings. I don't have the time or money to buy Mei the ring she deserves, but I have something that will work for now. I can afford perfect later.

I hold out the silver ring with an infinity symbol joining the two sides. "A placeholder until I can buy you a real wedding ring," I say, sliding it onto her ring finger.

She holds her hand out so she can look at it. "This is

perfect, Marcus. I don't want another ring. Only this one." Her smile glints off the silver. "I got you a ring, too."

Lin hands it to her, and when Mei slides it onto my finger, I smile at a mood band just like the ones Guo sells in her shop.

"So I always know how you're feeling," Mei says.

I look at it and meet her eyes. *"Hey, Mei Li Miller."*

"Not yet! Hurry up! I'm dying right now." She wiggles her knees. And then my eyes tell her exactly what I want to happen as soon as we get out of here, and her eyebrows rise to the heavens.

Guo clicks her tongue. "Please. Save the dirty talk for later. Leave me out of it." She chuckles, and Mei's face burns, but I'm gonna make these thoughts very public if Guo doesn't hurry up.

"So," Guo says with a grin, bringing us back to the actual moment. "Xiao Mei. Are you ready to not be Mei Li Zhang anymore?"

Mei blinks back tears, her smile faltering. "I never really was, so Mei Li Miller is the only version of me I want to be."

Guo searches her face, then nods once. "Today, you are changing your name for a new life—one you choose."

She and Guo share an unspoken understanding. "I'm so ready," Mei says.

Guo throws her hands in the air. "Then my magical paper and I say, 'Ta-da!' You two are legally married! You are now Mei Li Miller! And you!" She turns to me. "You are still Marcus Miller, but now you can kiss Mei Li as your wife."

I smile down at Mei, then lean in, putting all my feelings into a kiss that brings her to her tiptoes with her arms around my neck. We keep it up until Johnny groans, and he and Lin move away, making gagging sounds.

"Okay, yep—got it, Miller," he calls. "Or Millers. Whatever. Do this on your own time."

We break apart, and I reach for Guo, wrapping my arms around her. Mei joins our hug, followed by Johnny and Lin. A big, laughing circle of relieved, happy people as Jerry and Wen clap and laugh. Mei swipes tears from her face and Lin's as they hug and laugh-cry.

"Thank you, Guo," I whisper into her ear, and she waves her hand, dabbing at her face.

"Oh, you. I love you, boy. Now go before you see me cry."

I kiss the top of her head, hug Jerry and Wen, and grab Mei's hand. We take off running through the trees, up the path, Mei holding her dress, so she doesn't trip.

"You ready?" she asks, wiggling her eyebrows.

I hand her helmet to her. "Been ready since the night I saw you trip on the sidewalk."

Mei's eyes widen. "You saw that?"

"Oh, I saw it," I say, pulling on my helmet. She lifts hers and stops, inspecting the Sharpie design I drew on it with Wen's help—a replica of Mei's tattoo with my initials beneath it.

Her wide eyes rise to mine. "When did you do this?"

"Last night. When I couldn't sleep because I was too excited about today."

"Marcus, this is…"

"Our official logo." I smile at her and yank off my tie. I stuff it in Mei's bag that Johnny strapped to the back of the motorcycle over the streamers since only one bag fits in the seat compartment.

Mei puts on her helmet. I buckle it for her and tug the strap toward me, our lips meeting.

She squeals against my kiss, and I laugh, lifting her onto the bike. I slide in front of her and hold my phone above us to take a selfie. Mei flashes her wedding ring, her mouth open wide in a smile big enough for both of us. I type a quick text to Johnny and Lin on the same thread:

Marcus: Thanks for being here. Catch up later. Millers out.

I send the message, and when I reach for the key, Mei grabs my hand from behind. She sets my hand on her knee and pulls the Sharpie from my pocket. Concentrating, she writes **6-21** under my wrist bone, traces and retraces it until it's thick and bold.

I meet her eyes over my shoulder as she talks to me with hers. *"Official best day of my life. #1 spot forever."*

"Knew I'd take that spot." I grin and rev the engine before racing out of the side yard and down the driveway, our Just Married streamers flapping in the wind.

The only thing that's following us this time.

CHAPTER 10

Everything feels different. My arms are wrapped tightly around Marcus from behind, exactly like they were on our way to Seattle. But now, as we leave the city behind us, there's no question of what-ifs and maybes. No question of whether he wants me, because now he's all mine. Forever, officially.

I wrap my arms tighter around him, and he lifts one of my hands and kisses it. He laces his fingers through mine as he drives toward the undisclosed location. He won't even give me a hint. All I know is, our top-secret honeymoon spot is in the opposite direction from Stanford and San Francisco.

My mind floats back over this most perfect day and all the other surprises it held, like Lin and Johnny and Guo Mama. Lin brought me the most beautiful dress, curled my hair, and did my makeup. We laughed and cried, and she begged me to let her marry Marcus. I denied her request without hesitation, and my giddiness had almost sent me flying out the door toward him, but Guo Mama had pulled me aside, away from Lin, and asked if I'd told Marcus about Nick.

"No," I'd said, my voice shaking as anxiety stacked in my chest again.

"Why not, Xiao Mei?"

"Because this is the life he wants. And the life I want. I want to be with him, and I want to be part of him getting everything he wants." Tears welled in my eyes, threatening to streak my mascara, so Guo Mama smiled and said she understood. She'd brushed a stray tear off my cheek, warning me to be careful and stay safe. I promised I would, and then I followed her out of the house, Lin holding my arm to steady me when all I wanted to do was run to Marcus.

I rest my chin on his shoulder now, watching Washington blur past us, and I smile to myself as anticipation rustles in my stomach. On all the rides before, dread, fear, and uncertainty rode heavy in my thoughts since we didn't really know what was coming next. But now, I have a pretty good idea about what's next. There's no dread or uncertainty like when we were driving away from San Francisco. There are definitely nerves, but they're mixing with excitement and wanting, making a sparkler of my stomach.

My life's about to change again, and I notice everything like it's my last time as this version of myself—the rough road, the chill in the air that makes me huddle into Marcus's back, and my legs hugging his hips in a way that feels more possessive now that he's legally and officially mine. *Forever.*

The wind pushes my dress up my thighs, and Marcus glances down, gripping the handlebars a little tighter.

Anticipation splits me open a little further, and I would happily stop anywhere, but Marcus wants everything to be perfect. There's probably a hundred diagrams and checklists floating through his head while very different visuals float through mine. I wish he'd just let go for once, but he has his plans and surprises, and I have unbearable waiting.

I press against his back, my hands drifting up his chest. He puts one hand over them, but I slip one hand out, drifting it down his stomach, across it, my fingertips playing with the hem of his shirt and sliding under.

His stomach muscles tense, but he doesn't push my hand away, so I let it wander, testing his limits. Smiling, I bite my lower lip when his knuckles go white, surprised when he veers off the road and flips down the kickstand.

He hops off the bike, ripping off his helmet, and walks a few steps before turning back to me, face flushed.

I smile and shrug. "Why'd you stop?"

He closes his eyes and swears, fighting a smile. "Because you're driving me *crazy*. And you know it." The smile breaks through, and he runs his fingers through his hair. "I swear you're gonna get us killed if you keep doing that. And I really don't wanna die today. Not yet anyway."

I smirk. "Marcus Miller, I've played by your rules for months, and now there *are* none."

He takes my hands in his and pins them behind me. "Tell your hormones to back down a little longer and then, when we get where we're going, release them like the beasts they are." His smile catches the few rays of sun poking through the clouds. "I want them to run so free. So very free. But not until we're there."

"But I want you so bad right now." I look into his eyes and read his thoughts, which hover at the surface and send heat up my neck. Oh, he has plans.

He rests his mouth against my ear. "I'm gonna show you just how much I want you. Just not here on the side of a two-lane highway in the middle of nowhere. So, if you want more, you're gonna keep your hands to yourself until we get to where we're going." He lets me go and grins down at me as I groan.

"Seriously? How long until we're there? My hormones are wondering."

"Not telling." He wiggles his eyebrows at me, climbs back on the seat, and buckles his helmet. "Let's get outta here before Big Foot finds us. I hear he likes Asian girls, especially incredibly hot ones. Also..." He smiles at the road ahead of us, then turns it on me. "I'm imagining you naked, so the sooner we get there, the sooner it becomes reality."

———

Three agonizingly long hours and a ferry ride later, we're driving through a gorgeous town on a winding road, far from anywhere either of us has ever been. All new territory in every way. We had time to change on the ferry, and I opted for jeans and a loose sweater while Marcus switched from slacks to jeans but kept on his button down. I'd tried and failed a few times to talk him into finding a secluded spot on the ferry, but when Marcus puts his mind to something, there are no detours.

The sun is setting over the ocean, the orange glow slicing through the trees as we pass patches of forest that open to a rocky shoreline. Marcus checks his phone at an intersection, and we turn left toward the ocean. The road winds through more trees, and the lights of the town fade behind us. A few minutes later, we pull up to a gate.

I peek around him at the private driveway through decorative metal rails. "How did you afford a mansion?"

He shakes his head. "Overtime on three graveyards, that's how." He punches in a code on the keypad, and the gate swings open.

Marcus drives slowly through the gate and down the lane.

He rounds a corner to a beach house set on a hill above the ocean, completely encircled by trees.

"How did you find this place?" I ask. My eyes climb the steps to the front door and move along the wraparound porch, my nerves and excitement flaring.

"Spent hours on Wen's laptop while you were working your last day. And here we are…"

He pulls up to the garage and taps his phone screen. The garage door lifts, and he parks the bike, cutting the engine.

"And…here we are." Marcus hangs his helmet on the handlebars and grins over his shoulder at me.

I slide off the bike, hang my helmet on the handlebar, then slip back onto the seat, facing him. "So…release the hormones?" My stomach tightens, and the garage light flicks off as a breeze slips between us, ruffling Marcus's hair.

His nose brushes mine. We look into each other's eyes in the dim light from the sunset, and I scoot forward, sliding into his lap. I kiss him slowly, like I'm leading him down a winding path.

He melts into me, tugging me closer. His hands slip under my shirt, up my back, pulling the sweater over my head. One hand tosses the sweater over the handlebars behind me while the other glides over my bare skin, spreading fire.

Finally.

I deepen the kiss, unbuttoning his shirt, never breaking contact. We mold together, our mouths hungry and eager for each other until he pulls back, breathless, his mouth hot on my ear. "This bike's gonna know way more about us than it should if we keep this up."

I close my eyes as his hand runs up my neck, tangling in my hair.

"We have a whole house to ourselves. Where we can do

anything we want for three days, no interruptions." His smile spreads against my temple, and sparks zing through me.

He winds my legs tighter around his waist then holds me as he slides off the bike. I wrap my arms around his neck as he carries me toward the door.

"Should we grab our bags?" I ask.

He hits the garage door button, and it closes behind us as we walk up the steps. "I've got the essentials in my pocket..."

"What are you saying, Marcus Miller?" My fingers curl into the hair at his neck.

"I'm saying we might be doing things that don't require clothes, and I am very prepared."

"Do things like...?

"I don't know." He kisses my neck as he climbs the stairs. "Catch up on a couple TV shows. Bird watch. Make Thanksgiving dinner six months early."

I tighten my arms around his neck, laughing as he pushes open the door. Inside the beach house, a wall of windows overlooks the ocean, trees bowing all around it. An orange smudge of a fading sun hangs above the dark line of ocean in the distance, the only light coming into the room. We're nothing but shadows in the glow.

But my mind leaps to what comes next now that we're finally here, and fireworks explode in my stomach, hot and tingly. It was easy to flirt and drive Marcus close to the edge when we were on the road, but now...

My eyes meet his, our chests warm against each other. "So what should we do now that I've released my hormones? They're running all over the place, and I'm not even going to try to control them now..."

He grins, and I hold my breath when his fingers play with my bra, the only thing still between us. When the clasp releases, I slip it off and watch his face.

His eyes drop to my bare chest, and he swears under his breath, and rushes through the shadowy living area, his hands roaming my bare back, down to my backside. His mouth is hot, hungry, and I melt into him. When we reach the bedroom, he lowers me to the bed, his hands exploring my body.

"I want you, Mei." His hands find mine, fingers lacing together and stretching across the mattress as his mouth moves down my neck, lower. We've been in this place before, pushing limits, but now he's not holding back, and the heat builds between us until the weight of his body presses out a memory of Nick. I squeeze my eyes shut to push it back down, but a word crawls up my throat and out. "Wait!"

Marcus jerks his head up hovering over me, catching his breath while his hand runs across my face. "Are you okay?" He pushes himself to his knees above me. "What's wrong?"

"I..." I'm breathless trying to run from the memory of Nick throwing me onto the bed, his body suffocating. "I don't know." I whisper, and he searches my face before lowering his forehead to my chest.

"Did I scare you?" he asks. The question flits around me as I steady my breathing. "I'm so sorry, Mei. I got caught up in...everything. Didn't think about how triggering this could be."

"Please don't apologize," I say, tears gathering in my eyes. "Everything's great. So good—amazing—and...finally, we're here. I'm just..." I don't want to say the word because I've been the one teasing him all week long, frustrated that he wouldn't lose it over me, but now he's on the edge, ready to leap, and I'm the one backing away from the cliff. "I love you. I trust you. I just didn't realize..." Didn't know Nick is still ruining every perfect thing in my life. I thought I was over it after our week of making out and wishing and wanting to speed past his limits.

He looks up, reading my eyes, his face softening as his hand smooths my forehead. "You don't have to say it, Mei. I know there are things that still haunt you." His eyes hold mine in the gray light. "Also, if I'm being honest, I get that you're nervous because I am, too. Have been all day." His hand cradles the back of my neck, weaving into my hair. "At least I was until I saw you like this and my brain shut off." He smiles, kisses me slowly, deeply, like he's reaching inside me to stroke my panic. He pauses, his eyes staring into mine. "Let's slow things down, yeah? We've got forever to do this. So you're in charge—you decide when you're ready." He smiles against my neck and rolls off me. "I don't need any advance notice—I'm ready whenever. But you know I can wait, too. So, so good at waiting." He pulls me into him, his hand stroking my back, my head on his chest, and I wonder, not for the first time, how, in my world of bad luck, I ever got this lucky.

———

I smile at the dark ceiling, watching the moon throw shadows through the window. Marcus is sprawled on his back beside me, his arm over his forehead, breathing deeply in his sleep. It's a sound I fell in love with our first night in the cottage, even if it was from the top bunk.

We're definitely not in separate beds now. I roll into his side, reliving the last six hours. After my panic attack, Marcus held me, and we talked about our wedding day, the craziness of the last month, and how great it was to see Johnny, Lin, and Guo Mama. And then he'd told me all about the research he'd done for this moment—all the books with the covers torn off he'd read alone in his top bunk. He'd smiled into my neck, and I'd scooted up so I could hold his face in both hands as I'd kissed him.

"So now you're an expert."

He'd grinned. "Uhh…more like a well-read amateur. Who really, *really* wants to learn but is insanely nervous."

He'd gotten honest about his fears, and as he talked, I'd traced his mouth with my fingertip, drawn into his world. It had led to my own moment of honesty when I'd slipped out of the sheet he'd wrapped around me. His eyes had sparked, and we'd made out, our hands and mouths teasing until our nerves had sputtered and gone quiet.

I bite my lip, my smile widening at the ceiling. Marcus taught me things I didn't even know about myself last night. He was patient, gentle, careful, and when there was finally nothing between us, he created a new space in my heart, just for him. After, we'd lain facing each other in the dark, smiling and amazed at where we'd gone together.

My body is sore in new places, but I'm overflowing with love and gratitude. I feel bad for any girl who doesn't have a Marcus for her first time. Or all the times after that.

The moonlight still glitters above us, but thoughts of another dark room in L.A. move across my mind, blocking the light. I yank my thoughts back into this silvery, moonlit room where, last night, Marcus proved that he and Nick are two different species.

I wiggle my toes and run my fingers lightly over the words he wrote in Sharpie around my belly button after our first time: "WHOA" and beneath it "Day 1 of ∞."

I hold up my left hand, moving it around so the infinity ring glints in the shadows. My grin stretches my whole face, even though I should be sound asleep after last night. But my mind refuses to quiet, so I slide my hand over Marcus's bare chest, my eyes still on the ring as I rest my mouth on his ear. "Wake up, sleepyhead…"

I kiss his earlobe, and he stirs, mumbling something unintelligible. His hand slides across his stomach to my waist, and he rolls into me, his mouth pressing against my neck.

"Hey, baby." He kisses my throat, up to my chin, whispering as he goes. "Sorry I fell asleep so fast, but… kind of a busy night."

I run my fingers through his hair, holding him to me. "I have the perfect way to wake you up because I don't want to waste time sleeping…"

He pulls back, his eyebrows raised. I grab his hand and tug him up and across the mattress. Snatching one of the robes hanging on the closet door, I wrap it around myself before handing him one.

Pulling on his robe, he glances at the clock on the nightstand. "You know it's three AM, right?"

I nod, grinning as I lead him and his sluggish feet to the hot tub on the deck overlooking the ocean. Cool air weaves around my legs, the wooden deck smooth beneath my feet as I step toward the hot tub, reaching for the belt on my robe.

But Marcus grabs my hand and pulls me to him. "No way."

I look up at his face, which is surrounded by messy spikes of hair my hands created last night. "Have something against hot tubs at three AM?"

"I absolutely love hot tubs at three AM with a naked you, but hot tubs are meant to warm you up after you've taken a dip in the ocean."

"No time like the present for a swim?" I ask with my eyes.

He scans the quiet ocean and the private boardwalk to a dock on an inlet. "No time like three AM for a dare."

Goosebumps scatter over my skin when a breeze winds up through my robe. "Okay…."

"You'll get your hot tub time only if we drop these robes, run down that boardwalk, and jump off the dock. And you have to stay in for at least two minutes."

"Do you realize there are killer whales in that water? Right there?" I jab my finger at the ocean.

"Yeah, well, unlike Big Foot, they're not into Asian girls. I personally don't get it, but…"

"Are you serious right now?"

"You woke me up at three AM *not* for the reason I was hoping, so yeah, dead serious."

I step closer, hand on his belt. "Take your own dare, and maybe all your three AM dreams will come true."

He pulls his belt, and his robe drops to the deck. I shriek when he tugs my belt, trying to dart out of reach, but he yanks it before running down the deck stairs, a white streak in the dark. My robe slides off and I chase him down the steps along the cliffside to the boardwalk, laughing like a crazy girl at his white bum glowing against the dark smudges of trees. A few seconds later, a splash echoes through the air, followed by a string of curse words. My stomach knots. The end of the dock leers at me, and my legs tense, but Marcus chants from the water. "Faster, Mei! Don't stop. Get in this water NOW! HUSTLE, MILLER!"

I squeal, plunging into icy water. Fear about what's beneath me shoots me to the surface, and I burst out of lapping waves, gasping and shrieking. "So—*cold!*" I yell through clenched teeth.

Marcus whoops, swimming toward me, and pulls me against him as we tread water, sputtering and laughing. Moonlight shimmers around us like we're in a spotlight, just two silhouettes in a very, very dark ocean.

I tread faster, and Marcus laughs, our legs tangling.

"You ever done this before?" he asks, breathless.

"Never. And I won't, ever again." My teeth chatter, and I wind my arms around his neck, pressing my cold, wet body to his to find warmth. "What about you?" I ask through a shiver, and he holds me against him, his hand splayed across my back.

"Only with ugly soccer guys." He rests his forehead against mine, nudging my nose with his. Our legs and feet kick each other. "They didn't have anything I wanted to see. And I definitely didn't get this close to them. But you?" He smiles. "Watching you run down that dock like you owned the place kinda revved me up. If we didn't have to tread to stay alive, we'd be doing something else right now."

I wriggle out of his arms and splash him before twisting and swimming toward the dock.

"You wanna play, Mei?" he calls as he swims toward me, a gleam in his eye.

"You forget I'm connected to the mafia," I call back, changing direction to outswim him, but my stiff, jittery doggy paddle isn't fast enough.

He lunges, and I squeal when he hooks me around the waist and yanks my back to his chest. "You're going down, Mrs. Miller," he says in my ear, wrapping his legs around my waist and dragging me underwater with him.

We surface a few seconds later, his arms still around me. We spit salt water and swipe at our eyes, laughing and breathless. He turns me to face him. "What you gonna do now, Mei?" His hands glide up my legs to my thighs, and he grips them, wrapping them around his waist. One hand presses my lower back, the other keeps us afloat. "What's your escape plan? It's just you, me, and all the killer whales under us."

I squeeze my thighs against his ribs, and he groans, dropping his forehead to my shoulder. "You're gonna kill me. Gotcha." His hand slides along the curve of my back, flexing over my backside. I close my eyes when his mouth skims my neck, leaving a trail of heat, until something brushes my leg, and I jolt in Marcus's arms, screaming and thrashing. "Did you feel that?" I shriek. "Something just brushed my leg."

He bursts out laughing. "Yeah—my hairy leg."

"No! It wasn't." I push away from him and swim toward the dock, stopping only when I hear voices. I scan the beach and tree line, skidding to a halt on a couple walking along the beach, hand in hand.

Marcus swims up behind me, sliding his arm around my stomach, his mouth on my ear. "You can either stay in the water and get devoured by the scary sea monster feeling up your leg, or you can jump out right now and give those people the show they came to see. Your choice, baby. I know what they're hoping for 'cause I want the same thing."

"I'm so naked!" I hiss through chattering teeth.

"So very, very naked…"

The couple sits on the beach like it's the middle of the day and they're settling in to whale watch.

Or…

"Sunrise," I whisper.

"What?" Marcus's breath brushes the back of my neck as we tread, his hand skimming up my body.

"They're waiting for sunrise. They're not going to leave for at least two more hours."

"Then we risk becoming fish food. Although those sharks circling us earlier were smiling. Seemed super friendly, so we'll probably have a great time out here."

I tear away from him, frantically splashing toward the dock. Grunting and panting, I try to haul myself onto it without scratching my stomach on the weathered wood, giving all of nature and the sunrise couple a front row view of all my body parts.

Marcus belly laughs behind me, and his hand lands on my backside, pushing me up and onto the dock. He slides onto it beside me like he's some kind of seal and we scramble to our feet, and he grabs my hand, pulling me behind him as we sprint up the dock, right past the couple on the beach and through the trees along the boardwalk, not stopping or looking back until we jump in the hot tub and sink to the bottom together.

CHAPTER 11

Marcus,

I'm not sure there will ever be a place as beautiful as San Juan Island, and it has nothing to do with scenery and everything to do with the firsts we experienced together. Saying I'm the luckiest doesn't begin to describe what I feel for you, but until I find the right words, it will have to do.

Mei

Mei and I check into a cheap motel so we can save our money to go crazy on our new apartment. As soon as I get my scholarship money, we're using graduation money for fun stuff. I want to go on a shopping spree for some new clothes for Mei. I wanna TV. A huge one. And maybe a gaming console. If Stanford is gonna be our new home for the next four years, we're gonna make it ours. Whenever it's ready, which is hopefully very, very soon.

We drop our bags on the table, throw off the infested bedspread, and kick off our shoes. We sit next to each other on the bed, backs against the cheap, wobbly headboard.

We're sharing a bag of fries, our legs relieved to be stretched in front of us instead of molded to the motorcycle seat like they have been for the last ten hours.

Mei nibbles on a fry, taking in the dingy room, and I attack my double cheeseburger, famished from a day of driving, my fingers stiff from being wrapped around the handlebars. "I mean," I say, chewing and swallowing. "It's definitely not our place on San Juan Island, and definitely no place I ever thought I'd stay but…look." I wipe grease off my chin with a napkin. "It's like a time machine. Rotary phone?" I raise my eyebrow at her and nod my head at the phone on the desk. "I remember when Meemaw had one. That thing's a relic. Also, this place is basically a scientist's dream." I motion my burger at the bedspread slumped in the corner. "That thing's a gold mine of infectious diseases and biological specimens. And we're paying a mere $109 a night for all of this." I wiggle my eyebrows at her. "This is the life, Mei. Pretty sure it doesn't get better than this. Not even a little bit. We've arrived."

She rolls her eyes and laughs. I go on, loving the way she watches my face. "Plus, this place is so close to Stanford; I could run there and back every day, and if I miss you too much, I can run back during my lunch break for a little, you know…" I lean down and smile against her ear, whispering a few ideas, and she snuggles into my side, her hand slipping under my shirt to rest on my stomach.

I release a long, satisfied sigh. "We're gonna make some great prostitute and drug-dealer friends and be very happy here until our apartment's ready."

She laughs again. "It's definitely hard to be here after the last three days on a gorgeous island, in an amazing beach house. And that kitchen? I loved cooking in it almost as much as I love you, but you win because it never made me laugh or took me skinny dipping in the freezing, freaky ocean. Or stayed up all night doing other stuff." She smirks and devours another fry.

My stomach flips around, remembering how we only left the beach house three times—once to go skinny dipping, once to ride the island, and once to get groceries when Mei fell in love with the fully equipped kitchen and wanted to spend every second she wasn't with me in it. She went crazy at the store while I pushed the cart, my eyes glued to her because she was so excited and happy to create masterpieces. Our Seattle kitchen was too small for her to do what she really wanted to do, when she had the huge beach house kitchen, she became a gourmet machine, and I loved everything about it. Especially the topless tapas.

The memory smears a grin all over my face, and I smooth her hair off her forehead, kissing it.

"Promise we'll go back someday," she says while we both float in and out of memories.

"If you'd get busy making meth out of the bathroom, we could easily live in luxury. You could have any kitchen you wanted." I shrug. "All up to you, Mei."

She snuggles into her spot between my shoulder and neck, her face warm through my shirt. "I'm very motivated. But I'd rather be in a ratty motel with you than in a five-star hotel or gourmet kitchen without you, so I'm happy right here. Without making meth, even. But how about, while you're at practice tomorrow, I find us a place where we aren't afraid of being shot during a drug raid?" She traces a heart on my chest with her fingertip while I rub her back.

I lean my mouth against her temple, lips brushing her skin as I talk. "That's so boring. But okay, whatever. Go crazy and find us a place that's at least two stars." I put the bag of fries on the nightstand and scoot down on my side. Mei lies facing me, her fingertip tracing my face. "I mean—this is what we wanted, right? Just you and me?"

She nods, her hand moving down my chest to my stomach, and her fingers slide along the waistband of my jeans. My muscles tense. "We're so gonna make this work. We've got Meemaw's graduation money. Money from Guo. Our paychecks, very generous bonuses from Jerry. And we always have…the *diamonds*," I whisper in a British accent, and her smile breaks through the shadows in this corner of the time-stained room. We haven't talked much about the diamonds Mei took from Nick since they represent what she experienced at the hotel in L.A. They're carefully camouflaged and stashed in the tampon box in her bag. It feels like using them might release evil spirits or something.

I kiss the skin around her ear, and she grabs my hoodie strings. "Or, if we run low on cash, I can just call my boyfriend from yesterday. He told me he makes a lot of it…"

I snort. "Yeah, you could—you could call him Sugar Grandpappy."

A laugh bursts out of Mei, and she falls back on the bed, holding her stomach as she laughs. "I never knew you were an actor," she says, wiping laughter tears out of her eyes, "but your server impersonation was Oscar worthy."

On our way back down the coast yesterday, we'd stopped at a random restaurant, and before our orders arrived, I'd gone to the bathroom. When I'd walked out, some old dude was sitting in my seat across from Mei. I'd stopped, backed up, then snatched a check sleeve from the hostess stand before sauntering over to our table, pen behind my ear.

The guy acted like I was interrupting his private moment,

so I'd taken out my Sharpie and written on a blank bill: "Big, fat tip, Gramps: get the hell away from my wife."

I'd laid it on the table, walked away, and watched as the guy, being all chivalrous, checked the bill. And bolted.

"He was sitting in *my* seat, hitting on *my* wife. Should I have done something other than mess with him?" I roll toward her, smiling down at her. "Gotta give it to him, though—I fully get why he couldn't resist you."

She pinches my stomach under my shirt, and I yelp. I grab her hand and kiss it, running my thumb over the $100 infinity ring that's been on her finger for five whole days, and she says she'll never replace it. We'll see. Pulling the Sharpie out of my pocket, I turn her arm over and write a three-word inside joke on her wrist. I smile as she reads it and laughs, shocked I'd write it in a visible place, but I catch her eye.

"I can't believe how lucky I am," I tell her with my eyes, tracing her eyebrows with my fingertip, down her nose, memorizing her face. "I don't care if we're in a rathole—I get to spend every single day and every single night with you from now on, and I can't get over that." I lace our fingers together and hold them to my chest. "There's only one of you, and I got her."

We stare at each other, watching memories from the last few days play through our eyes. "Sorry I can't give you five-star hotels right now, but someday I will. I mean, a week ago we were wondering if we'd ever get out of Seattle and ware-houses and restaurants. And here we are."

She holds my head in her hands. "I'm feeling pretty great about it."

The sirens whining outside the drafty window and a door slamming a few rooms down can't slip between us—there are too many memories and plans taking up the space. Lots of hope. Big dreams. "But someday Mei, I'm gonna buy you the biggest rock so everyone will see you're taken, so I don't have to chase off old guys. Or young ones. And I'm gonna make all the stuff we've talked about happen, I promise. We're not starting out perfect, but I'm promising you in this nasty motel room in front of all the bed bugs and viruses and bacteria present, I'm gonna give you perfection."

CHAPTER 12

stare at the sidewalk and only the sidewalk as I walk back from the store, hoping my big sunglasses and Marcus's hoodie will be enough of a disguise if, for some reason, Nick happens to drive through Stanford campus on his way out of San Francisco. It's a stupid, irrational thought, but my senses have been in overdrive since we arrived. Guo Mama's words are on repeat in my head. We're too close to San Francisco.

The hazy sun's doing its best to break through the clouds while I hug a paper bag of groceries and wish Marcus was with me instead of at practice; I've been avoiding leaving the apartment by myself since we moved in three days ago, too afraid of what could be lurking on the other side of the door. But we needed something in our tiny kitchen; Marcus eats more in one day than I can in a week, and crackers, cheese, and bananas won't be enough to keep him alive another day. So, I talked myself through my irrational thoughts, grabbed $100 from our emergency envelope, and went to the store where I might have splurged on a few extras. Hopefully, having his favorite protein shakes magically appear in our pantry will keep Marcus from crashing after practice. He's been so tired from late nights and early mornings, but my days have dragged without him. By the time he gets home, I've got enough energy for both of us, eager to do all the fun stuff we've discovered during the last week.

I trudge up the stairs and balance the bag of groceries on my knee as I pull out my keys, fumbling them into the lock. I step inside at the same time Marcus jumps out from behind the door, yelling "Surprise!" I scream, dropping to the floor with the bag of groceries and covering my face.

He drops beside me, apologizing through his laughter, and I punch his arm as hard as I can, releasing the surge of fear.

"Ow..." He rubs his arm as he straightens. "What was that for?"

His eyes are mischievous, which only make me angrier. I punch him again and stand. "I almost had a heart attack."

He stands up, too. "Yeah, well..." He steps closer, backing me against the wall. "I'm calling campus police because I was minding my own business behind the door in my apartment when a crazy girl with dark intentions broke in. I can see them in her eyes..." He pins me against the wall with his hips, and I laugh into his chest, releasing the anger and fear swirling inside me. I melt into him, relief washing away my anger, and when I look up, his mouth crashes into mine, his lips guiding me to my tiptoes.

"Thing is, even though she's crazy, I'm totally in love with her and can't wait to spend all day with her," he says against my lips.

I pull back. "What happened to practice?"

"I told Coach I had other things I wanted to practice."

I pinch his stomach, and he flinches, then smiles. "Or...

Coach called it early today. Which means we get to celebrate the holiday."

"What holiday?"

Marcus squints at me, his best attempt at disgust. "I can't believe you don't know the significance of this day." His fingertips trickle down my sides to my hips, and my breath hitches, but I manage a whisper.

"July sixth?" I wait. "Am I missing something?"

"Definitely."

"Tell me."

Marcus leans in, his lips on my ear, and his hands slip under my shirt. "Mei-day!"

I wind my arms around his neck, encouraging him. "You're two months late."

"Any day I have no practice is Mei-Day. Mei Li Miller Day, any time, any month. And it's my favorite."

I close my eyes as his hands and lips wander. "And how…do people celebrate…this special…made-up holiday?" My mind swims, his fingertips leaving sparking trails on my skin.

"I'll show you, but first, the rules."

"Rules?"

He nods. "Important ones, so listen up. Number one." He holds up his finger. "You decide what we do, and two, you can't stop me from doing whatever I want for you."

———

The moon shines through the gaps in the blinds and pools over Marcus and me on our bed where we lay tangled in each other. His breathing is deep, and I smile and stretch, feeling very celebrated.

My feet are cold from the air conditioner, so I slip them

under Marcus's legs. He doesn't budge, but no surprise—we did a lot of celebrating.

The afternoon slipped away while we were in our apartment, but we'd spent the evening walking through the campus gardens, then checked out some nearby boutiques where Marcus said I could get whatever I wanted, no matter the cost. There's no way I was going to do that, even if we have extra money now that his scholarship is paying for things. I feel bad enough spending money on food for new recipes, even if Marcus will never complain. When we'd stopped in front of the Mediterranean restaurant I'd been dying to try, I looked at him and he'd just smiled and opened the door for me. He'd already made reservations under Mei Li Miller, and when I told him it was too expensive, he'd rolled his eyes.

"Nothing's too expensive on Mei Day," he'd said, his smile worth every dollar we shouldn't have spent but did.

Starting tomorrow, we'll be better with our money but today…was perfect. When we'd approached our apartment, I walked slower, reluctant to go inside, like I could drag the hours along behind us as we walked. But then he'd picked me up, spun me around, and given me a piggy-back ride up the four flights of stairs. Mei Day had officially ended a few hours ago, way too late but not long enough.

I snuggle into my pillow and stare into the purple haze, listening to Marcus's deep breathing and the hum of the air conditioner. Memories from tonight circle above my head, but a nagging thought trails them, sneaking between the memory of Marcus's smile that spread light over the whole day and his words whispered in the dark as he hovered over me. Thoughts of looking up my real dad don't belong in the sequence of private moments, but they flash behind my eyes when I close them, tugging me away from the Marcus tangle and out of bed.

It's not the first time these intrusive thoughts have pushed their way in, sending me off balance. But right now, they're spinning and toppling me.

I shrug on Marcus's t-shirt and tiptoe around the corner to the kitchen. Sliding into a chair at the table, I open Marcus's laptop we bought last week. We'd done well without internet for six weeks in Seattle—even our phones were too basic to have it. We also didn't want any news from home to creep into our life, but we have full access now in this new apartment. I've been fighting the temptation to look up Peter Mitchell, and tonight, I'm giving in.

The screen sings to life, and I type his name in the search bar. Nothing relevant pulls up, so I add Rhode Island and a Facebook link appears, along with a picture. It's the same picture Mama gave me when she said I should know him.

I swallow and click on the link, closing my eyes while I wait, unsure I want to know anything more. But when I open them, he's there, with his three blonde children that look nothing like me. They're all standing on a rock, the ocean behind them in a completely different life from mine. There are no shadows of unknown or unwanted children in his smile. His profile isn't private, so I click on more pictures, my hesitation stepping aside for curiosity.

There's Peter Mitchell, alone in front of a forest, holding up a sign I can't read. Him with his kids at a museum. On the beach. At Disney World.

He's a dad but not to me—to those kids who can't possibly be my half siblings. Everything about the pictures is too straight forward, collected, organized. There's no room for an old girlfriend and their long-lost child who looks nothing like him or his real family. I wonder about the story of Mama and Peter. Were they ever in love like I'm in love with Marcus? What would my life be like had they stayed together?

I'd read all their emails, scoured and studied them during lunch breaks at the restaurant. I'd tried to make sense of them because the relationship seemed serious until Mama sent a final email, telling him she needed to see him again and there was no response.

Unwanted.

Hurt uncurls inside me, and I shut the laptop; I have no right or reason to be hurt. He doesn't know about me. He doesn't know he could be living a different life, raising a different kid with a different woman who's trapped in a much uglier place.

None of it matters. Peter Mitchell doesn't matter. I may share the same DNA, but he's just a name. A profile on Facebook. I open the laptop again to clear the history, so Marcus won't find my search, then close it and crawl back into bed beside him.

I lay my head on Marcus's chest, and his fingers reflexively slide into my hair. I listen to his familiar heartbeat, its deep, steady rhythm reminding me that Marcus is my family. He knows everything about me. We have each other. We'll make our own picture-perfect family someday, and when we have kids, they'll never need to question where they belong.

CHAPTER 13

Marcus,

I asked Magic 8 if your very drafty, scandalous idea for Sunday afternoons is a good idea...

Want to know what it said?

Guess you'll find out on Sunday.

♥Mei♥

sit on the soccer field, surrounded by my new teammates, lacing my cleats and working to keep my thoughts on soccer plays instead of letting them run back toward the very sparse apartment with Mei inside it. Alone.

Our three days on San Juan Island may as well have been on another planet; we'd forgotten about Nick or Dad or Mei's family and all things past or future. It was just us, cruising around the island on our motorcycle, Mei's arms wrapped around me from behind. And then it was just us in a beach house where no one would've thought to look for us. If they'd tried, they would have seen nothing but silhouettes through walls of windows and shadows in tangled sheets.

My body buzzes with memories, then tenses, remembering we're not there—we're here, a whole lot more visible than our backyard cottage in Seattle or a beach house on a cliff surrounded by trees and a security gate. We're a little too close to San Francisco now. As much as I love Stanford and the team, I don't love that our old life and fears are just down the coast. Still not sure coming here was the greatest idea.

The whistle blows, and I finish lacing my cleats, setting aside thoughts and memories. I jump to my feet and run with my team toward the group of waiting coaches.

For hours, I run faster and kick harder to prove I'm worth a second shot. The whistle blows, and I rocket down the field for a huddle. I'm halfway there when a bright red streak outside the stadium catches my attention. A car shoots through the parking lot and veers to the curb by the gate, and I jolt to a stop. Aunt Audrey.

The soccer field fades, and my heart tries to beat its way out of my chest when Dad steps out of the car in a V-neck and jeans, his clenched jaw visible from where I stand a few yards away.

My brain throws swear words around, and my legs burn to run in the opposite direction. Fists clenched, I swallow hard, forcing down the hot, frantic heartbeat thumping up my throat.

Dad strides toward the fence, Audrey running after him in a dress and red Converse. The negotiator. She does it every day at work, so why not now, to keep her brother from killing his son? The look on his face is the bullet that could end it all.

There's nothing for me to blend into or hide behind, so I drag in a deep breath and haul myself slowly toward them. Like I've been caught being out past curfew instead of running away from potential criminal charges and Dad's orders. Getting married—to the girl Dad told me not to even date. No way he could possibly know that, but his fury march suggests otherwise.

My mind digs up words that might talk Dad down from launching his verbal grenade.

Oh! Hey, Dad. How's it going? It's been a while. Hope you didn't mind that I took off. Just needed some time. Distance. You get it, right? Oh, and by the way, I'm married. Yeah…last minute thing. Probably should've told you—invited you—but, you know how those things go…

Dad's eyes slam into mine and practically push me backwards, demanding answers. Not like Mei's eyes that are a soft, gentle touch, but like…anger and accusation and complete and total disappointment curled into a visual fist.

"Son, what are you doing?" He's chomping gum like he's punishing it. "I thought I made myself perfectly clear the last time we talked, but I quickly discovered I was dead wrong." His anger tumbles out in the thick Southern accent that lays dormant until he's mad. He fumbles with the gate latch, so amped up his hands shake. "You gonna tell me what's going on or just expect me to figure it out like I had to figure out where you were the last month?"

I jerk into motion, hurrying toward him, eager to take this explosive scene far away from my coaches and team. I slip around the corner of a neighboring building, and Dad trails me along the fence, right on my heels.

"You gonna keep running from things? That your new thing?"

I whirl around, my body rigid. "I can explain." But my mind goes static, my heart trying to pump more oxygen to my head and give me every chance to produce words that can actually explain any of this.

"You lied to my face and then you took off, knowing there were criminal charges on the line. With Mei Li Zhang, the one girl I told you to stay away from." He spits her name out like it's a bug that's flown into his mouth. His voice shakes, and I dig my toes into my cleats, bracing against the anger and hurt behind it, like walking against wind. "Did you think I wouldn't find you? That I couldn't figure out where you were since I find missing people for a living?" His jaw pulses, and he steps closer to me. But Audrey squeezes between us, facing Dad, and grabs his upper arm. "Ray, stop before you say something you'll regret." Her eyes are throwing darts at him. "Marcus is not the only male standing here who lied, remember that. Right? And maybe if you hadn't been so *freakish* about keeping him from girls, he would've just *told* you he was dating someone rather than sneaking around and running away with her. If you can't handle this, I'll take my car and leave you here to find a ride home. And I'm pretty sure Marcus won't offer you a ride on his motorcycle."

I stare at the cement, wishing Audrey didn't bring up the motorcycle.

Dad explodes, cursing at me. "If you're man enough to go out on your own, be man enough to look at me and the mess you've made of everything!"

My eyes skid through the heavy, tense air and slam into his. "How have I messed up anything for you? What have I ever done that put you out? I've never stopped you from doing anything you want and lying to my face about it. You're just mad because this is the first time I've done something I wanna do, and you had nothing to do with it. This isn't really about me at all—it's about you, like everything else. Me, making you look good and believing when you said that my mom was the bad guy, never you." Words that have been sloshing near the surface erupt. "And I never asked questions—never asked to meet her or find out why she really left because I didn't wanna make you uncomfortable. Instead, I did everything just right so you wouldn't leave too. So I didn't disappoint you like I somehow disappointed her. Did everything right so you were happy, no matter what I wanted."

Audrey's eyes widen, flicking between me and Dad. She's probably just as disoriented in the explosion as I am.

I swear at the ground, squeezing my eyes shut. The words that just tore out of me leave raw, bleeding spots inside. I'm crumbling under his fury and the hurt and disappointment in his eyes. I wanna give him an explanation—give him some relief. But then I'm mad at myself for caring because he didn't bother telling me about Kenna and his future plans that didn't include me, so why should I include him in mine?

I picture Mei's face during our shower earlier this morning, all lit up and laughing over something I said. I have to protect her. Gotta keep my mouth shut and be okay that Dad and I have our own lives that don't include each other. I have the life I want. He can have whatever he wants.

"I didn't sacrifice my life so you could wreck yours!" Dad's voice is quiet now, raspy, like my heated outburst burned his throat.

"Go ahead!" I yell, coming toe to toe with him. "Tell me how stupid and irresponsible I am, but at least I know how to keep a girl."

He stares at me, his jaw pulsing as he looks across the field, back at me. "You think it's my fault your mom walked away from us? Like I didn't know what I was doing or couldn't handle it as well as you obviously can?" He grabs something out of his back pocket and thrusts it at me. An envelope. "Let's see how you handle this since you've got it all figured out." When I don't reach for it, he drops the envelope and steps back. I keep my eyes on him for a few more seconds, then bend, picking up the envelope. It's addressed to me. The Clubhouse address. From Olivia Sultana, 3437 North Bayview Circle, Los Angeles, CA. Olivia. My mom.

My hands are sweaty, wrinkling the envelope clutched in them. I don't wanna open this. She's never talked to me. She's never sent a birthday card or Christmas present or acknowledged my existence. Unless Dad's kept it all from me. My breathing echoes in my ears, all my senses turning and running to hide from whatever's inside the envelope. What if my mom wanted to meet me, but Dad wouldn't let her? What if it's a letter explaining why she left?

"She showed up at the apartment. Was planning on coming to your graduation. But then, you know…you weren't there. So, she left that for you."

My fists clench and my feet flex, my legs ready to hurl me at him, but his eyes glint like they always did when he was onto a lead in a case. "But you can't run from this, Marcus. Mei Li will be deported, and you can't stop that from happening. I'd love to protect you from all of this, but I warned you, you took off, and now I have to make a phone call to let immigration know where to find her. It's my job." He shakes his head at the ground. "Don't want to do it, but here we are, so…I'll give you until Monday to figure out what you're going to do."

The ground drops from under me, a jolt rocking me on my heels. His words fly past me, a few sticking in my brain like arrows. But no—he's a liar. He wants me to give up my life… for what?

"Are you freaking kidding me?" I hurl at him. "You can't stand that I'm happy, so you find a way to sabotage it? It wasn't enough you ripped my mom from my life, you wanna rip Mei out of it too?"

"It's not me who will take her from you, Marcus. It's the law. There are things outside our control, and you chose one of them."

"And what does the law say about us being married?"

He tenses. "What?"

"We got married. Couple weeks ago. So, no one's taking her anywhere."

Audrey sucks in a breath, and Dad stares at me. "They can, and they will. Marriage can't stop that, and you're not the first one to try. A marriage certificate doesn't suddenly make Mei Li a citizen. This isn't your decision to make. I told you to stay away from her, and I meant it. Now I guess you'll have to figure out how to be with her from a different continent."

"We're not going anywhere."

Dad's jaw tightens. "And what would you do if you found out Nick had been released and was looking for her?"

"I'd say someone hadn't done their job in San Francisco, so I'll do whatever it takes to protect her. Even if that means you never see me again." I glare at him, my thoughts whirling so fast they kick up dust I can't see through.

"Hmm. Okay, well…you've got it all figured out. Good for you." Dad nods to the ground, then his eyes land back on mine, hard, not backing down. "Don't ruin your life more than you already have." His voice is defeated, an octave lower and worn out. "I love you, son, but you've got until Monday. That's the best I can do."

Emotions flood me and I'm choking, gasping, flailing. I want to slam my fist into his face for throwing those words around like they're a weather report. I want him to stop talking and telling me what I should and shouldn't do. I picture hitting him, how it would feel to put all my resentment into it, but I whirl away, sprinting around the corner to the field.

"Marcus!" Audrey yells, but I run faster.

Grabbing my bag from the bench, I take off out of the stadium, across the street, and through campus toward Mei. I need her right now. He's lying, just like he always has so he can get me to do what he wants.

I need Mei. Need to get away from Dad and figure out what I'm feeling and what I'm supposed to do with any of this. I just...

I swear, gulping in air, pumping my legs harder, and swiping at tears. I swear again because I don't wanna cry. Don't wanna let the fear or hurt take over. I can't lose Mei. I won't, law or not.

I ignore traffic signals, cross streets between cars, and jump medians to put distance between me and the show-down at the soccer field. Between me and the look in Dad's eyes.

After three blocks, I hit a red light and bend over to catch my breath, hands on my knees, nausea rising until I can't shove it back down and puke in a bush near a lamppost. When the light turns green, I take off again, sprinting the last two blocks, across the parking lot, and up the four flights of stairs. I pound on our locked door, afraid if I stop long enough to dig out my key, I'll fall apart in the hallway. "Mei, it's me. Open the door," I call, my voice wobbly, forehead against the faded brown paint. I slap the metal with my palm. "Please open, Mei."

The deadbolt clicks. When the doorknob turns, I push through the door and slam it behind me, backing against it. I drop my bag and pull Mei into my arms, my body shaking. Tears burn the edges of my eyes, attempting to wash away the look on Dad's face. But I can't shut it out, so I just hold Mei, the envelope from my mom still crumpled in my hand.

Mei leans back, searching my face. "Marcus," she asks, frowning. "What happened?"

"My dad knows where we are."

She stiffens. "What?"

I tell her what happened. I tell her how I ran. I tell her that I don't care even though it's a lie, but the one thing I refuse to let out of me is what Dad told me to do. That, I'll never tell her; she can never know. I'll never step back in San Francisco. We'll hide if we have to. Go somewhere far away if it comes to that. But I won't tell her.

My head pounds, and I drop to the edge of the bed, head in my hands. I stare at my cleats, my eyes tracing the laces so they don't see what's replaying in my mind.

I blink through the blurriness, but a tear drops between my feet, and Mei takes my face in her hands and lifts it up. "What should we do?" she asks.

"Nothing. This. What we've been doing. I'm not afraid of him or what he'll do." Except I am.

Her hand sweeps hair off my forehead and guides my head onto her lap. She runs her fingers through my sweaty hair, and I curl against her, not saying a word. She doesn't ask me to, and sometime in the shadowy minutes or hours that pass in silence, her hands close the gaping hole inside me.

————

My eyes fly open to pitch black. My face is tight, eyes swollen, my head fuzzy and heavy. Mei's curled up next to me, sound asleep. The message I wrote on her stomach last night in Sharpie peeks from under her shirt. I watch her sleep in peace without a clue what Dad threatened. I'll never tell her.

I shift carefully so I won't wake her up and glance at my watch. 3:27 AM. The fridge kicks on and hums, a TV in the next apartment drones, and my heart beats in my ears as I replay the moment with Dad. I examine every word, formulate what I should've said. What I shouldn't have. Then the envelope dropping to the cement lights up my mind, and I scan the darkness for it, running my hand over the bed. It lays on the desk, crumpled and abandoned. Mei must have pried it out of my hand. I wonder if she read it. I hope she did. She'll think that's why I was coming apart.

I slip off the bed, reaching for the wall when I wobble from getting up too fast. My feet are cold from being in sweaty socks and sore from running five blocks in cleats. Mei must have taken them off me last night.

The white envelope glares in the dark, guiding me toward it. I snatch it from the desk, ease it open, and pull out a card. I tilt it toward the night light in the kitchen: Congratulations, Graduate!

So just any graduate. Not her son, not a friend, just a graduate.

Inside, she's written a note. Her handwriting is straight, tidy. But there's not much of it.

Dear Marcus. This is a big day I didn't want to miss, even though I've missed a lot of other days. Congratulations. I'd love to talk sometime and hear about your plans. Don't spend this gift card all in one place.
Cheers, Olivia

I stare at the card, the words fading into the dark. I've never heard my mom's voice. Never seen her handwriting or how she'd approach me. Olivia. Not really my mom. But why did she come to graduation? And she and Dad talked—he has the card to prove it. What was that like, the two of them talking? Did Dad wish his life had turned out differently when he saw her face? Do I wish mine had?

I glance at Mei pulled into a ball on the bed, her hands pressed together under her chin like she's praying. And maybe she is. Maybe she saw my implosion and is worried about me. The weight of the argument with Dad and the inscription in this card and our new reality settle on my shoulders, so heavy I have to drop into the ratty chair by the window. I stare into the dark room, the clock on the microwave blinking blue spots into this murky place between night and morning. I'm hoping the day never comes. But one thing I know for sure—a promise to myself and the silence and the looming threats—She's not going back to San Francisco, and I'm not going anywhere without her.

CHAPTER 14

Marcus: Never been jealous of dogs before,
but they're with you, and I'm just so not.

Mei: They're all over me.

Marcus: Can I be all over you too?

Mei: If you stay on your leash and don't bark
and go potty in designated areas, yes.

Marcus: Wagging my tail.

The sun's breaking through the layers of puffy clouds as I sit on a park bench watching Alfie and Moose play. They love wrestling, and I love watching them even if I'm more of a cat person. I hope to convince Marcus to get one someday, but dogs come in a close second.

This has been our routine the past few weeks since getting my job as a dog walker. Walk, play, walk, play, treat. We're almost to the treat part, and that means Marcus will be home in four hours. In the meantime, I'll hang out with the other men in my life I see more than Marcus now that he's in preseason. Good thing all my furry clients are almost as cute as Marcus and love me almost as much as he does.

I let the sun soak into my bare arms stretched along the back of the bench. Fresh air, cute dogs, decent paychecks. I'll take this job anytime over working in a restaurant. Also, I didn't have to use my fake passport when I got the job since it pays in cash. Guo Mama gave us a red envelope of money at our wedding, but when we pulled it out after getting to the house on San Juan Island, there were two passports—for Darius Bromley and Peggy Bromley. Marcus was completely confused about how Guo Mama could pull it off. I wasn't. Either way, I don't trust fake IDs. I'm glad they're still tucked away with the diamonds in the tampon box in Marcus's duffle bag. I hope we don't have to use either anytime soon.

Alfie runs back for a drink of water in the bowl by my feet, and Moose comes over for an ear rub. I talk to them both in a voice only they understand, smiling, happy for this perfectly normal day in my new life. Not that normal has been perfect. Our apartment is pretty bare—one couch, a mattress on the floor, one lamp—except for the giant TV on the wall and shiny new game console under it.

I smile, remembering how Marcus had spent hours setting it up and how proud he was when we watched our first movie on it. Now he wants surround sound.

Thanks, Not-Mom-Olivia, for the gift card.

Alfie jumps up on my lap, wagging his tail, then jumps off and darts toward Moose, who wrestles him to the ground. I glance at my phone and stand, calling them over. They run up to me, and I ruffle their fur and put their leashes back on.

We head to the corner market. It's taken me a few weeks to get used to being so visible so close to San Francisco, but I feel safer with dogs at the end of a leash, even if they're too friendly to ever do damage to anyone.

On our way, I pass a teenage couple sauntering down the sidewalk with Slurpees, and a night on San Juan Island slips through my mind. We'd wandered down a quiet side street, taking drags on a shared blue raspberry Slurpee. Marcus kept stopping and squeezing his head between his hands, complaining about the heinous brain freezes, and I'd confessed I'd never actually experienced one.

"Whoa, whoa, whoa," he'd said. "If I'd known how inexperienced you are in the more important matters of life, I probably wouldn't have married you." He'd slid the Slurpee cup into my hand and nodded toward it. "Take a drag. Like it's a cup full of Marcus."

I'd followed his instructions, my eyes never leaving his, and when I'd inhaled half of the Slurpee, he'd snatched it from my hands and leaned forward, waiting for my reaction. I'd waited too, closing my eyes and pushing at my temples, pointing the way for an experience that never came.

I smile and tighten my hands around the leashes as I pass the couple, remembering every detail of what came after.

I saunter through the sliding doors of the market, and a familiar voice sings at me. "Mei Li!" Fay beams at me as she shuffles closer. "Are Alfie and Moose ready for their treats?" The eighty-five-year-old greeter and I have pretty much become best friends since I see her every day, and she always has doggie treats stashed in her apron pockets.

"They sure are! How are you today?" I ask, holding on to her arm.

"Oh, I'm having just the best day ever. Also, we got new

flowers. You should take one home for your hubby. It'll make his day."

I laugh. "Can he eat them or talk sports with them?"

She waves her hand. "Men like flowers, too. They just don't know it until they get them. I used to work in a florist shop and brought home flowers all the time for Dennis. It made his day! I'll hold onto the boys' leashes, and you can go pick out the perfect bunch for Marcus."

I hesitate. "Well…okay, then. Why not?" I make my way to the flowers and find the smallest, cheapest arrangement. Not that it matters, since Marcus seems to have no problem spending money, especially on me. Like buying me clothes and splurging on the most expensive restaurant on "Mei Day."

I change my mind and select the largest arrangement, then snag a few of Marcus's favorite snacks and go through self-checkout before heading back to Fay. I take the leashes from her. "Thanks for the tip." I hold up the flowers.

"Anytime. And here." She grabs my hand, slipping more doggie treats into my palm. "A little extra love for my boys."

Waving to her, I follow Alfie and Moose outside and toward the crosswalk. I give them their treats while we wait for the light to change. When it does, we cross the street toward our apartment so I can grab my water bottle and leave the flowers before taking the boys home and picking up my next fluffy clients. But as I step onto the sidewalk, my eyes catch on a car across the street. It rolls forward, veering to the curb, and stops. The black Mercedes throws my memory backwards where it lands in the front passenger seat. There are countless black Mercedes around Stanford, but there's only one with Nick stepping out of it.

A scream begins in my stomach and rises, getting lodged in my throat. My hand goes to my neck. Maybe he hasn't seen me. Maybe it's just a coincidence. But when his gaze turns on me, his black eyes pierce me over passing cars, and my heart plummets. I choke on air as his eyes pin me in place, and his smile creeps toward me.

I drop the paper bag with the flowers and snacks and yank Alfie and Moose in the opposite direction. We fly along the sidewalk, cutting through the grassy park and onto a residential street toward the dogs' house, not daring to look at the nightmare behind us.

I make it the two blocks and punch in the code to the owner's house. I shove my way inside. My breath is sharp against my lungs, cutting and slicing at me. I bend over until my stomach lurches, and I dart to the bathroom, throwing up in the sink.

My mind rewinds to rough hands ripping my dress, cold air, icy fear. Nick's hands around my neck, his body pressing me into the bed as he moves over me.

I vomit until my organs threaten to heave out of me, doing nothing to empty my head of memories. When I drop to the toilet, clutching the rim, a sob shoves itself out of me, gasping, frantic. He's found me. Us. The darkness rolling off him seeps into the bathroom with me, weighing me down, suffocating light and leaving only a decision to be made. But there is no choice. I have to leave. With or without Marcus.

"Mei Li?" a timid voice asks, and my eyes dart up to Poppy standing in the bathroom door, concern on her face. "Oh my goodness, are you okay?"

I swallow jagged fear and half nod, half shake my head.

"How can I help?" She and the dogs watch me, waiting.

But what can I say? I can't tell her anything about what just happened. I can't ask her for a ride home, or to stay here for the next four hours until Marcus is done with practice. I can't tell her that thirty minutes ago, my life was as close to perfect as it has ever been, and it just crumpled under Nick's presence. All I can do is ask, "Do you mind if I wait here for an Uber?"

Poppy's warm eyes meet mine. "Let me take you home instead."

But home is the last place I can go right now. "Actually… can you take me to the Stanford soccer field?"

CHAPTER 15

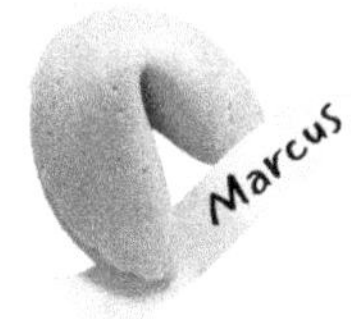

Mei: Sorry to interrupt practice, but there's
something weighing on my mind. When you
said Ghost Hunter's International wasn't real,
you were joking, right?

whoop to the sky, then spin and run across the soccer field to high-five my teammate, who expertly kicked my amazing pass into the goal. It couldn't have been more perfect, and all the coaches were watching. "That was INSANE!" I call to him, and he flashes me a grin, running to meet me.

"Stanford's never seen this duo before," he says, high fiving me with both hands. "This season's gonna be unbelievable."

Riding a high, we run toward center field, and he smacks my arm and points at the stadium gates. "Looks like we've already got ourselves a fan."

My knees lock, jerking me to a stop. Mei is on the other side of the fence, her fingers gripping it. Her face is red and swollen, and I try catching her eye, but she won't look at me.

Panic sweeps through me, leaving me light-headed, and dread creeps across the grass to yank my feet into motion. But the grass is sludge, holding me back from the reason she's here, looking like she's falling apart.

The earth pauses in its rotation, smothering the yells and whistles of the scrimmage behind me. I shove through the fog in my brain, easing into a run that turns into a sprint.

I skid to a stop at the fence, gripping the rail to steady myself. "What happened? What's wrong?"

Tears well in her eyes, and her hand goes to her throat. I kick my toe into the chain link, swing myself over it, and pull her into my arms. Her shoulders tremble. "Talk to me." My voice shakes as I cradle her against me. Her fingers grip the front of my shirt that's pasted to my chest with sweat. The longer she stays silent, the faster my heart beats until finally, I hold her at arm's length and duck to meet her eyes. "What is it, Mei?"

"He's here," she whispers. "I was walking the dogs and stopped in at the market to get them treats. It was less than five minutes." She swallows, choking out the next words. "I crossed the street toward campus, and he was there. Just… staring at me."

"Whoa—hold up. What do you mean? What are you talking about? Who's here? My dad? What did he say to you? I swear if he—"

She shakes her head quickly. "No…not your dad. I wish it was him, but it wasn't. I saw him, Marcus—he was following me. He saw me." Her voice breaks, and she drops her head, but I catch her chin between my fingers and tilt her head back so she has to look at me.

"Who was following you?" I press.

The answer swims in her eyes, sending ripples of fear through me.

I don't let go of her. "Did he hurt you?" I search her face, which is definitely swollen but only from tears.

She shakes her head. "I ran to Poppy's. She brought me here."

"How? It's not even possible for him to be here. He's locked up."

"It was him," she chokes. "He found me."

The night she stood in my room, bloody and bruised, flashes through my mind, and anger lights me up. I curse, letting go of her, my hands on my head as I visually sweep the field, my team—all there in a huddle. With one exception because here I am, once again, dealing with the aftershocks of Nick. Dealing with another mess he's making in our life.

"I'm calling my dad," I say, whirling around to face her. "We're not gonna do this. We're not gonna run or be afraid and let him—"

"No—we can't. I can't. You know what will happen, Marcus. And now Nick knows we're here."

Frustration boils in my chest, its heat rising in my throat. "Then what do you want me to do? Just let him find us? Let him rape you? Kill you? What, Mei? We never made a plan for this. Never talked about what we'd do if Nick found us here. Because he's supposed to be locked up." Even though… Dad asked me what I would do if I found out Nick was out. But Dad was just trying to scare me. No way Nick's out of jail.

She shakes her head and won't look at me. "He's not in jail. He hasn't been for a while."

"How do you know that?"

Tears roll down her cheeks, and I reach out and hold her face between my hands, wiping the tears away with my thumbs.

"The night you told me you got back into Stanford," Mei

whispers. "Right before you came into the restaurant. My mom called. She told me Nick was out. There wasn't enough evidence to keep him in custody. I should have told you. I know I should have told you, but you were so excited about Stanford. I couldn't ruin it."

I stare at her. Wait for understanding. Swear. "Not enough *evidence*?" I let go of her face. Step back, hands gripping the back of my head. Give myself some space. "How is that even possible? You called the cops. Told them what went down."

She nods, stiff and tense. "And when they got there, they found Nick in a puddle of his own blood, and he blamed me for it. Said I went crazy on him. Stole from him. Mama told me to stay away from San Francisco because he was asking about me. He's been looking. But after seeing how excited you were, I decided to be excited with you and hope and pray he would never find us."

Dad knew. He knew, and he didn't warn me. The thought turns to boiling rage. "No. No, no, no!" I curse to the sky, raking one hand through my hair. "We have to call the cops. We have no choice. We can figure out how to keep you in the States after Nick's in custody, but—"

"It doesn't work like that. The moment they know where I am, it's over. I've seen how it works. I've watched it. I'm on their radar for assault. They'll send me straight back to Taiwan or put me in jail here, so I'm leaving before they can. Nick knows people who will make sure I don't get out. But you don't need to come with me this time. Stay here. I'll find somewhere to—"

"Are you *insane*?" I burst, grabbing and squeezing her hands. "You're not going anywhere alone. If anything—"

Someone yells my name, and my head snaps over my shoulder, my focus going to the head coach who's staring at me, chomping his gum, hands on his hips. He already took me aside and talked to me about the day Dad showed up. Said I need to keep my personal life and soccer life separate and stay focused.

My legs tense, ready to hop the fence and run back to him. Instead, I yank Mei toward the bleachers, calling, "Be right back!" to my coach, and steer her around the corner and out of sight.

"I've gotta get back to the team. Hang out here. You'll be safe, and then, after practice, we'll figure it out. We'll find a solution, I promise." I search her eyes, but they fill with tears.

"It's only a matter of time before he shows up here, Marcus. He won't stop."

No way am I walking away from Stanford and giving up everything when there *has* to be another choice to ending this game of hide and seek. But is there really a choice? After what Dad said and now Mei…I'm not so sure anymore.

"He'll stop if he's locked up. It would take one phone call. You get that, right?" I wait, hoping she says yes to reassure me.

"There is no evidence to hold him. All the bruises are gone. There's nothing I can say or do that will keep me here with you. I have to go. And I won't ask you to give up every-thing to go with me. Never again."

"It's not about asking me to give it up. We're in this together. Remember our plan? Stanford's a big part of it. I can't just walk away. We can figure this out, I swear." I glance over my shoulder at one of my teammates running toward me and pull Mei to me, my mouth on her ear. "Hang out here, and when I finish practice, we can decide what to do. We'll figure out why he's following you. Come up with a plan to stop him. Please." I lead her around the bleachers to a bench. "Be there in a minute," I call to my teammate.

"Coach is flamed, dude. You can't just walk away." He

shoots a look at Mei, then back at me, shaking his head. "He told me to tell you that if you walk away again, kiss your season goodbye."

"Yeah. Got it—I'm coming." I turn back to Mei. "Stay here. He won't do anything with all of us here, and if he tries, that's the perfect way to get him locked up. It's only a couple more hours before we take a break, and then we can talk. Stay right here where I can see you. Yeah?"

Mei meets my eyes but says nothing. Finally, she nods. I let out a frustrated breath and run across the field to take my position. But the corner of my eye catches movement by the bleachers, and I look over to see Mei disappearing around the corner.

I take off at a sprint, focusing on her, ignoring Coach's yells for me to get back into position. I yell Mei's name, but she takes off running, so I yell louder and run faster, grabbing her arm when I catch up to her. I spin her to face me.

"What are you *doing*?" My chest heaves.

She's sobbing. "I can't do it. I won't. It's always going to be like this as long as you're with me, and I can't live knowing I ruined your life. The guilt will crush me. It's already started. You've got everything you need here, and I'm not going to hold you back anymore. I ruined your relationship with your dad and made you run away from your life. I love you so much, but I can't keep doing this to you, so…call your dad. Tell him everything. Just give me a head start so I can disappear."

I swear and grab both of her arms, pulling her closer and holding her in place. "No—stop, Mei. You're not even making sense right now. I can't even…" I curse again and let go. "What are you saying, Mei?" I squint at her like I can prevent the words she said from sinking in too deeply.

"I'm saying, if you stay with me, it's never going to get

better than this. Wherever we go, Nick will find us. You can't have Stanford *and* me. And I will never make you choose."

I take a few deep breaths and let them out slowly. "I just need you to sit on the bench and wait until after practice. Everything is happening too fast, and we're not gonna make any more last-minute decisions."

"Every decision we've ever made was last minute. Your team is waiting," she whispers but it's a hurricane, blowing everything apart, hurling it away from us. "Go."

"And if I do?"

"You'll win your season."

"With or without you?"

She looks at the ground and brings her tear-filled eyes to mine. "Without me," she whispers. "It has to be this way."

My heart pounds in my throat, ice water running through my veins, starting in my chest and flooding my limbs. "You're gonna *leave*? Like…you're walking away? From us? And me?"

Tears spill over onto her cheeks. "If I go, he'll follow me and leave you alone. If I don't, we'll both get hurt. Or worse. I love you way too much to let anything happen to you."

She's talking, but her words are droning through my head like a language I don't understand, and I turn my attention to my only available possibilities:

Chance of losing Mei if I call the cops: 100%

Chance of losing Mei if I turn and run back to practice: 100%

I look down, expecting my body to be half-submerged in the thick darkness of the decision, the weight from the atmosphere pounding me into the ground.

Mei's leaving.

Instead of figuring out a plan, she's walking away.

Without me.

My head snaps up. "So let me get this straight. If I call the cops, I lose you. If I let you run that way, and I run that way" —I throw my thumb back at the field—"I lose you. Am I right? Is it safe to assume that my only option is losing you?"

"For the last two months, I actually thought…" She shakes her head, swiping tears from her cheeks. "The last two months have been a dream, Marcus, but Nick just woke me up." Her whole body shrinks—folds in on itself, leaving nothing but her eyes, which deliver the ultimatum: *I love you, but I have to go.*"

My mind goes blank as I stare at her, my ears tuning in to the thud of someone's cleat connecting with the ball, my teammates calling to each other, their voices riding the breeze toward me, tugging at me. A plane drones overhead, and I wish I was on it, completely oblivious to the wreckage below.

A car horn blares and jerks me back to the moment, the ground opening between us, the gap filled with intentions and emotions and terrible, last-minute plans.

But am I gonna jump across that gap to Mei's side this time? The ground behind me is solid—turf and dreams and future. But on her side…

Uncertainty. Failure. Giving up. But also…Mei. I chose her once without Stanford, not knowing I'd ever get back in. Stanford didn't matter then. Why does it matter so much now?

Because I wanted Stanford way before I met Mei. It used to be everything before she took that spot.

But she's in that spot now, and Stanford could never fill the hole she'd leave. I gave up Stanford once. For Dad. Could I do it again for the one person I'll love forever, here or anywhere else? The girl I promised I'd love forever, no matter what. Is this included in "no matter what"?

Dad asked me what I would do if Nick showed up, and I

told him I'd run. I'd stay with Mei, choose her every time. Does that mean he knew Nick was out, and it was his way of telling me?

The whistle blows, and I know my time's up. Now or never. Do or die.

Do.

I turn and haul myself back to the bench for my soccer bag, keeping my eyes on my feet. I count the steps to avoid the soccer field that will forever remain stuck between my cleats and in the past.

I throw the bag over my shoulder as Coach strides toward me, his mouth moving, but my roaring thoughts drown his words. "There's an extra spot on your team," I call and walk away.

Mei is already across the parking lot. I stop, watching her, second-guessing my decision and wondering if I can handle this being my last memory of her if I turn and run back to my team.

Them or her.

Me or her.

Us.

She stops at the curb, waiting for passing cars. If she crosses the road, there won't be an us. That road will forever be our dividing line.

I take off running, my bag bouncing against my hip, and slide onto my motorcycle. I rev the engine and peel out of the parking stall. Pulling up to the curb beside Mei, I put one foot down. Her eyes roam my face, but she makes no move. "Get on," I say, my voice squeezing through my tight throat.

"Marcus, go back to—"

"Get on the bike, Mei. We have to go."

CHAPTER 16

'm stuck between a dream and a nightmare, my emotions stretched, frayed, numb. Hours ago, my life couldn't have been more perfect. I have Marcus. I'm married to him, not just dating, not hoping for someday with him. We were living in our first apartment—just ours, no one else's. He was living his soccer dreams, and I was cheering him on and figuring out how to make my culinary dreams come true in a new way. Now…we're no longer in that dream world. We're in L.A. We rode straight into the place I ran from after the assault, but this time I'm with Marcus on a motorcycle, idling at a sprawling entrance gate and there's still fear, no matter how far we've run.

This gate is like the one in front of our honeymoon beach house, but instead, I'm pretty sure the drive leads to a mansion, if it's anything like the other houses on this street. And unlike the beach house, I'm not looking forward to what's inside.

We really don't know where we're going, so maybe this is it? Maybe it's not. We have nowhere else to go, so why not here—a sprawling villa-mansion where Marcus's biological mom-who-he's-never-met-before lives.

After leaving the soccer field, we raced back to our apartment, parked right outside the doors to our building, and ran upstairs. We threw everything we own back into our weary bags. As Marcus was shoving things in his bag, an envelope dropped to the floor and he paused, staring it down. Then he'd snatched it off the ground, shoved it in his pocket, and said, "We're going to L.A." Those were the last words he'd said.

It was a long, silent drive from Stanford; we haven't had silence like this since the day we drove away from San Francisco with nothing but two bags and fear. Today, we still have only two bags, and fear has multiplied and invited loss along to take the place of hope.

Marcus's body was rigid the whole six-hour drive, like something inside him had hardened. I haven't touched him; I gripped my knees the whole ride instead, holding myself on the bike when what I really wanted to do was fly into the endless blue sky. He hasn't touched me either, and I'm afraid we both lost more than just Stanford. I'm not sure how we'll ever get it all back.

If I'm being honest, I'm okay with the silence because it's allowed me to think. Seeing Nick this morning was like drowning in air, mentally clawing at anything to pull me out and away. Memories have swerved toward me all afternoon, the ones I thought I'd buried hitting me head on. They rammed their way into my soul, and I'm thankful I was behind Marcus so he couldn't see me cry. The wind took my tears, and he'll never know. He has his own tears to fight, and I don't have energy for both of ours. My whole body is too full of hate toward Nick.

He obliterated my world and our dreams just by stepping

out of a car. He made Marcus choose between Stanford and me. I don't feel victorious to be the one he chose.

A man comes out of the guard shack in front of the gate, wearing a cardigan and tie. He asks us how he can help. Help is useless now.

"Hey. My name's Marcus Miller. Here to see Olivia Sultana." Marcus's words are flat, like they've been run over and he's peeling them off the ground.

"I'll give her a call. One moment," the guard says and goes back inside the shack.

Marcus's mom is inside the mansion. Maybe. We'll find out, if the guard opens the gate for us. If his mom chooses to allow two complete strangers inside her home, even if one of them is her flesh and blood.

Marcus looks straight ahead, waiting for the gate to swing aside and let us in. Maybe it will, maybe it won't. Nothing's gone as it should today.

But then the gate beeps, and Marcus's back rises like he's pulling air into his lungs. The guard waves us through, and Marcus eases the motorcycle past the gate and up the steep driveway to his mom. A mom he's never met or spoken to. She's as much a mystery to Marcus as my dad is to me. If the roles were reversed, I'm not sure I'd be brave enough to do what Marcus is doing. But we're also desperate. I wonder what he hopes to find behind the towering double doors of this Italian villa-style mansion overlooking L.A. Maybe he's just hoping to find hope because he left it all on the soccer field. I saw it in his backward glance. I left mine on the side-walk the moment I saw Nick, so neither of us can offer any to the other.

Marcus parks beside the cobblestone driveway and starts up the sidewalk, his posture stiff and hunched. I rush to catch up, and we climb the never-ending steps to the front doors together.

Halfway up, I grab his hand, yanking him to a stop. "Marcus."

He pauses, panic flashing in his eyes, chased by determination that hardens in his jaw.

I meet his eyes, holding onto them. "Whatever happens in there, with her, I'm in this with you. If you say we go, we go. You're not doing this alone, but if you'd rather, I'll stay out here." All I can give him is this one choice, now that I've taken everything else from him.

He pulls me into his arms and against his chest, his chin resting on top of my head. "I want you here," he whispers, choked. "I'm sorry."

I don't dare move, just soak in his voice rumbling through me, his arms wrapped completely around me, holding me to him until he draws back, and we take the few remaining steps to the doors together.

He stares at the doorbell for a minute, then rings it. He holds my hand so tightly it aches, but it's a relief to feel an ache somewhere other than my chest.

When the door finally opens, a tiny woman wearing a black pantsuit smiles, her eyes darting between us from behind white rimmed glasses. "May I help you?"

It takes me less than a second to realize this woman can't be Marcus's mom. Marcus must realize the same thing because he clears his throat and says, "Yeah, ummm...is Olivia here? I'm...her son. Marcus. I got her address from a graduation card she sent me. Just...stopping by to meet her." His words cut off at the edges like he was going to say something else but decided not to.

The woman searches Marcus's face before she gives us another warm smile. "I'm sure she'll be thrilled. However, she's not home right now. I expect her in about an hour. Would you like to come in and wait?"

————

We're sitting on the back deck overlooking L.A., both of us twirling our glass water bottles on the table opposite each other. Marcus is mentally rehearsing, lost between then and now, now and the minute Olivia gets home. He's holding back words I can see in his eyes before he shoves them aside. All that's going through my mind is how much I hate this town and being this close to what happened in a hotel not far from here…

The door sweeps open, and a female version of Marcus glides onto the deck. She hesitates, her dress and hair and miles of leg pausing, then eases toward us. I can't stop staring at her, but with a body and face like hers, she's probably used to it. It runs in the family, apparently.

"Marcus?" Her voice is low, rich, smooth. "This is a surprise."

Good or bad, I can't tell from her expression.

He stands, his chair scraping against the deck, one hand still clutching his bottled water. "Yeah…hi. I…sorry for the unexpected visit."

"Definitely unexpected!" The disinterested tone held up by fake cheer in her voice sits like a brick in my heart. He was unexpected from the beginning, and it seems nothing's changed. This is not how I'd want my long-lost parent to sound. This is not how I'd want Peter Mitchell to sound. After this moment, I don't ever want to hear the sound of his voice.

"Yeah, sorry, we just…" He rubs his neck. "I got your graduation card. Thanks for that, by the way." He looks up at her, and I wonder if he notices the resemblance. "Your address was on it. Thought I'd stop by. Hope that's okay, or—"

"It's definitely okay. I was so disappointed when Raymond told me I wouldn't get to meet you at your graduation. It was a last-minute change of plans for me to go anyway, and I had high hopes." She beams at him, then turns to me. "And you are…?"

"Mei Li." I say at the same time Marcus says. "This is Mei. My wife."

Olivia's eyes widen, and she tilts her head. "Sorry. Did you say *wife*? As in, you're married? Raymond said nothing about that…"

"Yeah. We're married." Marcus's response is clipped, cautious, like he doesn't dare take too many steps into this conversation.

"Wow." She plasters a broad smile on her face, throwing up her hands. "Lots of surprises today, I guess! Come inside." She flutters through the sliding door, waving at us to follow. Inside, she drops her bag on a table and sits on a white sofa, motioning toward the chairs across from it. "Sit down, sit down. I've got about twenty minutes before I have company coming over, but that should be plenty of time to get to know each other."

Catching up on eighteen years of life in twenty minutes?

Marcus lowers into a chair like he's sore or stiff, his hands gripping the arms. I observe Olivia and her long, toned legs between the slit in her dress—her glossy blond hair, dark eyebrows, and wide forehead which leads to round, impossibly blue eyes. She's beautiful. She's Marcus. He has all her angles, her perfectly sloped nose. I always thought he looked so much like his dad, but the only thing that's different between him and Olivia is how fake she is, inside and out.

The woman who answered the door sets a tray of drinks

on the end table. Olivia throws her an air kiss and grabs a bottle, leaning forward so her cleavage joins the conversation. She reaches out and touches Marcus's knee, beaming at him.

"It is so good to finally meet you. And wow—you've decided to take your own path in life. Good for you." She laughs. "Not the one I would've taken if I were you, but I guess you and I are alike after all, doing things other people don't want us to do."

Marcus stiffens but gives her a shaky smile and rubs the back of his neck, which must be raw by now. "Yeah. I guess."

"Well, you look just like me, so now I know what I'd look like as an eighteen-year-old guy." She takes a long drink and sets her bottle down. "Are you two in L.A. for long? If so, you're so welcome to stay in the pool house. Just remodeled it, and it's a perfect little getaway." She wiggles her shoulders suggestively. "But join Allen and me for dinner, definitely. He'll be devastated if he doesn't meet you. I'll have Isabella get you all settled into the pool house, and you have until eight so…do whatever. I'll even send some wine down with you so you can have a little pre-dinner romance." She looks between us, expectant.

"Uhhh…" Marcus glances around the room, his eyes darting to the front door. "Thanks. Yeah, pool house would be great. We'll get ourselves settled. But don't worry about the wine—we don't drink."

She raises her eyebrows. "Two teenagers who don't drink? Maybe you aren't mine and Raymond's child after all." She laughs, throwing her head back dramatically. "We used to have the *greatest* of times when we were wasted." She waves a hand. "Anyway…we'll skip the alcohol for you two, then. Do whatever you want. You obviously don't need my permission. I'll have Isabella fetch you when dinner is ready."

CHAPTER 17

The long, glossy dining table dividing Olivia from Mei and me pretty much sums up the slippery distance I feel with someone who supposedly gave birth to me. Cold, hard, no scars. Polished. Sharp edges. Since we arrived three hours ago, everything's felt like if I make one wrong turn, I'll meet the tip of that sharp edge and bleed out. The silence between Mei and me only added to the tension. So, when we got to the pool house, Mei slipped into the shower, and I didn't follow for the first time in weeks; I needed more space to think than even that thirty-person shower could offer. After she got out and I took her place, I stayed in until the water ran cold. After I was done, I sat on the back patio and stared into the bushes while my mind slowly, cautiously unwound.

Now I'm suspended in discomfort at the dining table, twisting the cap on my imported Italian soda that probably cost more than my Adidas. "Thanks for dinner," I say to Olivia. My leg bounces under the table.

Her gaze lingers on me. "Funny, you look just like me but

your mannerisms…it's like I'm looking at Raymond right now." She shoots a smile. "And if you're wondering what you should call me, it's Olivia. Just Olivia. No one would ever believe I could have an eighteen-year-old son, anyway."

Like I would call her mom after she strode into the dining room wearing a skirt I'm afraid will slide up and show me exactly where I came from.

"It's still just such a great surprise to have you here." She sips her wine, then sets it down, clearing her throat. "I only wish I didn't have to leave on Saturday to deal with a new line in Paris."

Turns out, my timing's always been inconvenient.

Her house help floats around the dining room, making sure our plates are full of appetizers that look like leaves, and even though they smell nasty, I pop one in my mouth so I don't have to talk. Is this what my life would've been like if Dad and Olivia had stayed together? Or if they'd split but I had to choose to live with one or the other? And what if I'd chosen to live with Olivia? I'd go to a private school. Drive a Ferrari. Eat gross food in fancy dining rooms. Be a total douchebag. I'm glad I didn't have a choice.

Allen, Olivia's boyfriend or agent or husband or whatever he is, keeps flipping his hair and smiling at the windows like the paparazzi are outside, just waiting to get a great shot. He's too old for that hairstyle, but Olivia can't keep her fingers out of it. Dad looks like a Scottish warrior compared to this mannequin-guy. I wonder how many guys there have been since Dad.

"So you really got married?" Olivia rakes her fingers through the back of Allen's hair like he's her puppy and raises her eyebrows at me.

I nod. "Yep. Really did. About three weeks ago. On the twenty-first."

She swirls her glass of wine and takes a sip. "Why?"

I choke down whatever I just put in my mouth and chase it with the whole bottle of soda. Did she seriously just ask that? Aren't rich models supposed to have manners?

"I mean, don't get me wrong. Mei Li's beautiful." Olivia gives Mei a tight smile, and I lean a little closer to Mei, like I can shield her from Olivia's judgement.

"Uhh…" I glance at Mei, who looks like she's concentrating on surfing the waves of awkward rolling through the room. "Because we couldn't stand being apart? Because we've been in love since day one?" Why does she think we got married? "Why are you two married or shacking up or whatever you're doing?" I motion between her and her man-pet.

Allen chokes on his food, and Olivia laughs. "Oh, we're not married. I don't believe in it. But if I did, I'm slightly older than eighteen. Even if I don't look it." She leans over and kisses Allen, and I find my plate fascinating and a perfect place to puke until she speaks again. "I've been eighteen, so I get it. I mean, I thought I loved Raymond for, like, ten minutes." She laughs and rolls her eyes. "I finally figured out I just liked looking at him. Getting pregnant definitely wasn't part of the plan, but I guess I looked a little too long." She flips her hair. "Don't get me wrong. I tried the whole mom thing. You were about ten months old when Raymond finished police academy and proposed, thinking we could be the picture-perfect family. But really, I didn't want any of it."

My blood runs cold. "I was ten months old when you left?"

She takes a sip of wine, staring at me over the rim of the glass. "Has Raymond never told you any of this?"

I shake my head, and Mei rubs my leg under the table.

"Really?" She leans forward, a smirk on her face. "What did he tell you about me?"

"Nothing."

She sits back in her chair, running her hand over her hair. "Huh. Well...yeah. I gave motherhood a go. But after ten months, I just knew it wasn't for me. And after Raymond proposed, I told him I felt the best thing we could do for you was give you up for adoption—let someone who wanted kids raise you. But he refused. So I controlled what I could and that was that."

My whole body tenses against the information assault, my stomach cold, her words acidic. I've never heard this version of my history. Dad said she left not long after I was born. But...ten months after? She wanted to put me up for adoption after ten months? Rejection echoes through my body, achy and empty, but before I can respond, Olivia continues.

"So maybe you two are Raymond and Olivia 2.0, and Mei Li just likes looking at you." She grins at us like she didn't just drop a jagged boulder in the middle of the table. She spears something on her plate with her fork. "You pregnant?" she asks Mei.

"Are you serious?" I blurt before Mei can say anything. "No, she's not pregnant. What kind of—"

"Why are you offended, Marcus? You wouldn't be sitting here right now if I hadn't gotten pregnant at eighteen, you know." Olivia tips her wine glass at Mei. "I wouldn't blame you if you were pregnant, Mei Li. He's gorgeous—perfect jaw line, amazing nose, perfect face, perfect height. All of it. And those blue eyes. A camera would make out with that face." She and Allen chuckle. He clinks his wine glass against hers and shrugs at me.

"I'll try not to be jealous since she's your mom." He throws his smile at me as an apology.

"Whoa, whoa, whoa," Olivia says, waving her hands. "Let's not call me 'mom.' I never wanted to be one but I have to say…I'm proud of my hard work."

I consider grabbing her glass and hurling it against the wall, and Mei must feel me tense because she slides her hand onto my leg and blurts, "I guess neither of us can resist Miller boys. And I've definitely been in love with Marcus for way longer than ten minutes. In fact, I love him so much, nothing could make me leave him." She takes a bite of a cracker with a glob of yellow on it.

I snap my head toward her, my eyebrows reaching for the 80-foot ceiling. "*Are you freaking kidding me? Did you really just say that? I love you so hard right now.*" We haven't talked in hours, and I've kept my eyes quiet on purpose, but I could jump on this rich person table and breakdance over that comment.

Mei sips her water while Olivia watches us.

"You two are adorable," Olivia croons. "Seriously. What did Raymond say about all of this, anyway? He's so opinionated about everything, and when I stopped by your apartment, he was so lit up about you not showing up for graduation, he was practically in flames. I can only imagine his reaction to this whole situation."

Hearing her call him Raymond all night has grated against my nerves. She doesn't know him. Doesn't know me. Doesn't know anything about us because she chose not to. Despite my anger toward Dad, she has no right to talk about him. I wanna stand between him and her stupid words. Protect him from her sharp angles and scratchy eyelashes and puffy lips. Kind of like I always tried to do but didn't realize why until now.

"Raymond gets it," I say even though he totally doesn't and never will. "He's getting married, too."

"Mmm." Olivia's lips are tight. "Interesting. He said nothing about that when I saw him, but Rozalynn will be so happy. She always wanted him to get married and 'settle down like a good little boy.' She just always wanted it to be with me but…no thanks." Olivia shakes her head too many times.

I'm coming unglued that she mentioned Meemaw, like she has any right to talk about her, either. I'm sick of deflecting her insults and hope the house help brings out food right now and rescues me from this moment.

But Allen clears his throat. "So, Marcus…what are your plans for the future?"

We just showed up. Like we were in the L.A. neighborhood and decided to drop in for a dinner party. I haven't mentioned we're homeless, and I won't. Meth labs are a more attractive option than anything Olivia has to offer. "Uhh, we're…" Wandering. Running. Fugitives? "Taking a summer road trip before school starts."

"Ah. That sounds perfect. Wish I'd done that when I was your age instead of focusing so much on making money." He smiles and rests his arms on the table like a normal person having a normal conversation. "Where are you headed in the fall?"

I swallow. Mei doesn't know that when we stopped for gas earlier, I called Stanford and found out I can apply for a leave of absence—put my scholarship on hold and maybe get my spot on the team back. Maybe.

"Stanford," I blurt, and Mei tenses beside me. But I refuse to say "maybe" or "I hope" because right now I could say anywhere since the answer today is nowhere. Someday, when this dumpster fire is finished exploding, I'll be back at Stanford. So yeah—that's the plan. After all this.

"Oh, very nice!" Allen says, beaming across the table.

"Congratulations. Do you know what you want to study? And what about you, Mei Li?"

Allen's asked us approximately a hundred more questions than Olivia, and actually seems to care, so I feel bad for lying to him.

"I'm pre-med," I answer, nodding.

"Culinary." Mei's voice is strong and solid, like she feels next to me. I rub her thigh under the table, and she puts her hand over mine.

"Wow. That's just great. Just great." Allen nods, but Olivia leans toward us.

"Or...I could get you both started in the biz." Her focus shifts from me to Mei and back again. "We could hire you both at the store, and Marcus, you could do shoots on the weekends. I'd love to show you off to my agent. He'll love your look. He has a type." She motions toward herself and bursts out laughing from either too much wine or too much of herself. I'm mad at Dad all over again for ever loving her. Even madder at him for telling me she came for graduation. I choke back anger and take a drag on my water.

"Oh. Wow. Yeah, that's...something I've never considered. Or wanted." I manage a shaky smile. It's the best I can do when what I wanna do is run. "Thanks for the offer but...not really my thing."

"Well, it should be." She flips her hair and adjusts the strap on her dress that shows way more of her than anyone wants to see. "You're obviously not following in Raymond's footsteps, so there's a big old world out there. You too, Mei Li. My agent is always looking for people of color."

I've never shoved food in my mouth as fast as I do when the helper lady sets down a plate of something unidentifiable in front of me.

Olivia smooths her napkin on her lap. "If you two don't have plans for tomorrow, I'll take you to the store, and you can meet all my people. It's in the Fairmont Hotel. I'll show you a bit of my world. Once you get a glimpse, it will be hard to say no to it."

Mei stands, tossing Olivia a weak smile as she picks up her plate. "I'm so sorry, but I'm going to call it a night and let you talk. Thank you so much for dinner." She scoots in her chair and disappears.

I watch her go, wondering what's wrong, my legs twitching to go after her, but Olivia continues the conversation.

"So how about tomorrow?"

My attention is with Mei, and I wish my body had gone with her, too. "Umm…sure. Yeah," I answer distractedly. But no way. Not a chance. We won't be here tomorrow—I'll make sure of that.

———

If I'd met Allen somewhere else, some other way, some other time, we'd probably be chill. I like the guy. Just can't respect him because he's with Olivia. After dinner, we went back into the white living room, and he'd asked me questions about soccer. Turns out, he played in college. Olivia got bored and scrolled on her phone while Allen and I talked, then interrupted so she could take me on a tour of the house, which could fit 100 Clubhouses inside it. At midnight, I told them I was tired, but instead of heading to the pool house, I came out here on the deck and just…sat. Alone in the dark. Letting my thoughts swirl in all the emptiness between me and the city below.

Less than a day ago, I was on the Stanford soccer field, running plays and living my dream. Now it's 2 AM, and all my dreams are dead, along with the one where I meet my mom and she's amazing and loving and wants me in her life. But she decided a long time ago she didn't. After she'd known me for ten months.

I close my eyes, clenching my jaw against the surge of pain. What did I think she'd be like? A mom who just steps out of the kitchen with freshly baked cookies and milk? Offers to read me bedtime stories? Throws a welcome home party for the son she's agonized over for eighteen years because "Raymond" intentionally kept us apart? Maybe an apology? A sort-of apology? A hint of one? Didn't happen. None of it happened. I wish Dad had told me the truth. It would've hurt a lot less to kill my dreams when I was young than it does now, after eighteen years of believing one thing and finding out the opposite. Dad's had eighteen years to settle into the truth that he has terrible taste in women, and I really did derail his life.

I pull out my almost-dead phone and navigate to the Stanford leave of absence form. All I can do is apply, then wait and hope and frantically pray that they accept my excuse: family crisis. I squint at the light beaming from the screen, my fingers stiff but determined to get this thing sent before I head back to the pool house and Mei. I'm not gonna tell her until I know the answer, yes or no. We can't go back until the Nick thing's settled anyway, and I wish that was as easy as an application.

I double-check the form and click the *Submit* button. Now I wait. They'll either tell me I can freeze my scholarship and my spot on my team or tell me too bad.

I push out of the chair and walk down the lit path to the

pool house like I'm at some kind of resort instead of trapped in a busted-up dream. I wanna run from all the debris behind me, the resentment building toward Mei and fear about where we go next because we're not staying here. I'm disgusted and embarrassed with myself for building Olivia and the Mom Moment up in my head.

I stare at the pool house door, my feet heavy, heart empty. Lamplight streaks through the cut glass on the door. Mei's on the other side, so why do I feel so alone right now? My hand shakes as I turn the knob and slip inside. I close the door behind me and lean back against it.

Mei's curled up on the bed, still in her clothes, even though she left a few hours ago. She sits up and swipes at her eyes when I shut the door.

I stop, hand on the knob like it's gonna hold me up. "You okay?"

She blinks at the ceiling and nods, her lip quivering, and I'm on the bed in two steps, pulling her into my arms. "What happened?"

She cries silently into my chest for a few minutes, her emotions leaking all over mine until we're clutching each other as we drown. "Talk to me, Mei," I beg.

"I…" Her voice is pulled under by tears, so I clutch her tighter, and she digs her fingertips into my back. "I didn't realize that coming back here…I didn't know it would affect me like this, but it's too close."

The words swirl in my head and drop one by one with a thud, kicking up dust, but no answers. "Too close to what?"

"The hotel." Her sobs deepen.

The hotel. L.A. We're in L.A. The last time she was here…

"The store Olivia mentioned? In the Fairmont Hotel? That's the hotel," Mei chokes. "I can't go there again."

I sit back on my legs, holding her by the arms. My throat's raw from the flow of emotions up and down it all night. "We're not going there, Mei. We're leaving."

"I'll be fine. We can stay. I just can't—"

"No. I wanna get so far from here." My jaw aches from being clenched for the last four hours. "She has a wall covered in pictures of herself." I picture the gallery of model photos. "She doesn't have room to love anyone but herself, and my dad told me I'm turning out to be just like her." I pause when my voice wavers. "But I won't be her. I can't even stand to look at her because I hate that we look so much alike. She wanted to give me away after knowing me for ten months. Who does that?" Silence crashes, a little of my emptiness spilling into the room. "We've been here four hours too long, and I'm so sorry I brought you here," I whisper to the bedspread and pull Mei back into my arms.

"Where do you want to go?" she murmurs.

I close my eyes. Back to Stanford. Back to my spot on the team. Back to the life we left this morning or the one before that when I didn't know Olivia. I want the future with Mei, but more than anything I want something solid around us, and right now, nothing is. "I don't know where, but we're getting out of here."

———

The sun has yet to show up, but we're still on I-15 in the middle of the desert, headed east. Toward somewhere. Anywhere. Nowhere, maybe. Not a studio apartment on a college campus that meant we'd made it somewhere and definitely not a soccer field that *proved* I'd made it somewhere. Away from L.A. where I never would have come if I'd stopped to think for one second.

When my eyesight blurs, I veer off the road and park under the lit canopy of a lonely gas station. I hang my helmet from the handlebar and shove the gas nozzle into the tank to top it off. Mei waits with it, and I go inside the convenience store, striding to the back and snatching two sodas from the fridge. I throw them on the checkout counter and rip some cash out of my wallet.

The cashier scans the sodas, glancing at me. "Long night?"

"You could say that," I answer, shoving the change into my wallet. "What's the nearest city?"

"Vegas. 'Bout an hour and a half or so…"

"Thanks." I grab the sodas and push the door open with my shoulder. Mei sits sideways on the motorcycle, watching me walk toward her, fingers spinning her ring in her lap. I avoid her eyes, afraid of what mine might say. "Guess we're going to Las Vegas," I say, handing her the soda and throwing my leg over the seat. I start the bike so at least there's some noise between us.

She hesitates before scooting behind me, her hands gripping the seat instead of my waist. I tear out of the gas station, thankful for the darkness of the deserted road and the way the yellow stripes rush at us.

When the haze of city lights stretches across the horizon, I speed up, eager for a distraction and a target for my attention.

Buildings pop up on either side of the road, and I turn off the interstate. Never been to Las Vegas, but I gotta figure out where we're going so my mind will stop pulling me backward to where we've been. Or comparing the looming mega-resorts to our safe, calm Stanford apartment. The never-ending asphalt and cement of Las Vegas to the soccer field turf.

My mind shifts to dark thoughts, and I shut it down, stopping at the first pay-by-the-hour motel we come to. I don't wanna think about staying for longer than that. But for now, I'm done thinking. Done with roads and motorcycles and Mei with all the extra space she's giving me on this seat. I just wanna go to sleep and wake up back in Stanford as if none of this ever happened.

CHAPTER 18

This motel is where people go to die.

We'd rolled into the pay-by-the-hour motel this morning at 5 AM, ripped off the comforter, and laid on top of the sheets, staring at the ceiling. The room was sweltering from the non-existent air conditioning, but it was frigid in the space between Marcus and me.

I'd fallen asleep at some point, and when I woke up, Marcus was gone. For a split second, I thought he'd gone back to Stanford without me. But then I'd seen the note on the nightstand, saying he'd gone to look for a place we could stay long term.

I'd showered, making sure not to touch the sagging walls or filthy curtain, and by the time I was done getting ready, Marcus had come back and told me he'd found a place. We'd grabbed our bags and jumped on the bike, not looking back.

In the late morning light, the streets of Las Vegas are gray and weary, like all excitement and energy drained when the electrical switches were turned off at sunrise. Now everything's getting beaten by the sun, including us, as Marcus parks the bike and we shuffle across melting asphalt toward the slumped stucco building.

We trudge upstairs to the second floor and stop at room 252, its door dented in the perfect shape of a fist. There's space at the bottom of the door for any and all desert creatures to crawl inside and join us. Or crawl out, depending on what currently lives inside.

We're about to find out.

Marcus unlocks the door and swings it open to reveal just how much $69.99 per day gets you in Las Vegas. My eyes jump across the cracked linoleum and threadbare carpet. The dingy walls. A sagging bed on a rusty frame that perfectly matches the feelings we're carrying with us. The quilted bedspread looks like it's been here since the 1970s and the sea green accent wall is chipped and faded. There's a tiny TV mounted on the wall, slightly crooked. A miniature kitchen is shoved in the corner, and the bathroom door is next to the beige fridge, which doesn't match the white two-unit stove or black microwave. I'm afraid to see the bathroom. I will spend any amount of money necessary on cleaning supplies and shower shoes. We're definitely going to need shower shoes.

It's a perfect hideout for drug dealers, prostitutes, or a couple on the run from a released rapist, human trafficker, and felon. Nick will never think to look for us here. No one will. If we die from murder, rat bites, or the secondhand smoke stuck to the walls, no one will ever find us.

"Ahhh." Marcus tosses his bag on the wobbly, faux wood table. "Home sweet hell on earth. So appropriate."

The anxiety that's taken up residency inside me flares, burning up my throat. "Not true." I take a breath and plaster on a smile, pushing away the tension wrapped around me. "It's way better than the last place, and we'll make it great! Make it ours. We know we can. It's better than—"

"Stop, Mei." He closes his eyes, shakes his head.

"Stop what?"

His eyes snap open. "There's no way to spin this into something good, because it's not," he growls, his jaw clenching.

"I wasn't trying to make it—"

"Yes—you are." His voice rises and so does my heart rate when Marcus swears. "You've been doing it since we left Stanford—trying to put a positive spin on everything, like you can fix it with words. But there's nothing positive about any of this. If Nick came walking by right now, I'd kill him."

I have tried to fix it—to help him see the tiny sliver of good—because I have to stay strong. But it's exhausting. This isn't what either of us wants, but I don't know how to make things better. He's got no idea how I feel because all he can do is think about himself—what he's lost, like I didn't lose anything when Nick showed up. But I lost Marcus, and I lost hope.

"What am I supposed to say?" I burst before I can stop the eruption. "I'm sorry a million more times? Because I am. I'm sorry we're here. I'm sorry you left Stanford. I'm sorry you lost your scholarship and your soccer team. I'm sorry we ever went to L.A. and that you had to meet Olivia. I'm sorry she's your mom and that you look like her and that she's the worst. I'm sorry your life isn't what you want and that you think punishing me with silence will make anything better."

"Oh really? You're being punished? Is that how you feel?" His words cut and anger slips from the gashes inside me.

"Yes! I didn't tell you to come. You chose to be here and now I get to walk on eggshells because you made the wrong choice. You act like you're the only one who lost things, but somehow, you forget that I had to run from my life, too. But I had to, you didn't. You could have stayed like I know you wanted to. So why don't you just go back and forget all of this ever happened?"

He turns away from me, grabs his bag, and yanks things out of it, throwing everything into a pile on the lumpy sofa.

I glare out the window while he silently opens drawers and hangs his clothes on flimsy wire hangers, then shoves his bag in the top of the closet.

The tension's too deep to wade through even if I knew what to say, but when the silence gets too heavy, it cracks my resolve. "Marcus, I—"

He shakes his head. "I can't talk about this right now. If I do, things are gonna fly out of my mouth. So I'm gonna go for a ride." He grabs his motorcycle key and heads for the door. "Maybe I'll find a job while I'm at it so we can stay here forever."

CHAPTER 19

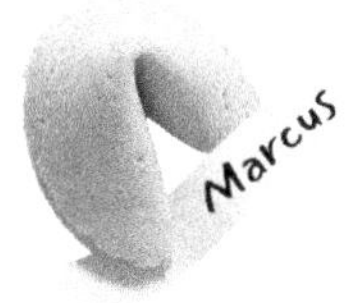

've never had to look for a job before. After today, I never want to again. Dad wouldn't let me work during school, even when I begged to work with Ty at his dad's electric bike shop. He said school and soccer was my job. And then it really was at Stanford. When I had everything paid for. Handed right to me. Everything, all of it. And now, I'm parking the bike in front of a busted-up wasteland of a motel, no hope in sight among the homeless people strewn across the sidewalks and beside dumpsters. All of them too consumed by their own misery to notice me just sitting here, idling. They've lost it all. I'm only one small step ahead, and that's only because I have enough money to cover a few weeks here. If Stanford rejects my leave of absence request and Nick never gets caught? Who knows.

I shut off the engine and stare at the almost-empty gas gauge. Just like me, almost empty, and it's gonna take a lot more than pulling up to a pump to get me up and running tonight. Or tomorrow. Any day after this.

I close my eyes, sink into the motorcycle seat under all the weight of the last two days. First the Stanford loss, then Olivia. Her super awesome news about wanting to put me up for adoption. Major rejection streaked all over the last 48 hours. Massive disappointment. I don't know why I care. I already knew she didn't want me, so what does it matter if I was barely born or ten months old? Why do I feel like I've failed at something just by existing?

I look at the motel room door, hoping Mei's just behind it. A bunch of cracked, crumbling asphalt and a dented metal door between us. I've failed at a lot of things lately. After our fight earlier, I wouldn't be surprised if she left. It's my fault, and I know it. I've gotta figure out how to not take all my frustration and resentment out on her. I made the choice to leave San Francisco. Stanford. None of this is her fault. It's Nick's. But I made the choice to stay with Mei, so now I gotta figure out how to be happy about it, or I lose her. It can all go away so fast like it almost did the first time we fought.

I put the lock on my ignition, make sure everything's out of the bike, and drag myself to the door, ignoring the guy ranting to himself on the second-floor landing.

I slip inside the murky motel room, close the door, and lean against it. Mei's curled up on the bed, one of my hoodies wrapped around her like I should be. I switch off the yellow lamp and sink into the chair by the window, absorbing the quiet. Light from the blinking neon motel sign seeps through the crack between the curtains. Its pattern numbs my mind, and I blink only when my eyes burn, demanding me to concentrate on immediate needs instead of "whats," "ifs," and "whys."

Leaning my elbows on my knees, I rub my hands down my face. I haven't said more than "I'm sorry" to Mei in over eight hours and that was in a text. Nothing else since I left her in this rathole while I looked for a job so we can afford more rathole time.

Yelling outside the window pulls my head up, and I crane my neck to see a guy and girl standing by some crappy car, fuzzy dice hanging from the rearview mirror. The guy's in her face, and she's pummeling his chest, but he grabs her neck and goes nose-to-nose, a string of profanities audible despite the drone of traffic on the interstate behind the building.

My heart speeds up when he slams her against the car. I stand, pulling my phone from my pocket to call 911, but stop when the girl yanks the driver's side door open and jumps inside before squealing from the parking lot, leaving the guy standing alone.

"That's right! Keep driving, 'cause if you stop, you're dead!" he yells at the disappearing car. He spits on the ground and lights a joint.

My heart's yo-yo-ing between my throat and stomach as I stare at him in his tattered jeans and baseball jersey. He takes a drag, white smoke curling around him like he has nothing better to do after assaulting and threatening to kill a girl.

Apparently, there are guys like that all over the place. We just ran from one. Nick's treated Mei like that before—worse, even. And he could've done it again two days ago. Mei had to be just as scared as that girl, but didn't have a car to jump into. I don't know. Mei hasn't really talked about it besides the basic details she told me in Seattle. And I haven't asked because I've been too caught up in my own issues.

The guy sits in the parking lot, face turned toward the sky. Smokes his joint, picks at asphalt. Talks to himself. The girl's long gone, and I hope she stays far away from him.

I ease back in the chair. Emotions push against my chest,

uncurl, knot, tangle, sink to the bottom of me. I lean forward, face in my hands, and let all the emotions push up and out of me. Swearing to myself, I swipe at tears. Swallow nausea from realizing not only what I lost when we ran, but what I almost lost if Mei hadn't run as fast as she did from L.A. If we hadn't left Stanford, I might be sitting alone on an empty soccer field like I was the first time I thought I lost her but this time, I wouldn't have been given another chance. If Nick had gotten to Mei, there wouldn't be enough soccer fields or scholarships in this world to keep me from taking myself out of it.

I watch her sleep in the purple haze in the room, my heart cracking and shifting. Settling back into its place. All the emotions leak out and burn as they trail down my face. When I get control of myself, I kick off my shoes, take off my shirt and pants, then slide under the sheets. Scooting next to Mei, I wrap her in my arms, and she stirs, her arms slipping around my neck, my wet cheek against her collarbone.

"I'm so sorry, Mei," I choke, holding her tighter. Her heart beats against my chest and I want to absorb it, pull it into me. "I'm so sorry."

"It's okay," she whispers into my hair, but her voice is flat, and I'm not sure she means it, because we both know nothing's really okay right now and may never be again. But from now on, I'm gonna try my hardest to make it that way.

———

The world's a little brighter this morning as I wrap my towel around my waist and step out of the bathroom, ruffling the excess water out of my hair. On the bed, Mei's scrolling on her phone. Probably reading San Francisco news like I do every day, just in case Nick's been picked up and it's safe for us to come out of hiding. We don't talk about it, though. Whenever I bring up Nick, she shuts down, so I back off. I don't wanna stir anything up that she doesn't want stirred.

She watches me walk toward her, her eyes sending an invitation I won't resist. I smile as I crawl across the bed and kiss my way to her lips. Yeah, today's definitely gonna be better than the last five days when we could barely look at each other and tensed every time we accidentally touched. She's tense now for a very different, way better reason.

Thirty minutes later, we drift back to reality together and I lean my forehead on her collarbone. "Ten minutes before I have to leave for my interview," I murmur against her skin.

She protests so I kiss her long and deep, then groan as I tear myself from her, glancing over my shoulder on my way back to the bathroom. I pause, turn around, then grit my teeth and shake my head when she laughs, knowing exactly what she's doing to me. Barking my frustration through a smile, I step into the bathroom and check the time on my phone, holding my breath when I see a new email. From Stanford. I click on it, my eyes skimming the response to my leave of absence request: APPROVED.

My whole body jolts, and I close my eyes, clutching my phone. Breathe through my nose. Okay. This is a start. I swallow the adrenaline because words and relief wanna burst out of me, but I'm not gonna tell Mei yet—not until I've got everything worked out. There are four more steps to take before we can get back to where we were. But we've got until August. Almost a year. Totally doable.

My eyes devour the academic advisor's email—she wants me to schedule a time to talk so we can go over details and process for returning, including getting my spot back on the team, which, unfortunately, can't be discussed until spring when scholarships go out. But there is so much hope sitting in these black and white words. I set the phone down on the counter and rub my hands down my face. Yeah. Today's already massively better than every day since we left Stanford, and it's only 8 AM. Today, hope finally caught up to me.

CHAPTER 20

Two Months Later

MARCUS'S SEPTEMBER GOALS:

1. Make Mei smile every day, multiple times a day (minimum of 10)
2. Find the tunnels under the city where people live
3. Make Mei laugh every day, multiple times a day (minimum 5 times—I can't be hilarious all the time)
4. Learn how to do a handstand since Mei can, and I hate losing to her
5. Make Mei happy every day (no minimum)
6. Take a motorcycle ride to Area 51 so I can prove there's no such thing as aliens
7. Make Mei really, really happy. A lot. (Unlimited times)

"I hate it when you work on my days off," I whine into my afternoon bowl of cereal. "I can only try so many new recipes. And who wants to clean or do laundry for fun? We really need to get on the same schedule."

Marcus puts the milk carton back in our nearly empty fridge and laughs. "Sounds like somebody's spoiled now, living in this luxury extended stay motel instead of porno-murder motel where you had to fight for survival all day." He picks up his bowl of cereal and sits across from me. "You got free cable with fifteen mostly working channels, and now you're too good for it, you and your quarter-operated washing machines." He shakes his head and I laugh as he goes on. "What more do you need than drug busts every night, prostitution rings on the daily? Or twenty-four-hour security since the cops are constantly out in that parking lot?"

"You're right—thanks for keeping me grounded." I push the floating marshmallows to the side of my bowl with my spoon, saving them for last. "But if I have to hear 'Exotic Dancer' One and 'Exotic Dancer' Two talk about how much they'd like to 'get with you' one more time while I'm pulling your underwear from the dryer, I'm gonna—"

"Ooh. You mean the strippers across the hall? I like where this is going."

I roll my eyes, scooping marshmallows onto my spoon, and devour them before taking my bowl to the sink. "Seriously, though," I say, scrubbing my bowl and setting it on the rack to dry. "It's like they think I'm deaf. Or maybe they don't care. Either way, it bugs me. And—AND," I say over my shoulder, "when you come home from work every night, they're lurking outside, ready to rip off your clothes before they go to work to take off theirs. Have you not noticed?"

Marcus's chair scrapes the floor, and I smile down at the

sink, ready to feel him behind me, and when his hands run down my sides, I relax into him, his laughter rumbling against my neck as he kisses it.

"It's not funny."

"You're right," he murmurs into my ear. "It's hilarious that you assume I've even noticed them when you're anywhere in this world." He kisses the tattoo on the back of my neck and rests his chin on top of my head, his arms draped over my shoulders. "The girl you should be worried about is the sexy one on the third floor. The Asian with the tattoo on her neck? You seen her?" He whistles and swears. "Can't stop staring. Think I'm in love with her. She does things to me…"

I smile and lean my head back, wrapping my fingers around his forearms. "You don't even know her."

"But I'm going to. I've told the guys at work about her, and they say I should make my move, but…I'm kinda nervous, you know? She's way out of my league, but I hear she likes white guys twice her size, so I think I might have a shot. What do you think?" He kisses the soft spot behind my ear, his breath warming my neck, and goosebumps rise on my skin. "Should I try and seduce her tonight? It's all I can think about."

"I've heard she's always hoped to be seduced by you, but I've also heard she loves gelato, so you should probably start there and see how it goes."

"Ooh—good call. You give the best dating advice." Marcus kisses my neck again before his hands guide me to face him. "Anything else you've heard she likes?"

I bite my lower lip, sliding my hands under his shirt, and his stomach muscles tense. "She's mentioned one other possibility…"

Marcus groans. "Is this other possibility something that can wait until after work so I don't get fired for being late?"

I grip the waistband of his pants and tug him to me. "Show me the gelato, and we'll see."

He kisses my forehead and snatches his valet jacket off the chair. "Tell her that after work, I'm gonna make that possibility a reality." He walks to the door. "I'll be home at one. Two at the latest."

I follow him onto the landing outside, but in a surprise twist, he turns and backs me against the doorframe, his mouth hot against mine. I gasp against his lips, and he growls and presses closer.

"You're dangerous," he breathes before our kiss works to a fever pitch, his body heat washing over me until we break apart to catch our breath. My legs tremble as the rest of me slowly drifts back to Earth.

"See you after work, wifey." He gives me one last lingering kiss and whispers, "Love you 365 forever."

Biting my lip, I lean against the doorjamb and watch him walk toward the stairs before my eyes collide with the two neighbor girls where they stand, stalled on the stairs, stunned.

I smile, then wave and hurry inside. Closing the door behind me, I lean back, my palms against the metal as I smile to myself. I'm so grateful to have the old Marcus back. So glad we're talking again. So grateful to be laughing again and giving ourselves to each other instead of locking ourselves away like we did for the first few weeks in Vegas. Even after Marcus apologized, things were still off. We had to move hotels a few times until we found this place, and he had a few interviews that didn't work out before The Palazzo job came through. All I could think about was whether Marcus would continue his plan to stay with me or turn back. But then, he got a job. We found this place and settled. It started to feel a little better between us. Then there was the night we heard someone singing right outside the window.

We'd rolled over in bed, frowned at each other, and gone to the window, peeking through the slit in the curtains. A man dressed like a chicken stood in a pothole in the middle of the parking lot, holding a Styrofoam egg high above his head and singing for someone named Crystal to come out and meet their baby. Marcus had lost it when chicken man started singing a lullaby to the egg. All of Marcus's locked away laughter and happiness had burst out that night and set mine free, too.

The guy kept singing Crystal's name, and we'd laughed until we were rolling on the bed, holding our stomachs and wiping tears. When we could finally breathe again, we'd heard screeching and darted to the window just as a woman wearing platform boots and nothing else ran toward the chicken man, grabbed the egg, and held it to her chest.

Marcus had clamped his hands over my eyes from where he stood behind me, his genuine belly laugh rumbling all around me.

I look around our room—our four bowls, four plates, two cups, and utensils stacked neatly on the counter. Toothbrushes next to each other on the bathroom sink. Marcus's Adidas in the corner by the chair, his shirt still slung over the lamp from this morning. A few books on the nightstand, a couple of Sharpies beside them. Empty wrappers and Buddha sitting beside Magic 8.

As gross as this place is, it's our home now, and while I hate the brown, leak-stained ceiling, rusted metal railings, and criminal neighbors, I love the moments of just us in our little world we've taken back from Nick and Olivia. Like the sheets covered in Sharpie messages we leave for each other.

Our clothes hanging next to each other in the closet. The collection of funny notes Marcus tapes to the refrigerator. The pickle jar we labeled "Mansion Fund" and fill with Marcus's wadded up tip money. The wilting flower arrangement I got on sale at work to brighten this place.

I glance at the clock, planning my next eight hours without Marcus. I haven't cooked in a while, so since I have the entire day to myself, I'll head to the store and grab some things to make a huge breakfast tomorrow. Night valet shifts mean working through dinner, and Marcus is starving when he wakes up the next morning. He'll be upset that I went out alone but will probably forgive me once his stomach's full. It'll be fine—the grocery store's a few blocks away, but I'll keep to the busy streets. Marcus and I are back to normal, and I want to put normal back into everything we do. I don't want to spend my days off stuck inside alone with Fear. Nick may have followed us to Stanford, but I'm not letting him ruin the new life we've created here.

———

1:53 AM and still no Marcus.

I put my phone back on its charger and roll over. Marcus called me around midnight to say he'd be working late. There was an event tonight, and they needed all valet drivers there to help. I'd whined a little about not seeing him in forever before we said goodbye, then I crawled into bed. I've been trying to sleep ever since. But my imagination is persistent when I'm alone at night with only my dark, lurking thoughts, wondering who might be just outside the door.

I close my eyes, breathing myself to relaxation. When my phone chirps, I roll over and grab it, blinking at the message:

Marcus: I have a surprise for you. Open the door and look down.

I crawl out of bed, throw on some pajamas, and undo all the locks before flinging the door open. No Marcus, but on the mat where he should be standing is a box from my favorite gelato place. I've never actually been, but Marcus has brought me home a different flavor after work almost every night this week.

I pick it up and bring it inside, and when I open it, there's a hotel keycard inside with a note:

If you want your precious gelato, come to The Palazzo, Room 1824. My driver is waiting for you at the curb. SECRET CODE: MARCUS IS SMOKIN' HOT LOVE. If you're not here by 3:30, kiss the gelato goodbye.

-M

My heart lifts and relief rushes through me, calming my nerves. I smile and rush to the closet to put on some clothes. I grab the keycard and dash out the door, stopping only to lock it behind me.

Taking the three flights of stairs down to the curb, I'm surprised to see a vintage Mustang idling in front of the building, and a guy about my age standing with his hand on the open passenger door. He wears an official Palazzo valet shirt.

He tips an imaginary hat. "Secret code, Mrs. Miller?"

I press my lips together and roll my eyes. "Are you really going to make me say it?"

He smiles and nods. "If you want a ride, yeah."

I blow out a breath, then rush, "Marcus is smokin' hot love."

"Yep—you're legit," the guy laughs. "You're the only one who would actually be caught dead saying those words." He helps me into the passenger seat and runs around to the driver's side. "I'm Patrick, and I'll be your chauffeur tonight."

"What shady deal did he make with you to do this?" I ask as I fasten my seatbelt, the smell of oiled leather settling around me. "I assume the car's not stolen."

He revs the engine. "Borrowed."

I raise my eyebrows, waiting for him to explain, and he chuckles. "Marcus and I park cars all night. We get a little lost sometimes." He puts the car in gear and glances at me, smirking. "But I won't get lost this time because I have strict orders to get you to The Palazzo in one piece or lose my manhood. So hold tight, because we only have ten minutes, and I prefer to remain whole."

Patrick squeals onto the street, and I grip the seatbelt with both hands as he stomps on the gas, taking corners at fifty miles per hour until we reach The Strip, and he's forced to slow to a snail's pace.

"So you're the one spending time with him when I'm not," I relax into the seat.

Patrick downshifts, the car crawling to a stop when the light turns red. "Dude, your husband's my freaking hero." He inches the car forward, focusing on the lanes of traffic, even at this hour. "I've only worked with him for three weeks, but I'm waiting for him to tell me he's Batman or something."

I look out the window, taking in the bright lights around me. "He's my hero, too," I say around the lump in my throat. This guy has no idea just how much of a superhero Marcus really is.

We drive in silence until my personal chauffeur pulls into

valet parking at The Palazzo's main entrance. He darts around the car to open my door for me, and I step out. I thank him, and then thank the doorman who yanks the towering, gold door wide open for me.

My gaze climbs the illuminated statue in the sprawling atrium, and I fight feelings of smallness with the thought that Marcus is here—somewhere in this hotel—waiting for me.

I follow the signs to the guest elevators, knowing I must look as awestruck as I feel. I've never been in a building like this and can't wait to find out how Marcus managed to get us here.

The elevator opens, and I step inside, scanning my keycard before pressing Floor 18. I watch the rolling numbers, anticipation buzzing through me, growing each time the doors slide open and couples stream in and out. When the elevator eases to a stop on the eighteenth floor, I walk out and stop to check my appearance in the mirror hanging above a gilded bureau. I've been so preoccupied with tracking down Marcus that I haven't thought to run a brush through my hair or put on anything nice. Though my "nice" is limited to jeans and V-necks, a jacket to cover my ratty tank top, and a toothbrush, would be helpful right about now.

Checking Marcus's note once again for the room number, I make my way down the hallway, my feet light on the heavily padded carpeting.

Outside room 1824, I wave the keycard in front of the reader, and it clicks. Pushing the door open, I ease inside, but halt in my tracks in the foyer.

The room beyond is lit up with electric candles that sit on every surface, their warm glow casting shadows across the carpet. I ease ahead, follow a path of flickering votives into the bedroom, which expands into a sunken living area with floor to ceiling windows. A tub of gelato sits in the center of the bed, and I read the note propped against it:

> *Happy 100-day anniversary*
> *365 Forever*
> *-M*

Warmth spreads against my back, and I smile as Marcus's hands slip around my waist from behind, flattening on my stomach. He presses his lips to the curve of my neck, creating a trail of heat. I close my eyes and lean back against his chest, letting his hands sweep away all my earlier worry and anxiety.

"Hey," he whispers against my ear, and I squeal when he picks me up and lays me on the bed.

"Mmm…not so fast, Marcus Miller. You have some explaining to do," I scold.

"Nothing to explain," he says in a British accent. "It was magic, and a magician never reveals his secrets, love. Though apparently, this magician is not efficient at filling a room with candles. It took forever."

I laugh, pushing him away, and roll toward the tub of stracciatella. "Suit yourself, but 'Girl with gelato does not become distracted by hot boy until gelato is gone,'" I say in my best Guo Mama voice, slipping my hands under the bulging tub and holding it up like a gift to the Gods. "If you think *you're* magic, wait until you see me make this disappear before your sugar-loving eyes."

I cross my legs, setting the tub in my lap, and pry the lid off. "You can stay if you want, but we're about to have a moment, and things might get a little crazy." I grab the spoon lying patiently in the box and dig in. "Mmmm…so good," I say, my mouth brimming. "I would share, but we'll see if there's any left over."

Marcus lays on his side, head propped in his hand as he watches me eat. "I'm sorry for making you worry, but surprising you isn't easy these days. Lots of planning and executing for my lady." His grin rivals the room full of candles, their glow resting on his face. He looks amazing in his white ribbed tank top and sweats hanging low on his waist. His usually messy hair is damp from a shower, blue eyes telling me everything I ever need to know.

I set the tub on the nightstand and take a picture of him with my phone. Then I push his chest, rolling him to his back, and straddle him.

"Done so soon?" He smiles up at me, his hands circling my waist. "Not that I'm complaining, but…it's your favorite."

"Second favorite." I grip the hem of my shirt, keeping my eyes on his as I pull it up and over my head.

CHAPTER 21

> Mei: Don't believe in aliens, huh?? If you
> saw the guy I just helped find vacuum
> sealed baked beans, I am positive you'd be
> eating your words. But not the beans. Never
> the beans. His name was Zertog (no last
> name). Believe.

back the Aston Martin into a stall and reluctantly step out. The smell of new leather and cologne that costs way more than my motorcycle makes me wish for just one day in the life of someone who has money to burn on valet parking.

After locking the car, I run back to the valet stand, swiping sweat from my forehead. Vegas in late September doesn't offer anything remotely resembling a cool breeze. I want to laugh at the thought of all my hoodies stuffed in my bag back at our place. I haven't taken them out since we got here two months ago, and I probably won't any time soon.

I reach the valet desk, dangling the Aston Martin keys in

front of Patrick. "Thought about stealing her," I admit as I tag the keys.

"Dude—you should. The owner is a total loser. He has a few of them. He could count it as his one and only charitable donation."

I smile and hang the key. "You know what I could do with the money I could get from that car? I definitely wouldn't be working here." I make a note in the logbook and laugh, imagining myself walking into The University of Anywhere's admissions office and paying my tuition in full. And then I think about the money I walked away from at Stanford. I pick up the logbook and shove it into its slot in the kiosk.

The Palazzo notepad we use to leave notes for the next shift slips out, and I lean down to pick it up, glancing at the last note someone scrawled across the top sheet. I freeze, and blood drains from my face.

I tear it from the pad and read the sentence over and over again. I hold it up so Patrick can read it, my knuckles white from clenching the paper so tightly. "Did you write this?" My voice barely squeezes through my throat.

He yanks it from my grip and scans the message. Shakes his head. "Nah man." He hands it back to me. "I'd never call you Mr. Miller." He pats my chest and heads for a car pulling up to our stand.

My heart beats so hard, I curl my toes to keep from puking.

TO THE ESTEEMED MR. MILLER,
YOU AND MEI LI SHOULD HAVE FOUND A
BETTER HIDING PLACE. I'LL COUNT TO 3...

I rip my phone from my pocket and dial Mei's number,

staring at the hotel's entrance, my eyes flicking to every movement, searching for Nick's face behind every column, every palm tree. After three rings, my pulse throbs, threatening to pick me up off the ground. Panicked, I stuff the note in my pocket and dart toward the parking garage and my motorcycle.

If Nick found me here, he probably found Mei first.

I dial her number again, the phone burning against my ear, matching the hot fear pounding through my veins. I beg God to please keep Nick away from Mei, and when she finally answers, a wave of relief crashes over me, leaving behind cold sweat.

"I'm guessing you called me at work to hear me tell you *again* how hot you are and how much you wish we were home right now?" The smile in her voice cuts through the thick fear inside me and I stop, my legs rubbery. I take a shaky breath as adrenaline recedes. Nick hasn't found her. Yet.

"Yeah," I say, straining to keep my voice steady as I ransack my mind for how much to tell her. The last thing I want to do is freak her out. I swallow hard and jerk into motion. "What time do you get off today?" I turn the corner, easing into a jog when my motorcycle's within view.

"In exactly one hour and…forty-three minutes. So, basically, not soon enough."

I hurry toward my bike, but my knees lock and I skid to a stop, almost dropping my phone. Another note waits on the seat. My mouth goes dry, Mei's voice on the other end's a blur of sound as I whirl around. My eyes sweep every dark corner, every pillar, every car.

"Marcus? Are you okay?"

My focus snaps to the note again and I step close enough to read it.

TIME'S UP.

I back away, my heart beating into my throat while I weigh my options. "Yeah. Yes," I choke, turning around. I start running back toward the valet stand. "It's just … any chance you could get off earlier?" Her silence gives me time to collect enough pieces of a likely story.

"Umm…I doubt it, but I could ask."

"Do it and call me back."

"Is something wrong? Why do you—?"

"Nothing's wrong!" I blurt, clutching the phone to my ear, my eyes landing on the black Rover parked closest to the exit. I lower my voice. "Everything's fine. Just ask if you can get off in thirty minutes. Let me know, and I'll swing by and pick you up. It's a surprise," I add. "No more questions." I close my eyes, mentally apologizing for the lie. It's a surprise, just not the good kind.

"Okay…I'll ask. Call you in a second."

I end the call and shove my hand inside my pocket. I yank out the motorcycle key and stare at it. If we take it, Nick will track us down. He already did. He's probably somewhere in this parking garage, waiting for me to get on the bike and lead him right to Mei. If I leave it, the bike will eventually be impounded. And that's that. Motorcycle gone. And if I call the cops to track down Nick, and they find out about Mei, she's gone, too.

My hands shake so bad, I drop the key twice before stuffing it and the note in my pocket and taking off toward the kiosk. I snatch the Rover key, sprint back to the garage, and click the remote engine start. I jump into the driver's seat and slam the car into reverse, taking the corner out of the garage at fifty miles per hour. My phone rings.

"What did they say?" I ask, working to keep my voice light, steady.

"I can leave in forty-five."

I glance at the clock. "Be there at 3:40." I end the call and clench my jaw, accelerating up the ramp and onto a backstreet to avoid The Strip and afternoon traffic.

My mind reels, and I ask for the thousandth time why Nick keeps this up. What does he want from Mei or us or any of this? We have nothing to give him. He can't have Mei. This goes beyond obsession.

I blast the air conditioner and radio, taking long, deep breaths to clear my head, but it's not enough. I park the car in front of our building and jump out of it, run up the stairs, and jam my key into the lock. But I don't have to turn it because the door swings open, and I jerk to a stop.

The room looks like a tornado plowed through it and lifted everything before dropping it somewhere else. Our clothes are strewn all over. The couch and chair are upside down, the nightstand toppled and torn apart. Our mansion fund in the pickle jar, shattered. What little money was in there, gone. My heart beats rapid fire and shorts out, restarts, and I'm standing against the wall, my eyes sweeping the corners of the room. Not a lot of places for someone to hide, but there's the bathroom. The only thing I care about in this place is Mei, and she's safe at work. For now. I close my eyes. I can't do this. But I could get him out of the picture completely. I'm twice his size. It would be self-defense. I've wanted to kill him more than once, and now…I could have the chance. He could be hiding in the bathroom. It's too much of a coincidence with the note for this to not be him.

Swallowing, I edge toward the bathroom, glancing around the room as I go. I ease open the door, my heart pumping in my throat, but he's not here. He's come and gone. But why? Maybe he's outside waiting for us.

I bend down and throw open the cabinet door. Tampon box is still there, untouched. I grab it and rifle through it, the diamonds cold on my fingertips at the bottom of the box with our passports. Whirling out of the bathroom, I yank our bags from the closet and shove the tampon box inside before sprinting around the room, gathering all our clothes. Buddha. Magic 8. Shoes, notes, books, chargers. I can't leave any personal touches for someone to find. I shove anything that says we were here in our bags and don't look back.

———

I stand against the Rover where I've parked along the curb at Mei's work, watching the sliding doors for her to come out and for signs of Nick. Everything was in fast motion until now, and it's slowed to a crawl. My thoughts are catching up to me. Like how much I never wanted to stay in Vegas, but how much I don't wanna leave it now because that means we're moving farther from Stanford. How much I wanna kill Nick. How much I question all our decisions up to this point. But they all make me mad and achy, so I shove them aside and use the few minutes I have before she comes out to practice being calm and rehearse the story I'm gonna tell her.

When Mei sails out the door, clutching her bag over her shoulder, I open the passenger side door, then close it behind her and run around the front of the Rover and jump in the driver's seat.

"Marcus," she says through a smile-frown. "You're going to get fired if you keep 'borrowing' people's cars."

I glance over my shoulder and pull away from the curb to screech out of the parking lot and into traffic. I grip the steering wheel. Check my mirror for signs of any car following us. I slam to a stop at a red light.

"What's going on?" Mei's voice is no longer filled with her smile.

"I…" If I just show her the note, it'll explain everything, but her reaction will haunt me more than walking away from my bike or starting over again. "Motorcycle wouldn't start." My voice shakes as realization claws its way out from under the avalanche of adrenaline. When the light turns green, I punch the gas pedal, ready to outrun any cop that dares pull me over right now.

"Marcus, what's wrong?"

The needle on the speedometer lays flat, and I glance into the rearview mirror, switching lanes to enter the freeway. Mei grips the door handle like she can squeeze answers from it.

I crank the radio's volume, letting the beat numb my mind; I want it to suffocate the anger awakening under the anesthesia of panic, and I grip the wheel tighter, my eyes boring into the car ahead of us like I can move it with my mind.

Mei cranks down the volume on the radio. "Are you going to tell me what's really going on? There's something you're not telling me, and it's not a surprise."

Oh, it was a surprise for one of us already, and it'll be one for her, too.

I veer toward the off ramp and exit to downtown Vegas. "I will. Just…when we get there." I search the signs, swear, and jerk the wheel, making a U-turn. I screech to a stop at the curb in front of the Greyhound station.

"When we get where?" she presses.

I bail out of the car, slamming the door, and grab our bags before Mei has gotten out of the passenger seat. But I can't wait—can't stand still—and open her door, holding out my hand to her. "We gotta go."

"You're scaring me."

That makes two of us.

"I'll explain everything, but please get out of the car."

"Tell me now. I'm not getting out of this car until—"

I turn and walk through the sliding doors toward the ticket counter. She's gonna fight me on this, and I don't blame her, but I can't do it right now.

The Rover door slams outside, and I flinch but keep walking as Mei's footsteps slap against the tile floor behind me.

The notes in my pocket hiss at me, and I want nothing more than to rip them out and shred them, leave my reasons for us leaving Vegas like a trail that will blow out the door and across the melting asphalt. I can't watch Mei fall apart again—see the fear that dilates her eyes and sinks so deep inside her that it pulls her with it. Gotta buy some time to make up a story about why we're getting on the first bus out of Vegas because the real reason, I will keep to myself. Forever.

"Marcus, talk to me," she bursts, grabbing my elbow as we cross the endless expanse of dingy white tile.

I shake my head, put my hand over hers on my arm. "We need to get on the bus. Then I'll tell you." My words are too sharp, but the whirlwind of the last hour subsides, leaving the debris of reality scattered around me until I'm wading through resentment and anger and fear.

She runs around me and stands in front of me. "Are we leaving?"

"Yeah."

"Like…on a trip?" Her eyes are all over my face. "Or for good?"

"For good." I close my eyes and swear. "Mei, I promise I'll tell you, but we have to get on the bus and we're running out of time. I'm sorry, I just…"

I step around her to the ticket counter, pulling out today's tips from my wallet, and slide the crumpled bills under the Plexiglas window to the cashier. "Two tickets to as far eastbound as we can go with this." Next time I'm running, it better be west and end in Stanford.

The operator gives us tickets and tells us which terminal and time for departure. We're going to Indiana. I hand the tickets to Mei and pull out my phone to text Patrick.

Big favor. Can you pick up the Rover at the Greyhound Station? Key's under the front left tire. Great working with you. Thanks for your help.

CHAPTER 22

Sitting on a bus that smells like fake coconut next to an anxious, shut-down Marcus is not how I imagined my Monday night going. When Marcus called me at work, I imagined something like us going home, eating takeout from the Chinese restaurant around the corner, then getting cozy and watching something on cable since we never have a night together.

But no. We're going to Indiana. I've never wanted to go there. I'm not even sure where it is.

The driver announces our next stop—Salt Lake City—and the bus growls to life and rolls out of the terminal. I turn to Marcus, who's staring out the window, eyes jumpy.

"Are you going to tell me what's going on now?" I say, tapping his knee.

He hesitates, and my anger surges. He can't uproot us like this without an explanation. I open my mouth to say as much when he turns toward me in the seat.

"An immigration officer came to my work." His voice is quiet and hollow.

I let his words settle in my head, but they don't make sense. "What do you mean…?"

Marcus's eyes go to the ceiling. "Some guy walked up to the valet kiosk this afternoon and flashed a badge. Immigration. Said he tracked us down. Tracked us down with our licenses when we applied for work and told me we needed to be in his office tomorrow by 9:00AM or he'll send the authorities to collect you."

Blood drains from my face, my hand going to my neck as I stare at Marcus. "We should have used our fake passports," I whisper. "When we applied for jobs. I can't believe they found us here. Everything seemed fine. No one asked questions. Why now?" I ask, squeezing my eyes shut. "We were finally getting comfortable somewhere." I swallow, and my pulse beats in my neck against my palm. "First Nick, now immigration officers?"

"I know," he whispers. "I'm sorry, Mei."

"Maybe I should turn myself in. How many more times are we going to have to run?" Marcus grabs my hand. "No. It's okay. We'll just…start over again. We've done it before, we can do it again." He talks to our hands now. "I hate this, too, Mei, but it's the only way. I don't want to lose you. I can't."

"I've ruined everything again."

"Stop, Mei. Please, just…" Marcus swears to the floor. "Let's just forget it and move on. Somewhere no one will think to look for us. We'll change our identities and our life. Again. But this time we'll do it right. We'll be safe. We'll use the stuff Guo gave us." He scoots down, knees against the seat in front of him as he looks out the window, his thoughts whisking him away from me.

I don't know if I can do this again. But there's only one way to stop it, and that's too far from Marcus.

I put my hand on his knee. "I'm sorry. So, so sorry, Marcus."

He nods to the window. "I know. And I'm not mad. I just…need time to think. And some sleep."

I watch him, then stare out the window at the desert sliding past us. I want to reach out and dig my fingernails into the hard dirt, slow this bus down, because I'm not sure what's next. I'm selfishly glad Marcus hasn't left me. I couldn't do this without him.

After a few minutes, Marcus's breathing deepens, and I close my eyes so I'm not forced to watch another life we thought we'd be living fall behind us once again.

CHAPTER 23

My stiff legs rejoice in an achy kind of way when I step off the bus and stretch, rolling my neck to loosen the last twenty-four hours of bus riding lodged in it. I take a deep breath of humid Missouri air and let it out, ridding my lungs of the sausage-and-pepper smell that's wafted from the guy in front of us for the last twelve hours.

I walk down the length of the bus to the storage compartments, pull out our bags, and throw them over my shoulder. Mei heads straight for the rest stop bathrooms, and I follow, not wanting her out of my sight even though we still haven't talked much since I made up the story about why we left Vegas. I can see in her eyes she doesn't believe me, but I'm gonna take what happened in Vegas to my grave.

She disappears into the women's bathroom, and I fish my toothbrush from my backpack and go into the guys' bathroom. I drop my bags on the counter and wash my hands and face. Layers of remaining Vegas grime and bus grit slide down the drain, leaving nothing but the same old me beneath them. The same old me that's in the middle of nowhere headed to nowhere—again—because of Nick, who showed up out of nowhere to complete the theme.

I toss my toothbrush back in my bag and click into my email to reply to the Stanford academic advisor. My response got delayed by a sudden relocation, and I hope a late response is better than nothing. *"I haven't had service for a couple days, so sorry for the late response, but yes, I can talk on Thursday at 3 PM,"* I mouth the words as I type. Not sure where I'll be on Thursday, or what time zone this is, or how I'll talk to her without Mei knowing, but I'll find a way to make this happen. Step two of four. Send.

I lean on the counter and close my eyes to steady the world that's been rocking with rolling bus tires for the last twenty-four hours. The miles we've covered rewind in my mind, pushing me farther from where I want to be. I think about what I'd be doing today if we weren't here. I'd be parking cars for the filthy rich and going home to unwind by winding myself around Mei.

Now, I don't have a job, I'm definitely not in the company of the filthy rich, and I doubt I'll unwind anytime soon. Not until I hear that Nick's been locked up, and we can go back to Stanford. Not to mention that Vegas Marcus stole a car and might have a criminal record. Good thing he no longer exists, and Darius Bromley has taken his place in the world. Thanks for the awesome name, Guo. Nothing close to what I would've picked, but none of this is what I would have picked. Except I did. I chose Mei.

I let out a long, weary breath, shoving away from the counter, and pick up the bags. Outside the bathroom, Mei's sitting on a bench facing the parking lot. I walk up to her and drop our bags, then hold out my hand. Her deep brown eyes meet mine, and she hesitates before taking my hand. I pull her to her feet and into my arms, wrapping them around her and burying my face in her neck. "I'm sorry I've been so distant."

Her hands slowly make their way up my back, and I kiss her temple. I lead her around the building to a shady, quiet spot that blocks the view of the bus and drone of its idling engine, and I back her against the wall. Cupping her face with one hand, the other on the small of her back. "I've been a total jerk, and I don't wanna be one anymore. I don't wanna run anymore. Don't wanna leave behind everything we start that sort of looks like a real life. So…when we make it to Indianapolis, that's it. We're staying there." Until Nick falls off the face of the earth and I work out the details with Stanford. I shove the thoughts aside so they don't accidentally slide across my eyes. "The only reason we'll move again is because we've figured out where we wanna be. For now, we're gonna get an apartment, and act like normal people." Except for my obsession with my email and checking San Francisco police reports. "As normal as we can be, being eighteen and married and living under aliases. We'll be newlyweds Darius and Peggy Bromley and it will be as normal as it gets. Except for the names. I think Guo hates us."

"Are you going to tell me what really happened yesterday?"

I swallow hard and look away now so she can't see the *Never* I know is in my eyes. "We might not have enough time to talk about it since we only have fifteen hours left on the bus…"

She relaxes into me, her shoulders dropping, her hand clutching the front of my shirt, pulling me to her.

I cradle her head to my chest, and her fingers slide into the belt loops on the back of my jeans. "I've missed you," she whispers, her voice swollen with all the words she's stored since Vegas.

"You mean that douche you've been sitting next to for twenty-four hours didn't do it for you?" I smile and rest my chin on top of her head, closing my eyes when her lips go to my neck.

She whispers, "I love you," and I take her chin between my fingers and lean down until my lips are telling hers how much I love her, too. She winds her arms around my neck and stands on her tiptoes, molding her body to mine.

My hips pin her to the brick wall and my body responds to her closeness. "I want you so bad right now."

"That's perfect because I've always …" she breathes, "wanted to be … *ravished* at a rest stop."

"You're about to get your wish," I rasp, one of my hands roaming beneath her shirt, and she's so into it, and my hands are taking the next steps when air brakes hiss as they're released and the clatter of a bus accelerating has me dashing around the corner in time to watch it pull out of the parking lot and away from the rest stop. Headed toward the interstate onramp. Where Mei and I should be right now.

"Oh, no way," I say to myself, then yell it as panic settles in. "No way, no way, no, no, no!" My hands are on my head. "Are you—?"

I whirl around and almost knock Mei down where she stands behind me, hand to her mouth. "Please tell me that's not our bus leaving."

I yell a string of curse words to the sky as the bus trundles out of view toward Indiana without us.

Squatting, I hang my head, raking my hands through my hair.

"How did we not hear the announcement to board the bus?" Mei asks desperately. "I didn't even hear—"

I throw a sharp laugh at the sidewalk and smack the cement with my palm. "Because all you could hear was me getting all hot!" I curse at the sky again. "I can't believe this." I swear at the asphalt again, close my eyes, then huff my way into a laugh that could easily turn into a sob.

"Is everything okay?"

My head snaps up to see an old lady looking at me from where she stands, dropping garbage into a trash can.

"It was getting to 'okay' before we missed our bus." How are we gonna get out of here without resorting to hitchhiking? With our luck, the first car to stop would be a freaking black Mercedes driven by Nick.

"Oh no!" The woman motions to her husband, who's near their open car door, doing a few rusty toe touches. She brushes off her hands and comes toward us. "Where are you two headed?"

"We *were* headed to Evansville, Indiana, but at this point … we're headed right here, to this bench within walking distance of these fine facilities." I huff and rub my forehead.

The woman tilts her head in sympathy and grabs her husband's arm when he shuffles next to her. "Gerald, their bus just left them." She pats his arm and waits for his response. He looks from me to Mei to the bags near the corner of the building.

"Ah. Believe it or not, the same thing happened to me back in the day. Made a cross-country trek to meet some buddies of mine and…well…spent a long night on a bench somewhere in Arkansas." He sucks his teeth and chuckles. "Didn't have a lady to worry about, though, so I don't believe I'll make the two of you have that experience." He throws a thumb over his shoulder. "Lucky for you, we have an empty backseat, and we're headed to Kentucky. We can drop you off in Evansville as we pass through. I normally wouldn't do this, but you seem like decent kids. Where you two from?"

"San Francisco," I offer, wondering if I should've said that much.

"Hmm. What takes you to Indiana?"

"Seems like a nice place to settle down," I say, smiling and scratching my head.

"Doesn't seem either of you are old enough to do any settling!" the woman laughs, adjusting her purse on her forearm.

"We actually got married a couple months ago," Mei says, shrugging.

"Married? Never would have guessed you're a day over sixteen, but I guess as I get older, everyone looks younger!"

The man laughs and nudges the woman. "Thought we were the only two crazy enough to get married as teenagers." He waves us toward the car. "Well, congratulations to both of you. If you'll accept the ride, we need to get on the road so we can make it to our grandson's tournament. We've got a bit of a ride left, so there's plenty of time for us to give you all our best marital advice."

CHAPTER 24

One Month Later

I sit on the steps outside our apartment building, my eyes wandering from my book to the sidewalk as I wait for Marcus to come home from work. Home. Yes. Definitely. It feels like it more than any other place we've been so far. Especially now that we have an apartment in a quiet neighborhood instead of a sleazy motel, jobs that pay enough (even if barely), and a routine that gives us time together. It took us a week to find this place. We checked apartment listings and went to a few until we both agreed on this one. It was perfect: great location, friendly people, didn't require background checks, and it wasn't Las Vegas. My mind has quieted since we moved in, even though occasionally, guilt drags it into a downward spiral, reminding me that while this is starting to feel like home, Marcus's heart never quite made it here from the Stanford soccer field.

It's surprisingly warm for early November. I wish it would snow. I've never seen snow, and now that we have an apartment with a working heater and fireplace, I'm ready for it. I think. Probably not, but I want to see it anyway.

My phone buzzes. I smile at the name on my screen.

Marcus: Hey—it's Darius Bromley. So ... I hope you don't mind that I'm texting you, but I got your number from that guy you're always with, and I'm wondering if you're busy tonight.

Biting my lip, I set down my book and type a response.

Mei: Sorry. I already have big plans tonight.

Marcus: Do they include a meteor shower and me picking you up at 7:30?

I check the clock on my phone. 7:28. My smile widens.

Mei: Hmmm... It's kind of late notice, but maybe I can rearrange some things.

Marcus: See what you can do. You won't regret it. I don't think you've ever met a Darius like this one.

The same rush of anticipation and cracking nerves I felt six months ago on my fire escape pulses in my veins. I set my phone in my lap, hand over my thudding heart. Exactly one and a half minutes later, Marcus is standing in front of me, a giant bag of gummy bears in his hand.

"Hey." He smiles, and it beams through my jacket, my shirt, and straight into my heart.

"Darius?" I stand, pocketing my phone, and wrap my arms around his neck.

"Wow," he breathes. "You don't waste time."

"Not when I like what I see."

His hands circle my waist. "Can't wait to see how the rest of this first date goes…"

I shrug and wiggle my eyebrows, then bend to pick up my book on the step. "How was work? And are those gummy bears for me, by chance…?"

"Work was long, thanks for bringing it up. Gonna be honest, refereeing indoor soccer games isn't as exciting as playing, but it pays rent and leaves enough to splurge on the finer things in life. Like these gummy bears to seduce you with while watching a meteor shower."

"Did you special order this meteor shower?"

"Yeah. Been waiting for ten years, but it's finally arriving tonight. Think I've figured out the best place to watch it."

He grabs my hand and pulls me up the cement steps and inside our apartment building, but instead of stopping on the third floor, he keeps going. We hit the fifth floor, and Marcus walks me to a door at the end of the hall.

"Found this last night while you were at work, and I was bored." He pulls the door open to a dark, concrete staircase that leads to the roof.

"Good find, Bromley," I say as he leads me to a pile of blankets and pillows on a flat section of the roof. "I wish Marcus would find cool things like this for us." I smile and plop down on the blanket pile. "He never does anything surprising or funny or interesting. And he's definitely not hot like you."

Marcus drops the bag of gummy bears and flops to his back beside me. I snuggle against him, enjoying the silence as the setting sun disappears and night replaces it.

Marcus rolls to his side, looking down at me. He pulls a Sharpie from his pocket and grabs my wrist, writing on it. When he finishes, he blows on it, then holds it up so I can read his message.

365-Forever

It's been a long time since he's written anything on me, and I kiss the words, then grab his neck and pull him down on top of me. His hands and lips work their magic, and I wrap myself around him until all I want is to be locked inside our apartment, but the more he kisses me and the hotter his whispered thoughts get, the more I don't care where we are. His mouth's on my neck, hands on my back, holding me against him. I'm on his lap, sweaters and hoodies dropping to the blanket. Cold air brushes against my skin, and his mouth's on my neck, hands on my back, holding me against him. His fingers knot in my hair, and I push him to his back just as sirens whine to life on the street below. My head snaps up. I almost forgot we're on this rooftop—the rooftop of a large apartment complex where a lot of other people live.

"Darius and Peggy are going to get charged with indecent exposure if they don't stop."

He groans, his arms spread wide across the blanket beneath us, and he sighs loudly to the sky.

I laugh, propping my chin on his chest. "Pause button?"

"Think my pause button's broken. Only rewind and fast forward." He mimics punching a remote button, pointing it toward me.

I laugh and sit up, grab the bag of gummy bears, then

snuggle in beside him, looking at the sky. "Guess we can take out our frustrations on these poor, innocent gummy bears."

He groans again but nuzzles my neck, and I flinch and smile when the stubble on his chin rakes across my skin. He slings his arm around me, holding me closer to his side, and I grab a handful of gummy bears and pop a few into my mouth. But they're smaller than normal and I stop, holding one up between my fingers. "Ummm… Marcus? Where did the rest of the gummy bears go?"

"Are you so distracted by my body that you missed this?" He picks up the bag, shaking it above us.

"No—there are only heads. Lots and lots of gummy bear heads. Where did their bodies go?"

"Didn't realize you're so picky." He works to keep a smirk off his face.

"I only eat whole gummy bears, bodies and heads intact."

"You're vicious."

I pinch his side, and he squirms, grinning.

"What did you do to them, Marcus?"

"Look…I had a really long break between games. I was starving, so I opened the bag and ate a few." He pauses dramatically, looking at me out of the corner of his eye. "Maybe a few more than a few."

"But why just the heads…?"

"Because…the heads taste the best. Plus, I feel weird eating the butts."

I lean up on my elbow, looking down at him, then burst out laughing and fall to my back again. "You are so *weird*! Who thinks of stuff like that?"

He smiles and rolls into me, his hand on my neck, fingers threading in my hair. "I must not be too weird since you were about to get me naked on this rooftop."

"Oh, you're definitely weird," I murmur in the slit of night air between our faces, "but I just so happen to be madly in love with weird. Can't get enough of it."

We make out under blankets and eat gummy bear bums, taking breaks to watch the stars shooting through the darkness above us until the temperature drops.

When I shiver, Marcus gets up and pulls me to my feet, and we gather the blankets and pillows and tuck them under our arms as we walk across the roof to the door, hips bumping against each other.

"Someday, Mei, we're gonna have our own house and our own roof where we can do whatever we want."

"All I really want is you, but…I'd probably really like you on a roof doing whatever we want too."

Marcus tries to turn the doorknob, but it doesn't move. He wiggles it again and swears. "It's locked. Not even kidding." He knocks while I try the knob like it just might open for me. "Okay. So let's look for a ladder or…something." He turns, surveying the roof for inspiration.

I grab my book, grateful I used a bobby pin as a bookmark. "Can you shine your phone on the doorknob?"

Marcus frowns but gets his phone out and illuminates the lock.

I hunch over the doorknob and slip my bobby pin into the hole. I wiggle it around until I hear the dull thud of the lock sliding away.

Marcus peers over my shoulder and whistles. "Just when I think I know you…"

"When you have a cousin who's shady, you learn shady things that are useful sometimes." I smile and swing open the door, and we're back inside the building, skimming down the stairs to the second floor and our apartment.

"That was hot, Mei," Marcus whispers as he unlocks our door, his hair standing at angles from static and my hands.

Inside, he tosses the blankets and pillows on the couch, drops the key on the counter, and presses me against the door in the dark.

His mouth is hot against mine, the rest of his face cold as I whisper against his lips, "Unpause."

CHAPTER 25

Mei: If Santa were real, know what I would ask for?

Marcus: Wait! Santa's not real?

Mei: Uhhhhh……no. I mean, yes! What?

Marcus: I'll never trust again.

'm a freaking Christmas elf.

I stand back, admiring the tree I just decorated. Yeah, it's one of those small, grocery store trees that's, like, two feet tall. It doesn't have all the cool ornaments like my Clubhouse Christmas tree—weird sculptures Dad and I created from broken stuff. But I spent thirty minutes sorting through a bag of Skittles, picking out only the reds and greens, then gluing them to branches, like real mini-Christmas ornaments. The tree may be small and flimsy, but it's our first, and it's glorious. Just like the past three months have been. I didn't think we'd still be in Indiana. I have a virtual meeting scheduled with the Stanford coaches in March, which will be in person if all goes as I want it to. Eight more months before I can pick up where I left off. Even though Nick hasn't been locked up yet...

There's been no sign of him, though. No sightings, encounters, no threats, so no reason to not plan on going back to Stanford. Maybe he got run over by a semi-truck or fell in a hole that dropped him in Hell. Got amnesia and forgot his obsession with Mei, which I still don't get. I mean, I'm obsessed with her too, but not like that. Take a hint, loser, you're not her type.

Until I know Nick's in custody, we'll just be a normal Peggy and Darius living this slice of a dream. If Nick's wasting space on this planet somewhere, he's gonna make a misstep and get picked up; it just has to be before August. Once that happens, I'll tell Mei about Stanford. For now, I'm holding onto hope.

I check my watch. Twenty-eight more minutes until I need to pick up Mei from work. She didn't wanna work today, but I'm kind of glad she did, so I had time to create the most magical Christmas Eve I could with basically nothing. Now I have just enough time to get the fort ready for some serious Christmas Eve movie-watching and other festivities.

Using the sheets off our bed, the three blankets we own, and a couple of extra bath towels, I construct a pretty decent fort that engulfs our living area. I'd be doing the same with Dad tonight if I were back in San Francisco. I've always been in charge of design while Dad was construction so there are usually a few secret tunnels, some extra rooms off the main fort, and an architecturally sound roofline. Mei and I don't have enough sheets, blankets, or pillows for all that, so this one-room fort in a one-room apartment will have to do.

I unwind the dollar store lights I picked up yesterday and

plug them in to make sure they work. The store only had green left so our fort might look more Teenage Mutant Ninja Turtle than Christmas, but it'll look pretty cool in the dark.

As I string lights across the fort ceiling, Dad slips a little deeper into my thoughts, and I wonder if he's making the fort with Kenna tonight. If they'll sleep in it like we always did, but then I'm grossed out thinking about what else they might do in the fort, and I slap the thought away. I don't even know how to picture her, anyway. In my mind, she's just a smear of anger across my last San Francisco memories.

Nope. Not thinking about that tonight. Only gonna think about Christmas Eve and the gift I got Mei that might be the best thing I'll ever give her. I dipped into what's left of Meemaw's graduation money, and the smile on Mei's face when she opens my most excellent gift is gonna be worth way more.

I make the comfiest floor bed I can manage with only a couple of blankets, throw our pillows inside along with the Oreos and iced mini gingerbread men cookies I bought and arranged on a plate. A couple candles in the corner, some tinsel around the door opening, and then I crawl out of the fort, survey the room to make sure everything is ready, and head out to pick up Mei and start our very first Christmas together.

———

I wake up at 10:30 AM to a dark, cozy fort and a cloudy Christmas morning. We haven't slept in for a couple weeks because of work, and neither of us moves from where we're wrapped around each other on our makeshift floor bed. Mei practically jumped me when she saw the tree and fort; she's never had a Christmas tree. Or a fort, which almost collapsed last night when things got a little rowdy.

I smile, remembering the background noise of whatever Christmas movie was playing on TV while we were distracted with other things. I'd grabbed a Sharpie and written MM under Mei's tattoo. When she asked what I'd drawn, I told her, and she'd said someday, she'd make it permanent. Maybe I will too. If Santa were real, I'd ask for matching tattoos. And piles of presents, so when Mei opens her eyes, there'd be glittery stacks all over this place.

But I'm playing Santa this year and can't wait another minute to finally—FINALLY—give Mei the gift I've been working on for two months.

"Wake up, Mrs. Claus," I whisper in her ear, pulling her tight against my chest. My fingertips graze her warm, bare back and her leg slides up mine. She mumbles something incoherent, and I slip out from underneath her, tuck the blanket around her, and crawl out of the fort to get the gift I wrapped in a cereal box and a bunch of paper grocery bags. It's much warmer in the fort so I hurry back inside, kneeling over her and kissing her neck until she squirms and smiles against my skin.

"I can't wait another second," I say into her neck. "I'm bursting with monumental secrets."

"Secrets...?" Her eyes are still closed, but her smile widens.

I flop down beside her. "Big ones."

She opens her eyes and props her head on her elbow, yanking the blanket over her bare chest, which normally I would passionately discourage, but I'm too excited about her gift. "Not the prettiest wrapping paper you'll ever have, but what's inside makes up for it." My mouth stretches to its limits in a smile, and she glances from me to the box and begins carefully dissecting it.

"No," I say, putting my hand over hers. "Rip it open. Like…just rip it. Go crazy on it."

She smiles and sits up, pulling the box into her lap and tearing open the flaps. She pulls out the paper chef's hat I had to scavenge for last week. Her eyes roam it, then land on mine, eyebrows raised.

"Do you know what it means?" I ask.

"Umm…you want me to make you Christmas breakfast?"

"Not even close." I take the hat and put it on her head. "This hat means I signed you up for a 12-week culinary course. Starting January 4th." I was hoping we'd be back in our studio apartment at Stanford by then, but…

Her eyes search my face, her hair sticking up in all directions, making the moment more dramatic. "Marcus, are you—?"

"So serious, Mei."

She presses her hand to her chest, tears welling.

I wrap my arms around her. Maybe she didn't want this. Maybe I should've asked. But I've seen her scrolling through recipes on her phone, and she's been experimenting in the kitchen on her days off, humming as she cooks. "You okay?"

She nods. "I'm so okay," she sobs into my shoulder, sniffing and shaking as she cries. "I cannot believe you did this." She surfaces, swiping her eyes and wiping her nose.

I crush her against my chest, and she laughs through tears and pinches my side.

When I squirm, she smooths the spot with her hand and crawls into my lap, wrapping herself around me. "I love you so much."

"If you cry a little harder, I'll probably believe you."

She squeezes me until I squeak, then pulls back. "This is a

complete shock. The perfect kind of complete shock, but…my brain is having a hard time catching up to this."

"So I surprised you."

"You will never top this gift," she says against my mouth.

"Never?"

"Ever."

I lean back enough to meet her eyes. "So I win best gift forever."

"And ever. But I'm pretty sure you're going to love my gift to you. At least I hope. I'm actually really, really not sure, but even if you hate it, it's the thought that counts. Remember that."

"You're really selling this." I say, tucking her wild hair behind her ear.

"There's symbolism behind it. Hold on." Mei scrambles off my lap, throws on a shirt and pajama pants, and seconds later, the front door opens and closes. I frown, wondering where she's going, and flop onto my back. I stare at the fort ceiling, smiling to myself while I wait. That surprise couldn't have gone better, so whatever she gives me is gonna be the best thing ever because today can't go wrong.

A few minutes later, the door opens, and Mei's light footsteps cross the room. Her shadow bends, and the blanket wall beside me moves. I sit up just as a tiny, furry head pokes through the crack, and a grey kitten pauses, then skitters toward me, meowing.

I gawk at it. Mei ducks inside the fort, her face beaming. "I hope this place allows pets. Didn't exactly check first."

"You…got me a cat." I flinch as the cat crawls into my lap and turns a circle before pawing at the string on my pajama pants.

"Okay, so listen—yes, I got you a cat, but there's a reason. A really, really good reason. I was at work two days ago, and one of the girls told me she and her husband were driving down the highway when they saw this little guy running on the side of the road, wet and shivering. They took him home only to find out her husband was extremely allergic. She was going to take him to a shelter, but I just thought…he's a runaway. Like us. And all he wants is a safe, happy, warm place, just like us. And we have that now, even though we were once runaways too." She picks him up and holds him to her chest. He licks her neck, and she laughs. "His name is Charlie, short for Charleston. After his daddy."

I choke, shaking my head. "Whoa, whoa—I am not a cat dad. I'm not even a cat friend."

Mei holds Charlie up to her face and says to him, "We'll see about that, won't we Charlie?"

CHAPTER 26

Mei: I'm fighting feelings of extreme jealousy.

Marcus: About my mad crossword skills? My undefeated streak of taking out the garbage before it reaches the top of the can? Tell me. Suspense is killing me!

Mei: I'm jealous of Charlie.

Marcus: He's pretty good at killing crickets, and you're just not, so yeah, I get it.

Mei: I pay him big money to kill those crickets. I'm jealous that he loves you more than he loves me, and I'm the one who rescued him from homelessness and certain death. He's a Marcus Snob now, and it's hurtful and annoying because I used to be the only Marcus Snob.

Marcus: Oh. Yeah. That's true. He does love
me more than you, but I think it's because
we both have hair on our chests and you
don't. For which I'm very, very grateful.

Mei: You told me you aren't a cat person.
But it doesn't look like that to me. All I
wanted was a little softening toward him, but
this? THIS?!

Marcus: He's growing on me, okay? Let it
happen. Let the bros be bros. If you listen
closely, he'll meow-whisper that he loves
you. I've heard it, so think of it this way: now
you have two men who can't live without
you. One with green eyes, one with blue.
Take your pick.

Mei: He sleeps on your feet now.

Marcus: Confession: he's helping me get
over my stuffed animal phase. It's
embarrassing, and I didn't want you to
know, but it used to be a problem, so he's
helping a brother out. No more teddy bear.

Mei: He's a total brat. You're spoiling him.

Marcus: Turns out, I like cute, small things
around. In fact, now that we have Charlie,
I've solidly landed on wanting 4 kids. I hope
they're fuzzy like him.

Mei: 4??????? Are you volunteering to be
the pregnant one??

harlie paws at my feet as I dry a bowl and put it in the cupboard, then I scoop him up. He nuzzles into my chest, purring. It's so nice to have him around when Marcus isn't, and I'm just happy I got to keep him. It was a close one since Marcus has never had a pet, and I wasn't even sure how much he liked animals. I wish I would have recorded Marcus's face—eyes wide, completely still for the first time since I've known him, like Charlie was going to rip his throat out or something. But by Christmas afternoon, Marcus patted his lap for Charlie to come sit, and by that night, he was talking to Charlie in a new voice, kind of like a boy voice mixed with high-pitched old lady. That's when I knew Charlie had a forever home.

I finish cleaning the dishes, my movements slow and sluggish like the rest of my body has been all day. I picture the bed, my pillows, warm blankets, and wonder if I should take a quick nap. I've been so tired lately. Yes, we stay up late, and some of my shifts have been earlier, but I'm full-body exhausted, like I'm coming down with the flu and want to sit and cry for no reason. It could be the long winter and the piles of snow in every direction, surrounding us like barriers. When we got to Indiana, I was so excited about seeing snow for the first time. I'm so over it all. Maybe I really do just need a nap.

I dry my hands and shuffle into the bedroom. The door to our closet is partially open, so I push it as I pass, but it won't close. I investigate.

Marcus's duffle is blocking the door. It must have fallen off the shelf. I bend to pick it up, and it's heavy, even though we emptied our bags when we moved in. Marcus must have left a few things in his.

I place the duffle on the bed, unzip it, and peer inside at a few of Marcus's books that lie abandoned, untouched. We did a lot of research of our own, and by the time we left Vegas, he didn't need books anymore. I smile, picking up one of them and flipping through it. I stop on Marcus's notes and… sketches. Diagrams. I turn the book, tilt my head, and laugh out loud as I take a picture of his notes with my phone and send it to him as a reminder of his pre-wedding assumptions.

Mei: Oh really…? Is that how it works…?

Setting my phone aside, I pick up another book and finger through it, stopping on a Q&A., like he was quizzing himself on what he read. I pick up the last one, scan the title, and am forever grateful he didn't shy away from it, but before I can read anything written inside, a note slips from the pages and drops on my feet.

I snatch it up and unfold it, ready to see more Marcus diagrams, but it's written on The Palazzo notepaper and the handwriting isn't Marcus's:

TO THE ESTEEMED MR. MILLER,
YOU AND MEI LI SHOULD HAVE FOUND A
BETTER HIDING PLACE. I'LL COUNT TO 3…

My mouth goes dry, and my hands shake, the pads of my finger burning against the paper. I can feel bruises on my face, around my neck. My throat tightens, and Nick's hands are around it again. My body throbs with the memory of his face, his dark eyes, empty except for anger and hatred. I force away the memories and remind myself, once again, that they're of a past life. But this time, they're not so easily shoved away because they've crept into my new life and twisted around my bright, happy, recent memories. Nick wrote this in Vegas—that means he found us. And if Marcus has this note, he knew. He packed us up. He left the motorcycle. He picked me up at work, and with no explanation, drove us to the bus station in a stolen car where we left our life behind to, once again, start another.

Marcus kept it all from me. He lied to me. For months.

Hot tears burn my cheeks, my chest tight as my lungs struggle to find air. But there isn't enough, and when my stomach lurches, I scramble to my feet, dart to the bathroom, and throw up in the toilet.

CHAPTER 27

Two days of power outages postponed too many indoor soccer games and wrecked my paycheck. No games, no ref. No ref, no money, and I really wanted that TV like the one I bought at Stanford and had to leave behind. There's always the diamonds. I've never wanted to dig through Mei's girl supplies so bad. But then again…how am I gonna haul a TV back to Stanford with us when the day finally comes? Hopefully. Five months and counting. Still no reports of Nick rotting in jail.

I walk past a guy about my age sitting on a bench, soaking in the weak sun rays as he studies and devours a Little Debbie. I'm starving, and the Little Debbie makes my stomach rumble, but I almost falter in my steps when my eyes land on the guy's chemistry textbook; it's been months since I've touched a textbook. Been too busy studying Mei, and she's definitely my favorite subject, so I'm not complaining or anything. But still…I miss it. Miss a life that slipped through my fingers because of some loser we can't shake. If Nick didn't exist, I wouldn't be walking down this random street in the middle of nowhere Indiana hoping he gets locked up or shot soon so I can make it back to California in time. If Nick no longer existed, I'd be running the field, going to class, and then going home every night to study chemistry *and* Mei. We could've had everything. We *had* it all. I might be able to get it back, but my motivation has been wearing down with every passing week.

My legs are heavy and my head throbs with loss and resentment that always stirs during this walk home, unsettled by students and progress and futures. Brutal reminders of this wasted time. But every time I walk through our door, I remind myself that Mei's way more than enough, and I have to be enough for her, too. From the moment I met her, I couldn't stay away, so now…here we are, but at least we're together.

I swing open the apartment door, close it behind me, and drop my keys on the counter. Charlie jumps up to greet me then flops to his side, begging me for a belly rub. I give in like I do every day, and his purr vibrates the countertop. I catch sight of Mei lying on the couch in the fetal position and abandon the belly rub. "Oh. Hey. What are you doing home? Weren't you scheduled for this afternoon?"

"Not feeling well."

"Ooh …" I hate seeing her like this but don't wanna get too close; can't afford to get sick right now, even though she would never act like this if I were the one not feeling well. She once spent three hours pulling cactus needles out of my butt in Vegas after I'd basically fallen asleep on my feet during a hike and slid through a cactus patch.

"Stomach virus? Or was it my bad attempt at Mexican last night?"

She sits up, and her face is blotchy, eyes swollen. "Not sure."

"What happened?" I kick off my shoes and go sit beside her, but she stands and walks toward the kitchen table. I visually follow her as she picks up a piece of paper and holds it up. My eyes skitter across it. I freeze.

"Want to tell me now why we left Vegas?" Her tone is cold, sharp, and I'm suddenly achy, like I've fallen in a cactus patch all over again. This time, though, I'm wide awake, my brain flicking through the series of events that led her to finding the note. She sent me a picture earlier of the sketches I'd drawn in my books. I didn't even think about what else was in them. Now I'm gonna puke. I'd prefer that to talking about the note in her hand.

Instead, I vomit words. "I was working, and I found that note on the valet desk. I freaked." I shake my head, swallowing as I relive the moment. "Stole a car, called you to make sure you were okay. Then I went to our apartment. The whole place was trashed. Like Nick, or whoever, was looking for something. You? Me? I don't know. Didn't know what to do, so I packed our stuff and picked you up, and now we're here. I didn't tell you because I couldn't have handled the look in your eyes. Maybe it was selfish, yeah, but I wanted to protect you from it." My chest relaxes, like pulling out the words created new space where I can breathe again.

"So you lied." The accusation barely makes it out of her, like she's afraid of it.

My eyes snap to hers. "Mei, I—"

"Even when I begged to know the truth, you lied. There was never an immigration officer." Her voice is louder, fury seeping into it. "I knew...I knew it was something else." She clutches her stomach, breathing hard and staring at the floor before darting to the bathroom.

I jump up and follow her, but she closes the door, locks it. "It was the third time, Mei. The *third time* that loser stole our lives." Feelings and information I've pushed down rise, and my chest is full again. I want the extra space back.

The toilet flushes on the other side of the door, and I wait, pressure building. I'm tired of feeling bloated with things I never wanted and things I'll never tell her and things I don't understand, like why Nick won't give it up. Why she lets him shove fear down our throats and acts like it's just the way things have to be. I hate thinking it, but I've wondered if there's more to the story she's not telling me. Her accusations erupt in me like fire as I talk through the door. "I had everything, Mei—a dad, a scholarship, a life I wanted. I had it all, and Nick took it, and you were never going to stop him, so I made the choice not to tell you. Because I've never understood the whole Nick thing with you and never will unless there's more to that story. Is there?"

I close my eyes, my back against the wall. I know I'm being a jerk; she was going to find out eventually, and now she knows. And on top of it, she doesn't feel well but neither do I. It's getting harder to drag up anything but tired, stifled resentment. And there's more that I haven't told her. Like Dad's ultimatum at Stanford. That I'm still enrolled there, and I plan on keeping it that way.

The toilet flushes again, the faucet runs, and then Mei's voice splits the tension from inside the bathroom. "I know. You had it all. But I lost things, too. There are things I miss, and I'm sorry you miss your dad, but—"

"Should I *not* miss him?"

The door opens, and she leans back against the counter. "Of course you should."

"Yeah, well that's good because I do. I miss it all."

"Marcus, I get it. I miss things, too. You're not the only one who gave up a life and hopes and dreams."

"There's a difference between us, and you know it." I throw my arms out and walk to the window, my back to Mei.

But silence is the only response to my outburst. And it makes me angrier. I rub my forehead where loud, obnoxious thoughts crowd my mind. But they're right—it could've all been so different. It could have been so, *so*—

I swear. *Loudly.* But it feels too good coming out that I say it again, louder, slamming my palm into the wall. Anger oozes from me, and if I don't direct it at something inanimate, I'll hurl it at Mei again.

"Marcus…"

I whirl around. "No—don't." I don't want her to calm me down. I want to rage; I've been talking myself down and controlling my irritation for too long, and it's too big now. She pretends the past never happened, but I can't. This is my chance to empty myself of all the negative, heavy feelings I've dragged around and added to every time we've had to start over.

"Things didn't have to be like this, but here we are, hiding out in some random town so the Chinese mafia won't find us, pretending they don't exist. We never talk about it. You don't talk about it, or what Nick did to you, or anything that happened before us. And I know it's all in there." My body's rigid, the heat from my rage scorching my throat as it comes out from deep inside. "Why is he following us? Did he threaten you? Did he warn you? We have to talk about this."

"No, we don't. And I don't know why he's following us. If I did, I would've stopped him long ago."

"There's a reason. There's gotta be a reason. He's not just doing it for fun. What did he do to you? And why will you never talk to me about any of it?"

"Because there's no point. Whatever he did is in the past,

and I've moved on, but you're stuck in the past. Like you never left Stanford. Maybe even San Francisco."

Words push against my chest, fill my mouth, blur my vision. I did leave myself at Stanford, and I'll be back. I'm not doing this life forever. "Our life could've been totally different right now."

"So what you're saying is...all of this is my fault." She steps out of the bathroom toward me. "Because I won't talk about all the bad things that happened in my life before I even knew you. Because I don't want to give the past air to breathe, because if I do, it might come back to life. And you're mad about it because your life doesn't look exactly like you want it to. Or maybe you're mad because you chose to come with me and don't want to take the blame for that."

I close my eyes. It's easier to be angry when I can't see her, but it's still red hot against my closed eyelids, and it has nowhere else to go. But then she steps in front of me, and I open my eyes to hers. They're sad. Hurt. Betrayed. And my anger deflates, slumps inside me and solidifies like a rock in my stomach. "I've tried to make things perfect, but perfection isn't possible in this scenario, Mei. I've given this *everything*. What more do you want from me? How should I feel about giving up everything? Should I be happy about it? Should I not want what I had? What I still could have? Because I do. I want it every single day."

I swear, trying to catch my breath, but there's fire in my chest. I bolt past Mei and inside the bathroom so I can break down in private. I've held it in for so long, it's grown into an unmanageable beast, and it hurts coming out, clawing and scratching and thrashing.

But none of it hurts as much as the look on her face just now. I hurt her bad—Mei, the one thing I still have. Isn't she the only thing that really matters? The one thing I chose. The girl I wanted so bad, I gave up my world for her.

This isn't her fault. I'm the one who was so desperate to keep her that I came up with this stupid plan. But I've still almost lost her, more than once. To Nick—to the guy who intentionally hurt her. Like I just did.

She's right: I lied to her. But I've also lied to myself about how everything I lost didn't really matter to me. No matter how much I love Mei, the life I wanted still matters to me and I don't wanna let it go. I still want it. And I hurt Mei because I'm thinking only of myself and what I want, just like Nick.

Cold realization trickles through my veins, into my chest and up my throat, and I rip the small mirror off the wall, unable to look at myself. What have I done?

Exactly what you said you'd never do.

No, I love her. I've proven it over and over.

But the words I just threw at her didn't sound like love.

Panic takes control and I stumble from the bathroom, afraid I'll find an empty living room like I did all those months ago at The Clubhouse. The night I thought I'd lost her because of more stupid words I said.

But she's there, crying silently on the couch, Charlie in her arms. Wrecked. Again. But this time, it's all because of me.

CHAPTER 28

For the millionth time, I push away memories of my argument with Marcus two nights ago, but they're persistent, relentlessly piercing holes in me. My life is slowly leaking from them, and I'm desperately trying to patch them, but I don't have anything strong enough.

Marcus usually picks me up after work, but he had late games, so I'm hurrying home on well-lit public streets, grateful for the time to think, even if it's freezing. San Francisco is chilly year-round, but nothing compares to the biting wind and snow flurries dusting my nose.

But the real chill I'm feeling has nothing to do with the temperature.

Everything I'm experiencing—the body aches, the nausea, and feelings of inadequacy—are a byproduct of *us*.

Marcus is right: I don't talk about what happened with Nick. I want to pretend it never happened. If I do, it will fade and lose any power to destroy me. It's my decision if I want to let the past out, and I don't. I think Marcus finally gets it because he's been trying so hard to make it right ever since our fight, working to show me he's happy, even if his words during our fight said otherwise. But the harder he tries, the more obvious it is that something has to change. Also, the harder he tries, the more clearly I remember what I saw in his eyes before I shut down.

Resentment.

I knew we couldn't live in our happy little bubble forever; sooner or later, we would pay the price for all our hasty decisions, and now, I'm afraid of the cost.

I rush into our tiny studio apartment and shut the door, rubbing my arms to get the blood flowing again. Our apartment isn't much warmer than outside, though, since we set the thermostat at a cozy sixty-five degrees to keep the heating bill low. Our argument the other night heated it up enough.

On any given day, at least one of my female co-workers is complaining about some misunderstanding she had with her significant other, and I know it's normal. Marcus and I are no exception. We even had a small argument on our honeymoon after I told Marcus I believe in the Loch Ness Monster as well as Big Foot and aliens. He'd passionately argued against their existence, and we'd quickly learned there are some subjects we should avoid.

I open the fridge and pause, staring at a note from Marcus propped against the orange juice: a lopsided heart-shaped pie chart divided into six sections where he's written things he loves about me, including percentages. Picking it up, I smile, my heart and body thawing a little. Allison at work told me if couples don't fight, it means one person is holding too much back and will explode someday. Marcus and I haven't held much back lately. But…that also includes the good stuff. I bite my lower lip and smile, remembering our day off last week, still hoping and praying our neighbors weren't home.

I position his note on the windowsill, and it pulls my

mind back to a night in Vegas when Marcus and I disagreed about drink coasters. Marcus is pro-coaster while I think they're pointless, and that disagreement led to other ways we saw things differently. It sucked the hope out of the stale, hot motel room, and Marcus had left to go for a very frustrated run, and I'd retreated behind the closed bathroom door.

About thirty minutes later, a note had slid under the door with a pie chart and question: *Chance of Mei forgiving me?*

I'd grabbed a pen and written: *87%*, sliding it back under the door and waiting until it came back with another note: *Possibility of me earning the other 13% if I promise to watch those 3 (stupid) movies I vetoed last week and do that other thing we talked about yesterday that I can't bring myself to write here?*

I'd held in a laugh, written *100%*, then opened the door. His arms had wrapped around me and when I'd protested about his sweaty shirt, he'd held me tighter until we were both laughing. I forgave him then and every time since. But forgiveness hasn't stopped the tormentors in my mind from whispering how unhappy Marcus *really* is behind his brilliant smile. They tell me he's better at hiding things than I ever imagined he could be, that I'm not good enough for him, that I destroyed his future, his relationship with his dad, and one day, I'll destroy us.

I fill the teapot, set it on the stove, and turn the unit on high before picking up Buddha and rubbing his belly. Tonight, I'm going to talk to Marcus—really talk to him. I want him to say all the things he might be holding back to protect me.

Placing Buddha back on the table, I grab Magic 8. Shaking it, I ask the question that's been on my mind since our fight:

Will things get better between Marcus and me?

Turning it over, I wait for its all-knowing response:

Ask again later.

Rolling my eyes, I set it beside Buddha. The teapot whistles, and I pour the steaming water into a cup and drop a tea bag in. I need to talk to someone real—sort my thoughts before Marcus gets home so my emotions don't sweep through and scatter them. I've almost called Guo Mama multiple times this week, and now Marcus won't be home for two more hours. Plenty of time. I haven't talked to Guo Mama since we left Seattle. When we got here, we bought new cell phones and promised each other we wouldn't call or text anyone from our past, which includes Lin, Johnny, and Guo Mama. But Marcus lied to me about Nick, so maybe me calling Guo Mama won't be that bad.

I dial and hit send before I can talk myself out of it.

"Wei?"

"Guo Mama?"

"Xiao Mei?" she blurts, and I smile, picturing her standing in her shop with the phone to her ear. "It is so good to hear your voice. Everything is okay, yes?"

"Probably?" I say through a light, noncommittal laugh. "Maybe? I think so…?"

"Are you in danger?"

"No." I shake my head. "No. We're fine."

"What is it, my beautiful girl?"

I sigh and throw my head back, talking to the ceiling as I lean against the counter. "Please don't tell anyone I called. And you have to delete this number when we're done talking, but I just…things are a little…heavy…between Marcus and me. I need some advice."

"Tell me everything."

I let it all stomp and sprint and roll out of me—the moving around, fear of Nick, Marcus's resentment. Guo Mama listens, waits for me to run out of breath and then speaks.

"You two are doing something more difficult than most couples. It has never been easy for you to be together, has it?"

I swallow a lump in my throat. "No."

"The very best things never are. When things are easy, you should be cautious. Easy never sticks." She pauses. "You want this to stick, yes?"

I nod, circling my throat with my hand. "Yes. So bad. I want it to be the stickiest," I say through a weak smile.

"Ah, yes. You are a smart girl." She chuckles. "You are both so very lucky to have each other, so keep going. Keep doing whatever it takes to make your marriage work. Sometimes you will give 100%, and sometimes Marcus will give 100%. You are a team. A very beautiful team, if I do say so myself." The warmth in her voice melts over me, softening some places inside me, but also drawing attention to the hard places.

"I don't want to be the one who always takes, but I also don't want to always give more, either. That's what Mama did, and I don't want anything like that. Ever. I never want a life like hers."

"Then do not create that life. You have choices, Xiao Mei. Your mama did, too. She did what she thought was right at the time. Maybe it was the wrong choice, but you are different. Talk to Marcus. Tell him all these things you are telling me. Marcus loves you so very deeply, and I know you feel the same. You are meant to be together. Do whatever it takes, and when you are on top of this hard time, you will have a better view and see."

CHAPTER 29

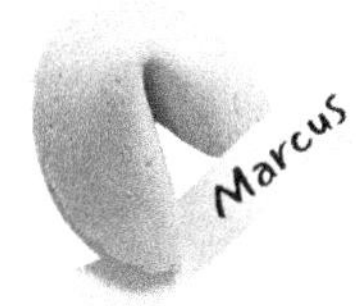

Marcus,

I've been thinking. I don't want you for just today or tomorrow or for the next 50 years. Any chance you're available forever? Check your schedule and get back to me.

Mei

t's gonna be a great afternoon. Mei and I were at least stable when I left for work this morning, and we laughed and talked like normal. A great date idea is growing in my head, and I need to figure out some details. I said what I needed to say, she knows what she needs to know. Do over number…who knows. Lost count. I feel like one of those old guys who chuckles and smiles and tells anyone young and inexperienced that marriage is work. Thing is…we're young but far from inexperienced. Feel like I'm forty by now.

I unlock the apartment door and throw my keys on the counter. Charlie jumps off his windowsill hammock bed we made him and trots over to me, stretches, then sits at my feet and meows. After I pick him up, ruffle his neck fur, and talk to him about his day, I open the cupboard and give him what he really wants: the treats Mei made fun of me for buying because I wouldn't spend the money on Oreos but couldn't resist getting Charlie a little something that didn't smell like dead fish.

Charlie rubs against me then eats the treats right out of my hand. I set him down, kick off my shoes, and put the milk I picked up on the way home in the fridge. Changing my mind, I take it back out, drink half of it, and put it back. Leaning against the counter, I check out the text Mei sent on her lunch break again and smile. Things are definitely back to normal if she's sending texts like this.

I send her a selfie of me with very raised eyebrows. I add exclamation points and grab a couple of protein bars from the cupboard. She'll be home in two hours, and I wanna plan something special for tonight. My cooking isn't exactly special, but it would be nice for her to come home to something that's intended to be delicious. A night together will be perfect since I've been getting home late, and she hasn't felt awesome. I still haven't gotten whatever she had, so…fingers crossed.

I put in my earbuds and zone out to music while I do my best to make jambalaya. The whole place smells like onions, and that's gonna pretty much kill the mood when Mei gets home. I open the door, trying to air out the apartment. Charlie perches in front of it, too scared to step beyond the door frame because the neighbors across from us have a dog that has a bad case of little dog syndrome.

I keep my eye on him as I sauté and chop and read the recipe I found online that looks the most like Meemaw's. If there's anyone I'd run to, it would be Meemaw, and I'm living closer to her now than I ever have since Dad and I moved to San Francisco. But I can't call her; Dad would know where we are. She'd tell him everything, no matter how I made her promise. She can keep secrets—she kept the one about Mei and me getting busy in The Clubhouse as far as I know—but she wouldn't keep Dad in agony for my sake.

My mind floats toward San Francisco and home and what Dad's doing right now, and I turn up my music and sing along. When we're back in Stanford, I'll call him and try to work things out. I mentally draft what I'll say to him but get distracted when Charlie darts across the living room and under the couch. I look over my shoulder and freeze. In the doorway stands the greasy guy who was feeling up Mei months ago in the alley behind the restaurant. I haven't seen him since, but there's no forgetting Nick's ugly face.

I grip the knife in my hand as I yank out my earbuds.

"Did I come at a bad time?" He sneers, leaning against the doorjamb. "I probably should have called first. Left a note, maybe?"

My heart changes rhythm, my blood reversing in my veins, going from cold to boiling.

"Aren't you going to invite me in and tell Mei Li I'm here?" He laughs and steps inside the apartment.

My fingers flex around the knife, and my feet tense, ready to rush the nightmare as he kicks the door closed.

"Get the hell out." My phone's behind me, and I'm not gonna turn my back to get it. I swallow.

"Why would I do that when I've come so far to find you?"

"I said get out. Last chance." My whole body tenses. "Because if you don't, you're dead. I've been fantasizing about killing you since the first time I saw you."

"Ah. The detective's son, a murderer." He laughs and rubs

his temple, one hand still in his pocket. "I've been fantasizing about a few things too, but it doesn't involve you."

My fingers wrap around the knife handle. Dad always taught me never to use a weapon I didn't know how to use effectively. I've never knifed anyone, so I drop it on the counter and rush Nick, grabbing the collar of his jacket and ramming him into the wall. I'm double his size, and I've been working out. I don't need a knife.

Our faces are inches apart as he spits threats, and when they turn to Mei, all sense fades. I hurl him to the ground, flying over him and crashing into the couch. Something metal clatters across the floor, and my head snaps toward a shiny, black gun spinning on the linoleum. I scramble after it, but Nick's faster, one foot stepping on the gun, the other slamming into my face.

Hot pain sears the inside of my nose, stars bursting and circling in the blackness smothering my mind. My arm is yanked from behind, my shoulder ripping from its socket, and Nick drags me to my feet.

I yell a string of profanities, agony welling and overflowing as red, pulsing rage. Twisting, I launch myself at him, bulldozing him into the door, one hand locked around his neck, the other hanging limply at my side.

He rips my fingers off his neck and shoves me. I hit the ground hard, and he lunges for me, but I roll out of the way. Using my good arm, I haul myself across the floor, focused on my phone on the counter. The sound of a gun being cocked sends me to my stomach, bracing for the bullet that will end everything.

"Get up," Nick orders from behind me, breathing heavily. "I won't ask twice."

Blood streams from my nose and drips down my lips. I'll kill him. First chance I get, he's dead. I use my working arm to push myself to my feet, then turn slowly, my stomach ripping apart when I straighten. My body is on fire, blood dripping off my chin as I meet Nick's hollow eyes.

He raises the gun, aiming it at my chest from where he stands across the kitchen. The refrigerator clicks on, its hum growing louder in my empty, whirling mind, my thoughts shoving me toward the door, the kitchen window—out. But even from across the room, the gun's cold stare needles through me.

"I came to reclaim what's mine, and I have a strict policy to leave nothing behind." Nick's finger moves on the trigger.

"She's not yours," I growl through gritted, bloodied teeth. "Never has been, never will be."

Nick laughs. "You think I'm here for her? She stole something from me, and if you give it to me, I won't kill you."

Footsteps echo outside the door and, afraid it might be Mei, a rush of adrenaline sends me sprinting toward him, but a deafening roar ricochets off the inside of my skull. My ears ring, and a flash of heat cuts through my leg.

Someone screams, and my teeth crash together when I hit the floor, my hand clapping over the hole in my jeans where red bubbles are soaking through the denim. Nick flies past me and bolts from the apartment, his footsteps rumbling down the hallway as my eyes slide to our neighbor lady, who blurs before fading to nothing.

CHAPTER 30

The end of my shift can't come fast enough. I'm still laughing at the selfie Marcus sent me of his shocked face after I sent him a text during my break, detailing the dream I had the night before. It had nothing to do with restocking canned beans, and the prospect of going home has my head floating far, far away from aisle eight. Only forty-three minutes until—

"Peggy?"

I glance up at my manager whose penciled-in brows are furrowed. Sylvia hesitates as if she's not sure how to say what she's about to say, and dread snakes in my stomach. "There's someone on the phone. Your neighbor, I think? Says it's urgent. There's been an accident of some kind. With Darius."

I don't hear anything else as I run to the break room and grab the phone where it's sitting upside down on a folding table. "Hello?"

"Peggy, it's Amy." Amy. Not neighbor—apartment manager. My mouth goes dry as she talks, my mind sorting information into any place that means Marcus isn't really at the hospital because he was shot.

Shot. Like…with a gun. That's what she said, but my brain rejects it, and my body takes over. Hanging up, I grab my coat and bag and rush from the break room, through the store, and out the front sliding doors. Silvie is on my heels, asking me if everything is okay, but I just shake my head and keep running until I reach the curb. I have no car, no way to get to the hospital except to keep running.

I take off, but Silvie calls my name, her voice a ripple on the air that reaches me. I slow, and her hand grabs my elbow. "Peggy, stop—I'll take you. Where is—"

"Deaconess Midtown Hospital," I choke, and she nods and puts her arm around me, steering me toward her car at the very far end of the parking lot.

My legs can't feel anything as I slide into the passenger seat. My mind spins, trying to gain traction while Silvie pulls into traffic, but I'm shaking too hard, my coat and bag still gripped in my hand. Silvie doesn't say anything until she pulls up to the emergency room doors. "Do you want me to go in with you?"

I shake my head and thank her, and then I'm hurling myself through sliding doors, scanning the ER waiting room. Police officers are talking to a paramedic, a doctor, a few nurses. I step to a desk in the center. "Marcus Miller?" I blurt, my voice loud, uncontrolled, and edged with panic.

The woman turns to her computer, types, and looks up. "We don't have a Marcus Miller here. Maybe at Gateway?"

Fear and realization hit me at the same time, and I shake my head. "Sorry. I…I'm looking for Darius Bromley."

She studies my face. "May I ask your relation?"

"His wife."

She blinks at me, like she's trying to think of words. "Your name?"

"Peggy Bromley."

"Okay, then…" She types again. "Looks like he was just brought in about thirty minutes ago, so let me look up his status." Her fingers fly across the keyboard, the sound like gunfire against my skull. "Looks like he's in ER room three. Let me make some phone calls. Have a seat over there, and I'll let you know when you can go back."

"Is he okay?"

"I don't have any other information, I'm sorry. But I promise I'll let you know what I find out. Just take a seat. Won't be long."

I hesitate, then find the chair closest to the desk and perch on the edge of it, watching everything around me. I cling to my coat and bag, hanging onto something to get rid of this feeling that I'm dangling over the edge of something horrible. Police talk to each other, filling out forms. Are they here because of what happened to Marcus? A doctor and two nurses walk through the emergency room doors together, and I want to follow them, find Marcus.

If I don't get a grip on this moment, I'll plummet into the darkness below me. So I stand and pace the waiting room, my eyes jumping around every corner, trying to collect information, but the woman behind the desk calls my name, derailing my thought.

"You're free to go back. Room number three. I'll buzz you in." She clicks a button, and I toss a breathless "Thank you" to her as I hurry through the opening doors and locate the flimsy curtain of Room 3. It waves with movement from the other side.

"Marcus?" I dash around the curtain, stopping short when I almost run into two nurses working on an IV drip attached to his arm and two officers standing by his bed. The male officer turns, but I rush to Marcus, my frantic eyes on his bloody, swollen face. "Are you okay?"

He starts to say something, but the officer speaks over him. "Thank you for your statement, Mr. Bromley. We'll do our best and keep you informed."

"Thanks," Marcus says, his voice crackly and hoarse.

When the officers leave, I turn to Marcus, my breath catching in a hard ball in my chest. "What happened?"

Before he can respond, a doctor breezes through the curtain into the room. "Looks like we're cleared for surgery, Mr. Bromley."

My heart jolts, and I grip the bed railing as the doctor steps toward me, hand extended. "I'm Doctor Faulk."

"Peggy," I say, shaking his hand.

"My wife," Marcus adds, and the doctor nods.

"Nice to meet you, Peggy. I'll give you two the overview." He studies a computer screen. "Your shoulder is fine. It was dislocated, but we put it back where it belongs, and there's no lasting damage there. As for your leg, looks like the bullet exited but fractured the tibia. I've called in an orthopedic surgeon, and he'll fix the bone and remove any fragments. Seems pretty straightforward, so the good news is, surgery shouldn't take too long. Maybe two hours at most. The surgeon's on his way now, so they'll get you prepped." He motions to the two nurses working in the corner, pulling out drawers and packages. "You're welcome to stay until they take him to the O.R.," he says to me. After giving a few instructions to the nurses, Dr. Faulk leaves the room. My fingers lace through Marcus's, and I run my other hand over the bruises on his knuckles while a nurse on the other side of his bed adjusts his IV.

When the nurses leave, I turn to him. "What happened?"

"Nick." Marcus's eyes dart to the curtain, away from mine. "He showed up at the apartment. Told him to leave, he shot me. Now I'm here." He closes his eyes.

"Are you in pain?" I whisper, my voice still catching up to the moment.

"They gave me something, and I feel okay right now. Pretty good, actually."

"What did he want?" I press my lips together and wait to hear what I've wondered for months.

Marcus's eyes move to the curtain again. The wall. The blanket covering his legs. "Diamonds."

My throat tightens, but I squeeze out the words, my fingers on my neck. "He said that?"

"He said he wants what you stole from him. So yeah… basically. Right before he shot me."

Dr. Faulk comes back in with two different nurses. "You ready? They'll take you to the O.R., and you'll be back in no time with your leg as good as new." One of the nurses smiles and steps past me to wheel the bed from the room. I squeeze Marcus's hand before he slides through the curtains and away from me.

I follow a nurse to the waiting room where I stare out the window at the fake potted plants lining the sidewalk. If they can't keep real plants alive, why are they a hospital? Plants should be easy compared to people.

I close my eyes and breathe in through my nose while my mind twists around Marcus's words until it's all too tangled and heavy, and I drop into a chair. I get lost in the swirls in the carpet, and my mind does the same, collecting questions and fears. How did Nick find us? We were careful. And why the diamonds? Is that all he's wanted this whole time? It doesn't make any sense. He has cases of diamonds—a warehouse of expensive things Why couldn't he leave us alone?

Why couldn't he move on, let me live my life that I so obviously didn't want with him?

Anger stretches against my chest, tightening my throat, and tears spill, hot as they streak down my cheeks. This has gone too far. It went too far long ago, but I didn't stop it and look what happened. If I'd known all he wants is the diamonds, I would have given them back forever ago. I'll do it now, if he'll just leave us alone. But he won't. He'll find ways to punish me, even if he gets what he wants. He'll never be satisfied. It's only a matter of time before he's back, and what will he do then? I thought the diamonds were my escape route. But Marcus is in surgery right now because of them. And me. He's far from home because of me. He lost everything because of me. He could have died because of me.

———

My mind is hazy and sluggish when a doctor strides toward me almost two and a half hours later to tell me the surgery went very well, and that Marcus will be in a brace for a few months. He won't be running on it anytime soon, but it will heal, and he'll be as good as before. The doctor tells me he was lucky. The doctor doesn't know anything.

He leads me down another echoey, white hallway to Marcus's recovery room, telling me that he'll have to spend one night here for observation, and I'm welcome to stay in the room with him.

Marcus is unconscious when I step through the door behind the doctor, who checks a chart, then turns to me. "Pull up a chair and get comfortable. He'll be groggy for a while. And you never know what he might say as he comes out of anesthesia." He smiles, pats me on the shoulder, and disappears through the door.

I pull a chair to the side of Marcus's bed and grab his hand.

"I'm sorry," I whisper, fierce, like if I push the words out hard enough, they'll penetrate his anesthesia fog. "I'm so sorry, Marcus."

I rest my head on his arm and let the tears puddle on his skin. Everything has changed again, but I don't feel like he's lucky; the doctor had no idea what he was saying. Marcus came face to face with Nick and barely escaped. He's unconscious in a hospital bed and will wake to find that he can't run, much less walk for who knows how long. He goes on runs every day, even in the snow, but now he can't. He can't go to work. He can't do anything but sit and think about how Nick has ruined everything all over again. How I've ruined it all because I ignored it. And he'll have plenty of time to wonder what might happen next if he stays with me.

Marcus stirs, and I lift my head as his eyes flutter open. They move around the room, land on me, and stay on my face, trying to focus. "Did you see that horse? He put his nose in my crotch because I'm wearing this dress." Marcus's hands fumble with his gown as he laughs, sloppy and delirious.

I smile. "I didn't see it."

"Well…you're really small, and he was huge, so I'm not surprised." His bleary eyes flick to me and he frowns, "What did they do with my underwear? Did you take them? Because I don't think they'll fit you. But I don't want to wear this dress anymore. Johnny'll never let it die."

I try to hide a laugh, and the nurse who steps into the room smiles at me.

"The horse thing is a new one," she says, patting his arm. "Your underwear's safe and sound."

"Oh, okay." Marcus relaxes into his pillow. "Okay. Good. I just don't want to wear this dress anymore." His eyes drift closed, his breathing slowing. A few minutes later, they pop open again, scanning the room before stopping on me. He studies me, his eyes more focused this time. "Hey." His voice is husky, his words more solid.

"Hi," I whisper.

He clears his throat. "I'm still in the hospital?"

"Yeah. Overnight."

He nods, closing his eyes again. "Why you so far away?"

"I'm just letting you wake up. A horse was chasing you, so I figured you might be kind of tired."

He frowns. "A horse?"

I smile and grab his hand again. "Just something you said when the anesthesia was wearing off. How are you feeling?"

"Tired. But happy I woke up to your face. I missed it. Wanna join me in this hydraulic bed?"

I crawl in next to him, gentle to not jostle him as I lay my head on his chest. Tears escape, and I'm grateful he can't see my face. He's silent and I wonder if he's thinking about how none of this would have happened if he hadn't met me. Then he sighs, his body relaxes, and his breathing slows and steadies, leaving me to wonder alone.

CHAPTER 31

Beeping pings off the inside of my skull, and I blink through the purple haze. I swallow, but my throat is dry and scratchy, my body heavy. The smell of rubbing alcohol stings my nose, and I wince. I look down the bed at my legs, one in a brace to my upper thigh, the other bruised but in one piece. My brain is static. Invisible hands press me into the bed and won't let up. I had this same feeling when I got my tonsils out at nine years old. I run my hand through my hair, which yanks the IV sticking out of the top of my hand, and I swear.

Someone squeezes my other hand, and I roll my head to the left.

"Hey."

I close my eyes. Sink into the sound of Mei's voice. I'm okay. Everything's good, even if my head weighs 400 pounds. "What time is it?"

"Almost 7:30 in the morning."

I scan the room, wrestling with the fear and anger that anesthesia didn't take away.

"You slept all night. Even when the nurses came in to check your vitals. Are you in pain?"

I shake my head once. "No. Just wanna get out of this bed, but..."

"You get to go home this afternoon. If you can walk and pee."

"Perfect. Now if only I could actually walk and if only we had a home to go back to."

She presses her lips together, staring at her hand wrapped around mine like she'd forgotten why I'm actually stuck in this hospital bed, and I just reminded her.

"You know we can't go back to our apartment, right, Mei?"

She stands and leans over my bedrail, burying her face in my neck. "I'm so sorry, Marcus," she breathes, and I slide my arm around her. Her weight presses against me, grounding me in reality.

"We gotta move," I say.

Mei pulls back, meeting my eyes.

"We can't risk Nick showing up again to finish us off. We can't stay here. Like all the other places we couldn't stay." My words are still too big, too hot, coming too fast, so I close my eyes and focus on pushing them down, but I'm too tired. "I'm so sick of running and hiding and worrying. This is all so stupid. And I don't wanna do it anymore." I'm too exhausted to resist the truth bobbing at the surface. It's found my weakest moment and slipped out.

She smooths her hair away from her face, acting like nothing happened. "What do you mean?"

"I mean, we're going back to Stanford. I've been talking to my academic advisor since we left. I'm still enrolled, and I might be able to get my scholarship back. Maybe. I'll find out in a couple days." I swallow. "All I know is, I'm not staying here anymore. I'm not doing any of this anymore."

She searches my face like my words are scrawled across it, illegible. I'm surprised she hasn't seen them before now. But maybe she's looking at me like that because she didn't hear me, so I say it again. "Done running and hiding and pretending." The moment with Nick seeps from my memory, a hot trickle through my whole body. My lungs ache, my leg throbs, my face burns.

"When you say you're done, are you talking about—?"

"All of it. I can't do it. I don't want to. Can't even run anymore anyway." I flex my toes to remind my body I still have a leg, but pain shoots up my shin and through my thigh, and I hiss through my teeth.

Mei stares at our hands and I can almost see the thoughts circling her head, wondering when to land. Wonder if she'll say what she's thinking since I can't see her eyes.

"You know this is what I've always been afraid of, right, Marcus? You getting hurt? This is why I gave you so many chances to run the other way."

"You think I would've run, knowing you'd get hurt? Not a chance, Mei. But I don't wanna do any of this anymore." I throw my hand toward my leg, the room, whatever waits for us once we leave this hospital. "I wanna get out of here and out of Indiana and away from it all." Our eyes meet, and we stare at each other, but hers are metal doors she's hiding behind. I let out a long breath and reach for her. I slide my hand around the back of her neck, threading my fingers in her hair. "I'm sorry, Mei, I—"

Someone taps on the door, and my head snaps up as two officers step into the room.

"Hello again, Mr. Bromley. Hope you're feeling better today than yesterday."

Mei stiffens beside me, her eyes on the cops as I pull my hand away.

"I can think of a few things that would make my life a little better right now, but hey—I'm alive, so we'll start there," I say.

They chuckle, approaching my bed. "Mind if we ask you some follow up questions about yesterday's events? We don't feel like we got a full report since you weren't in any state to answer a bunch of questions."

I'm really still not. It's like my mood took a dive during surgery, and I'm trying to swim through the tension and frustration, but I'm drowning "Uh, yeah. Sure. Not going anywhere for a few hours."

Mei grips the bedrail. I'm gonna have to be very careful with my answers; can't say anything that will make them suspect Mei.

They stand at the end of my bed, so I have to talk over my brace like it's part of the conversation.

"Are either of you connected in any way to your attacker, Mr. Bromley?" the shorter officer asks, leaning casually against the end of my hospital bed. "Any reason he would enter your apartment specifically?"

My eyes dart to Mei, who's shaking her head. "No. No connection to him," she says.

I swallow the inevitable bitterness that always comes before a lie. "Nope. Just the chosen one, I guess."

The officer glances at Mei before throwing out another question. "Are you aware of any reason someone would break into your apartment?"

Mei's response is immediate. "The only thing I can think of is that whoever lived there before us was involved with him in some way."

I'm impressed with her quick thinking, but the officer is looking at me. "Mr. Bromley?"

"We have nothing anyone would actually want." Minus that very battered, expensive box of tampons throwing a shiny beacon from the cupboard.

"We're just trying to piece together why the attacker zeroed in on your apartment complex, your apartment."

"We have the same questions," Mei says, nodding, and the officers shift their attention to her.

"Mrs. Bromley, would you mind stepping outside for a few minutes while we question your husband? We like to do this one on one usually, though this is a unique situation. We'd love to ask you a few questions when we're done with your husband."

Mei's jaw tightens and her throat bobs. "Sure. Yes. No problem." She stands and walks stiffly out of the room, glancing over her shoulder at me as she rounds the corner into the hallway and disappears, leaving me alone to clean up this mess.

Or, at the very least, not make it any bigger.

CHAPTER 32

Marcus's words nip at my heels as I walk down the hall away from him and the two officers who want to uncover the truth. But I know the truth: Marcus is done. He wants something he once had but gave up for me, and where he wants to go, I can't. When he said he was done with "all of it," did he mean me, too? No matter how I want to look at it, our problems trace back to me. I'm included somewhere in "all of it." Maybe he's been pretending all along. About us.

But no. There's no way. I know he loves me. He's just tired. And sad and in pain and…done. I don't blame him. I'd like to be done with fear and hiding and pretending and remembering and running, too. I've said "I'm so done with this" in my head a few times during the past couple of months and never once meant done with him. It was all frustration and loss speaking, same as Marcus, I'm sure.

I stop at the vending machine at the end of the hall; maybe I'm shaking because I haven't eaten in who knows how many hours. I pull a dollar bill from my back pocket and push it into the slot with shaky fingers, but it pushes back out. It's too crumpled. I pull the dollar tight and rub it against the corner of the machine, glancing over my shoulder when someone comes up too close behind me. My heart drops, and the dollar flutters to the ground.

"We need to talk." Chaz's eyes corner me, pressing me against the vending machine glass. "But not here."

He takes my elbow and steers me toward the elevators, and my throat tightens as if I'm already suffocating. Like Chaz's hands are already around my neck like he'd threatened all those months ago in L.A. He pushes me through the elevator doors into a space too small for both of us and his threats. He's stiff beside me as he slaps the "1" button, watching the doors close, our reflections a smudge in the metal like the panic smearing my insides.

"What are you doing here?" I choke as the elevator bumps to a stop and the doors open. "And how did you find me? Did Nick send you?"

He stays quiet, his grip on my elbow all he needs to say about his mood, and walks me down the hallway, through the lobby, and out the sliding doors into early morning haze.

Cold bites at my bare arms as we turn the corner, and Chaz veers toward an alcove facing a parking lot, then turns me to face him. "I'm only going to say this once, so pay attention."

"Whatever it is, I don't want to hear it."

"You have no choice."

His comment ices my veins.

"Nick wants the diamonds, and next time he gets the chance, he'll take them and leave both of you dead," Chaz says.

"He has thousands of diamonds. Why does he care about them so much?"

Chaz glances around like someone might overhear, and my eyes sweep the concrete pillars, the shrubbery. Did Chaz lure me out so Nick can finish what he started?

"He got himself in too deep, like I always knew he would. But this time, I won't be there to pull him out. Xander's locked up because of him, and it's way past Nick's turn. You want him in prison, I want him in prison, so do what I tell you, and he'll rot there."

"I want him dead," I say, trembling. "I want him dead so he can never find me or Marcus again. I'll kill him myself if you'll tell me where he is."

"That'll just leave bigger problems for all of us. He wants the diamonds."

"Okay, but why does he—"

"They're evidence against him. Evidence that will take him and a few other influential people down. He wants them back before you turn them in, and they trace back to him."

I sift through Chaz's words, try to connect the dots and predict the meaning for me, but he goes on.

"I want to disappear; you need to disappear. Do exactly what I say, and you'll be rid of Nick forever and back to your pretty little life in no time."

———

When I finally get to our apartment, yellow tape is across the door. I duck under it and walk inside. I can't stop or I'll think. I'll second guess my decision. I'll doubt Chaz and put Marcus in danger. But I have to stop because there's blood all over the floor. It's streaked across the linoleum, smeared by the door. Dried next to the kitchen. I stare at it, my hand over my mouth. This could have been it for Marcus. Our life could have ended here with Nick's gun. I'm not giving him another chance.

Charlie eases out from under the couch, meowing, and trots toward me. He stops to smell the blood, and I scoop him up and bury my face in his neck. He saw the whole thing, and even though he could do nothing about what Nick did to Marcus, I feel better knowing he was here. And he's going to stay with Marcus until I get back.

According to Chaz, Nick won't be anywhere near here, but neither of us knows where he could pop up next, so I'm going to do what Chaz asked. There's something inside me that believes he actually wants to help me. The sooner I do what he asks, the sooner I can get back to Marcus and give him the life he wants. The sooner I go, the sooner we can start over, no Nick. That's all I've ever wanted. I just can't tell Marcus, because if he finds out what I'm doing, he'll call the police. Nick will disappear without getting what he deserves, and I'll never get back into the country.

Chaz told me this will take a few days, five at the most. Then I can come home and beg Marcus to forgive me for keeping him in the dark. He'll forgive me eventually, and we can start again, just like we have before, but this time we won't have to run. For now, though, he can't know. He'll try to stop me. I'll hear his voice and back far away from Chaz's plan.

I set Charlie down and plunge my hands deep inside the sofa cushions and pull out our passports. Sorting through them, I find one for Peggy and my original one for Mei Li Zhang. Then I shove the others back inside the cushions and head to the bathroom. I open the cupboard and pull out the tampon box, frantically shoving away Marcus's words "I'm done with all of it" and replacing them with Chaz's "You'll never have to deal with Nick again." I have to remember why

I'm doing this. Marcus will understand once I get back and tell him everything.

I stuff the box inside my duffle bag along with all my clothes and the envelope of cash from my dresser—savings from my paychecks. Marcus's is stashed in a kitchen cupboard, and I won't touch that. He'll need it to get back to Stanford where I'll be with him next week. Five days.

I glance around the apartment one last time while Charlie weaves between my legs. My heart leaves a trail of shattered pieces as I move toward Buddha, snatch him, and drop him in my bag. My hand hovers over Magic 8, and I pick it up, asking a silent question:

Am I doing the right thing?

I hesitate, then flip it over, promising myself if I get a negative response, I'll change my mind and make another plan. But as the message bubbles to the surface, my heart cracks and there's no way I'll ever be able to put the shattered pieces of it back together:

It is decidedly so.

With trembling hands, I place Magic 8 back on the table. Charlie jumps up and purrs, rubbing against me. Tears drop into his fur, and I pick him up again, nuzzling him closer. "Tell Marcus I'll be back. He's gonna need you. I love you both." I set Charlie on the table and turn toward the door, but I close my eyes. I have to tell Marcus something. I need him to know I'll be back.

Grabbing a pen and the unopened electricity bill envelope on the counter, I force my hand to stay steady and write a few words. They're not enough, but will have to do. I've shut my phone's location off so it can't be traced; I can't have any flags on either of my passports or I'll never get back into the country. I can't call him. If I hear his voice, there's no way I'll go through with this.

I drop the pen and grab my coat and bag on the way to the door, not looking back. If I do, my love for Marcus and the memories we've made will devour what little is left of me. I might not be back in this place, but I'll be back to Marcus, ready to start our new life without Nick.

Scraping together what little courage I still have, I turn on my phone and google a phone number, then push send.

Even if I have to leave, there's no way I'm leaving Marcus alone in a hospital, and there's only one person I trust to take care of him until I get back.

After a few rings, someone answers. "San Francisco Police Department. How may I direct your call?" the voice on the other end of the phone asks.

"Detective Miller, please."

"One moment."

There are a few clicks, then a beep. Another. Five more before the same voice tells me he's out of the office for a few days, and can they take a message? I close my eyes, relay the message I've rehearsed for the last twenty minutes. "Can you tell him his son is in Newburg, Indiana at Deaconses Gateway Hospital? He's been shot but is fine and needs to come home."

CHAPTER 33

"Mei's here somewhere. The police wanted to get her statement, so she can't be far," I tell the discharge nurse after she gives me the green light to take my useless leg and go home. Not that we have a home anymore. But first, I gotta get out of this hospital before I can figure out how we're gonna get to California. My zoom meeting with the Stanford coaches is in two days. I wanted it to be in person, but there's no way now.

"I'll check again," the nurse says, moving the IV stand behind my bed. "Maybe she was in the bathroom or grabbing something to eat. Can you try calling her? Either way, you are free to go as soon as she's back."

Can't run, can hardly walk. Can't go look for Mei, and the longer she's gone, the more seriously I emotionally spiral. I know I hurt her with my words, but she's gotta be here somewhere. Unless the cops found out who she is and hauled her away, just like Dad said they would.

All I can do is sit here and replay our conversation and wonder how I'm ever gonna play soccer again and where we'll be in two days when I'm supposed to have my virtual meeting with the Stanford coaching staff. My thoughts drop into worst-case scenario while people do things for me, including looking for Mei and watching me pee like that nurse just did before she signed discharge papers. I avoid eye contact with her when she leaves. Grimacing, I lean over the railing to grab my phone from the plastic souvenir hospital bag on the bedside table.

I'm relieved to see it still has 27% battery, so I dial Mei's number, but it goes straight to voicemail. I dial again. Same thing. Her phone's dead. We've been here for almost twenty-four hours. Clicking on the locator app, I squint at the screen, my eyes hazy and heavy from no real sleep. I blink, check again. Her location says she's at the apartment. Like, the place where Nick showed up and shot me. Or at least she was forty-seven minutes ago. Swearing, I scan the room for crutches, but they're in the farthest corner by my bloody shoes and bag of bloodier clothes.

No way Mei would go back there. I check the location again. No updates. She wouldn't go back. Would she? To pack our stuff, maybe? Grab her charger? But then her phone wouldn't be dead.

I ease back against the upright bed and pray the nurse finds Mei coming out of the bathroom or grabbing something to eat in the cafeteria. The sooner she gets here, the sooner we can get to a hotel. Or wherever. Somewhere I can rest enough to look normal and act normal during my coach meeting. I flex my leg again, just to make sure it's still there. The ache and throb reassure me it is, but will it run again? The doctor said yes the last ten times I asked him, but what if he's wrong? What if—

My focus snaps to the window, and I hobble to it. Where's Mei? A woman in high heels strolls past the window, crying as she talks on the phone, a guy sitting on a bench, staring at his feet. Those people can walk but they've got other problems maybe bigger than mine. This place is charged with agony and unfairness. Maybe Mei couldn't take it anymore. Or couldn't take my words. Maybe she's finding us a place to go. But it wouldn't take this long.

I check the clock. It's been over an hour and a half since she left me with the cops. The worst of the worst-case scenarios snakes through my mind. Maybe Nick found her. He could have forced her back to the apartment to get the diamonds. Forced her to do other things. He could've—

No. I squeeze my eyes shut to cut off the thought. Then again, worst-case scenarios always seem to be just around the corner. I wanna get out of here, but I can't even move around until someone comes to get me out of this dress and onto my crutches so I can be done with this place and find Mei myself.

I swear at my leg like it's the one to blame and not Nick. Never thought I'd be shot. Should've taken the knife to him when I had the chance.

The nurse breezes back into my room, no Mei. "Were you able to get ahold of her?"

"No…" Panic rises, swirls, but I steady my voice so she doesn't suspect anything. "Her phone's dead. Probably went home to get her charger or something." I wave my hand like I couldn't find the right brand of peanut butter and not because my wife's missing. "I'll call our neighbor to come pick me up. Maybe she's seen Mei."

But I don't call a neighbor—I order a ride and a different nurse helps me change and get downstairs into the car waiting at the curb, then hands me my bag of bloody clothes. I obsessively call Mei on the ride back to our apartment. But after attempt twenty-five, I stare out the car window as a stranger drives me back to a crime scene. I pray in the backseat, whispering to myself and to God. I wanna yell at the driver to go faster, but he's an old man, and there's too much traffic for a Wednesday afternoon.

When we get to our complex, the driver goes the extra mile and helps me out of the car and up the three flights of stairs that were no problem twenty-four hours ago.

When we get to the landing, I tell the driver I can walk from here. I thank him and hobble down the hallway, pretending I'm relieved to be home instead of freaked out of my mind to open that door and find Nick standing there, waiting for the final round. I shove my key into the lock, yellow police tape still dangling from the doorjamb. I stumble inside, one crutch at a time. "Mei?"

The place is empty—no Mei, no Nick, everything where I last remember it being, including the dried smears of blood. There's still food on the counter from when I was making Mei dinner before Nick showed up. Powder on the floor where the police did whatever they did after I passed out in the blood puddles and was hauled to the hospital. It's like Mei hasn't been here, so where is she?

"Mei?" Not sure why I'm calling for her—I can see the whole apartment from where I'm leaning against the wall, trying to stay balanced. When only silence answers, I crutch as fast as I can across the blood-streaked floor to our room and the tiny closet, my breathing loud in the silent apartment.

I yank the door open and take stock of the shelves. Her bag and coat are gone. I drop my crutches and use the wall to steady myself as I hop to our rickety dresser and open the top drawer where Mei keeps her clothes. It sails out of its slot, empty.

I drag in air, but too much panic rushes in with it. She was so quiet after we fought two nights ago. It was our worst one yet, and we've had a few. I tried to get her to talk, unnerved and groveling for forgiveness, but she'd fallen asleep, and I'd kissed her neck, pleading with my lips. I'd held her the rest of the night, whispering "I love you," even though it wasn't enough; I just wanted those words to be the only ones ringing through her head when she woke up. Hoped they'd erase the ones I'd hurled at her earlier.

I'd watched her sleep because I couldn't stand myself for what I'd said, afraid if I blinked, she'd disappear. But in the morning, she'd smiled her sleepy smile, and I'd made us breakfast before work like I did every morning. I thought we were good. But what if she's had enough and left?

No.

In Vegas, we'd promised each other we'd make our situation work, no matter where or what. So no—there's gotta be another explanation. My eyes go to the bathroom door, its knob still missing from when I slammed it after losing patience with our life again. I hobble over, but the counter's empty—no flat iron, no toothbrush. I grimace and swear as I bend over and throw open the cupboard. The tampon box is gone. Diamonds—gone. Nick wanted them. Maybe she took them to give to him? No. She wouldn't.

My breathing is ragged as I turn to the sofa and rip off the cushions, pulling out the envelope of documents. The pain racing up and down my leg is nothing compared to the pain that floods my chest as my heart plummets. My stuff is there, hers isn't.

Leaning against the couch, I wrestle cold, creeping panic, then jerk into motion toward the door. I have to move—keep moving until I find her, no matter how slow. Nick didn't take her. She left. Took everything that belonged to her. Everything but me.

She wouldn't leave, though. We promised each other. Then maybe Nick did take her—made it look like she left willingly. Desperation overtakes me, and I press my palms to my eyes and swear in the silence, trying to catch my breath and rational thoughts. Nick wouldn't have waited for her to gather everything. He would've taken what he wanted and left the wreckage, like he has on her face so many times. Like he did to me yesterday.

I hop on one foot toward the door, pain shooting up my leg. I grab the card table as I pass and stop. Magic 8 is there, but Buddha—who hasn't moved since we placed him there four months ago—isn't. Nick wouldn't have taken Buddha. But Mei would have. And that's her writing on an envelope where Buddha was. I snatch the envelope. My eyes devour the words, but my mind rejects them, so I read the note again. Again and again, until the period at the end of her sentence marks the end of this life, too.

Mei left me.

My words left her black and blue on the inside, and she left.

I gulp in air like I've been kicked in the gut. Like my body's collapsing, lung by lung, rib by rib, folding itself away from this moment.

———

I'm lying on my back on the couch, staring at the ceiling that's gonna cave in any minute. Smother me, break me. Take me out of this reality. I don't even bother to blink, no matter how much my eyes burn; they can't match the throbbing, twisting ache in my chest. In my whole body. Wish I'd lost my leg so there'd be one less place to hurt. I don't close my eyes because if I do, I'll see the words she scrawled on the back of our electricity bill:

Marcus, I know this isn't the life you want so I'm fixing it. I love you 365-forever, Mei

I swallow, clutching the note and my phone for dear life, like they'll save me from falling off this Mei cliff. She left me. She left our life and our future and us, thinking that would fix it. I had it fixed, except for the Nick part. I had a way out of it. But she packed her bags and took off. Left a note to let me know she's fixing our life. By leaving. What does "fixing it" even mean? I wanted to leave this particular version of our life, but not without her.

Where did she even go? There's nowhere safe for her to go. Nothing she can fix, only more things to break, and I pray she'll at least stay in one piece.

I forget how to breathe and when my chest screams for air, I take sputtering breaths, like I might actually be dying. I almost died yesterday. Pretty sure it's happening today.

Charlie headbutts my chin and paws my chest, and I let his claws dig into me because it feels good to have different pain. He lays between my shoulder and neck, and I reach up and hold him to me, gripping my phone tighter. I've called her countless times from this couch and gotten the same result every time: nothing. I've been on the receiving end of her nothing before and know exactly where it leads—to days and weeks without Mei. The only thing that brought us back together last time was me finding her bloody and beaten after Nick got to her.

I'm afraid of history repeating itself, but worse this time. Where do I even start looking for her? Or will I just lay here on this couch, waiting to see if she ever comes back? Let the days slip past, including my coach meeting tomorrow? Who cares about that now? I just want Mei here. I want out of this place, this situation, this moment. But I don't have a way of making any of it happen. Except for one. One number I can call.

I've dialed his number countless times too but couldn't bring myself to hit the call button to tell him everything in my life shattered with my leg.

Tears rush my eyes, and they're hot, loaded with anger, betrayal, loss. They drip off my face as I look around the empty, silent apartment, gathering memories.

There were nights we spent exploring each other—nights that melted into mornings when I had to skip sleep and tear myself from Mei to hit the shower and get to work. We've talked for hours in this place. Laughed our heads off until Mei had to run for the bathroom or pee her pants. Spent Saturday mornings eating dry cereal and watching our favorite childhood cartoons, pretending life wasn't complicated. We've stared at the glow-in-the-dark message I wrote on the ceiling for Mei and talked about our future.

I think about this ratty couch I'm slowly dying on, where we spent an hour last week facing each other, trying to find a word that rhymes with orange for her crossword puzzle. We devoured five grilled cheese sandwiches between us and drank the last of the hot chocolate, trying for the perfect chocolate 'stache.

I move my leg and swear. Wipe my face with my shirt and come undone until the apartment's full of shadows, thoughts and memories of every moment spent here. Charlie curls up on my chest like he's afraid, too, and he doesn't purr like he normally does.

"I don't know what to do," I say to him, my voice ragged. "This has always been my biggest fear, and I thought I knew what I'd do if it happened, and it's not this." How ironic that I can't even run after her, even if I knew where to run. I can't run away from here, either, no matter how much I need to. I don't have anywhere to go. Except backwards.

I dial my last resort number again and push send.

The beeping stops, the air on the other end expands. "This is Miller."

Tears well in my throat, clogging it, but his voice pulls pain and sadness out with one word. "Dad?"

CHAPTER 34

stand in front of the floor-to-ceiling windows that look out over the airport tarmac, watching planes take off, land, and roll to their gates. One of them is mine, ready to take me far away when all I want to do is run back to Marcus.

I look down at the two wrinkled boarding passes Chaz handed me when I agreed to do this. He told me he would have my flight records wiped along with his so Nick couldn't track us down. The plan is for him to text Nick and tell him where I'll meet him with the diamonds but get me on a plane to Taiwan with them instead. Chaz will also be on a plane to somewhere no one will ever find him.

Pulling my phone from my pocket, I stare at the dark screen. I turned it off when I left the hospital, but…

I press the power button, and the screen comes to life. I choke on my own air as stacks of missed texts and calls from Marcus appear on my screen, one by one. My fingers flex. I shouldn't read them. I should delete them so I stay strong, but I'm not and don't want to be.

Marcus: Where are you?

Marcus: Nurse says I can go home.

Marcus: Mei? I'm sorry about what I said
earlier. Let's figure out where we're going.
Come back to my room.

Marcus: Your phone shows you're home???
I really hope it's wrong because it's not safe
there.

Marcus: MEI??????

Marcus: Where are you? Call me.

Marcus: Did you really leave? All your stuff's
gone. Don't do this. We can talk about this.

Marcus: What do you mean by fixing? How
are you going to fix anything by leaving?
That fixes nothing and busts everything into
thousands of pieces.

Marcus: Where are you? I'll come to you,
just answer your phone and we can talk
about it.

Marcus: Please don't do this.

I squeeze my eyes shut, clenching my phone in my fist. I don't want to do this. I should call him. Just once, to explain. He knows I'd never leave him, but if I call and tell him my plan, he'll try to stop me. He'll call his dad or the police, and Nick will go free again. That, and if the cops get involved, my time apart from Marcus could be much longer than the five days I'm giving it now.

I stare at his picture on my phone: a close-up of him lying on his side of the bed at The Palazzo, his blue eyes talking to me. If his eyes could see mine now, they'd tell him everything I can't.

But until this is all worked out, I have to go to Taiwan alone, and Marcus can't know.

CHAPTER 35

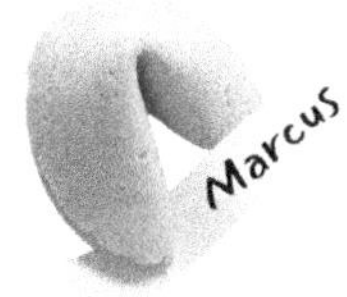

Dad's not singing to the Led Zeppelin song blasting from the car speakers like he usually would. He's just staring out the windshield while I lie in the backseat, gazing at the roof of the rental car he picked up after he landed in Indianapolis late last night. Or this morning, or…whenever. Don't know what day or time it is, just that everything is lost. Mei. Our life together. My third chance at Stanford. The meeting was supposed to be this morning. And here I am, taking up the entire backseat while Dad drives me back to San Francisco, Mei-less. Broken in so many ways. And I can't bring myself to care. I have too many questions and no answers. No motivation to call Stanford and beg for a fourth shot. I want everything to stop. The pain, my thoughts, this car that's taking me in the direction I wanted to go a few days ago, but now none of it even matters. Not even Stanford. Yeah, the car's speeding forward, but I'm going backwards off a cliff. And that's fine—I prefer not to see my final moments. Though honestly, Nick pretty much killed me.

Dad heard about Nick being in Indianapolis before I

called him. Guess he had a few of his guys keeping track of Mei and me since we left Stanford. Apparently, he knew I wasn't going to show up with Mei when he told me to. And he never turned us in. Just kept an eye on us from a distance. I should be mad, but I'm too relieved I don't have to tell him everything that led to this point and relive it. He knew stuff about Nick and knew Nick would be after Mei. His informant called him after Nick shot me, then the department secretary handed him an anonymous message, detailing where I was, and Dad was on a plane two hours later. There's only one person who knew where I was. She didn't wanna deal with me, so she called my dad.

By the time I worked up the courage to call him, he was on his layover, pacing the airport. He sobbed when he heard my voice. I sobbed when I heard his, and when he finally made it to me, he'd hugged me for ten minutes. I'd cried for all ten. All the awful things we'd said to each other—and all the things I hadn't said before I left San Francisco—got flattened in that hug.

Dad had helped me pack whatever was left and carried everything to the car while I'd picked up Charlie in his carrier. He hasn't been himself since Mei left, and I totally get him.

When the apartment door closed behind me, I'd locked the old anger toward Dad inside. Tried leaving every Mei feeling and memory behind too, but they clung to me.

We won't get home until tomorrow. Lots of cross-country driving time for Dad to ask questions, but he still hasn't, so I lie in the back, waiting. I don't even have a clue where to start the conversation.

Dad clears his throat. I tense, focusing on the pain in my leg that no Ibuprofen is touching. He changes lanes, speeding through whatever state we're in. Thankfully, not Indiana anymore. If only all my hurt and memories had stayed there.

"What's going through your head right now, son?" He turns down Zeppelin, and I want to laugh for the first time in days. Nothing's going through it. Everything's jammed inside it, wrestling for room, but there's no place to go. All I can say is, "Not sure."

He nods, stretching in his seat. He's been driving for nine straight hours, only stopping for bathroom breaks for all three of us and to load up on caffeine.

"Embarrassed you had to keep me balanced while I used the urinal," I add.

He gives a half-hearted, one-syllable laugh. "You forget, I potty-trained you. At least now you know how to aim." I can see his jaw working from back here. "Marcus, I…"

I hold my breath. Is this where he tells me he told me so? Or that I brought this on myself? That he knew Mei was trouble, and why didn't I listen to him instead of getting myself messed up?

"I wish I could've helped you sooner. With a lot of things."

I release my trapped breath. Didn't expect that. Not sure what to say. I have comebacks for everything else but that. Not sure how I feel about it.

"I'm so thankful you're alive." His voice cracks, and I blink back tears that were waiting for an excuse to break through.

"Why didn't you turn us in?" I ask, swiping at my eyes. "After you came to Stanford and gave me a deadline I didn't keep?"

Rain drops fall on the windshield, and Dad flips on the wipers. Silence fills the car until he finally responds. "Because you're more important to me than my job. What you want matters to me. Even if it means bending some rules, M.C."

That's all it takes. I lose it, and I'm fine with the tears sliding down my face. I've lost everything else, so why not all my dignity? Those initials—the nickname I haven't heard since I left San Francisco—pushes out all the tension, and we both cry silently for miles.

When I can finally speak again, I say, "Thanks for coming, Dad." I swipe my eyes again, my face raw. Sniffing, I wipe my face with my shirt, my chest a little less tight.

He laughs and sniffs. "Uh, yeah. I've wanted to show up at your door more than a few times."

I don't blame him for staying away. Not after what happened between us at the Stanford soccer field. Not after I betrayed him and went to Olivia's. Even though he doesn't know, I do, and I hate myself for ever blaming him for protecting me from her.

But maybe if he'd shown up in Vegas or Indiana, I wouldn't be like this right now. Maybe I would've been ready to listen to him and put my life back together before it exploded for good.

When I don't respond, Dad keeps talking. "But I knew you needed to be on your own. Make your own choices. I'd like to know all about your last seven months. We've got fifteen hours of driving. And I'm not worried about you getting mad and running off again. If you do, I'll definitely catch you this time."

A laugh huffs out of me. "I'm gonna give up running permanently. That's all I've been doing since I left San Francisco. I'm done."

"Maybe, once your leg heals, you can just ride your motorcycle instead."

My neck tenses with yet another confession that needs to

come out but doesn't know how to find an exit big enough. I picture the bike parked in The Palazzo parking garage, abandoned. Definitely impounded by now. "I don't have it anymore." The words scrape up my throat, shame scorching every place they touch

"I know. Because I've got it."

My heart trips. "What?"

He nods in the front seat. "Yeah. It was registered to me, so I got a call from a security company in Vegas."

Thoughts skid across my head, brake, U-turn, and speed around my brain like they're on a racetrack. "So you…went and got it?"

"Had it shipped. That's how we figured out Nick was on your trail. You never would've left it otherwise."

I run my hands down my face. He keeps things that are abandoned. He kept me when Olivia walked away, and he kept my bike when I walked away. I almost spill everything about meeting Olivia, my heart in my throat, but I swallow. I don't wanna talk about her right now. "You can keep it. It's yours."

He's quiet for a few seconds. "We can talk about that later. And you can tell me how it ended up in a parking garage. Or you can wait on that, too."

"Later." I push away memories and sadness and loss. I shove them so far down, they're like a rock in the bottom of my stomach.

"Figured."

The rain pelts the roof and Dad slows, flicking the wipers to the fastest speed. I have to say…pretty impressed you made it this long and far. You did a great job of flying under the radar. Coming from a guy who finds people for a living, I'm impressed."

He uses "you." Not "you and Mei." There is no more

"us". She's still under the radar after throwing me right in front of it.

My chest combusts, and I'm breathing fire. I clutch my shirt over my heart and try to roll to my side to absorb the shooting pain in my leg. The question I've been avoiding floats in the pain, rising to the surface. If I don't let it out now, it'll gnaw at me until it tears its way out. I clench my teeth, breathing through my nose, and let words slip out. "Do you know where she is?" I can't say her name.

"No." Dad's answer is tight, clipped. "No flags, no trace. Yet."

I nod like I can slide his answer into place, like the final puzzle piece in my acceptance. "Okay."

"Look, Marcus, I—"

"I don't really wanna talk about her right now," I choke.

His eyes are heavy on me through the rearview mirror. "That's fine. I get it. You know I do."

He definitely gets it. He knows all about this feeling. But does he know I went and saw Olivia, the reason he knows it? Not bringing that up now or maybe ever. I don't wanna talk about her, either. Or hurt him more than I already have.

"Listen. There's something I need to tell you. Not sure how, actually." He turns on his blinker and switches lanes. "I might've known where you were during the last six months but… didn't know how long you'd be gone. Wasn't sure if you'd come home or call eventually or…I just didn't know." He shrugs. "I wanted to give you space. I knew that's what you needed—to make decisions on your own. So I made some decisions of my own, too." His confession hangs in the air, waiting for the rest of whatever he's going to drop on me.

When I don't say anything, he shifts in his seat and goes on. "We should talk about Kenna."

My stomach ices. Her name means betrayal and the end of

my life with Dad as I knew it. It's a name that happened on the same dark night that set my life loose like a wild animal, chasing me to this moment. It means someone who came between Dad and me, and I—

"You're gonna see a lot of her."

"Why's that?"

He runs a hand through his hair. "We got married. I would've told you—asked you—but…" He shrugs.

I roll to my back again. Death blow delivered.

"I didn't know when I was gonna see you, Marcus." Dad's voice is tight, edging around the corner from driver seat to backseat. "Didn't know if I should wait or call you. So—"

"When?" I cut him off, staring at the roof and wishing I could eject through it.

"Almost two months ago. November 30th."

Mei and I were in Indiana. Dad's married, I'm married. Am I?

My next question bubbles. Not like gum or soap bubbles. More like lava, boiling hot and turbulent. "Did you move? From The Clubhouse?"

He shakes his head. "No. She moved in. You'll meet her when we get home."

Home? No such thing. My brain powers down, and I close my eyes, hoping when they open, I'm in a different place, different life…or even better, that they never open at all.

CHAPTER 36

The police station is busy, swirling around me just like the past two days, which are a blur in my head. They cloud reality as I take the elevator to the third floor. I don't know what I'm doing or why I took Chaz's word for anything; this could all be a trap, but traps seem so much more straightforward than the last two days of my life.

The elevator dings, and the doors open. I walk to a circular desk, and the lady behind it glances up and offers her help in Mandarin.

I hesitate and respond the best I can. "I'm looking for Detective Chang. Is this the right floor?" The words barely make it out of my mouth, still anchored to the pain lapping at my insides, but the woman stands and tells me to follow her.

Swallowing a bitter surge of fear, I adjust my satchel on my shoulder and grip my duffle bag as I trail her through cubicles to a back office. She motions to a chair next to the office's closed door, but I can't sit; if I have to run, I want a head start. I'm glad the door's closed because I'm not ready to find out where I really am, who Detective Chang really is, and how Chaz knows him. Will he put me in a cage like Nick tried to do?

The woman knocks, and a few seconds later, it opens. When I look up, my eyes land on a tall Taiwanese man in a dark suit and orange tie. His short hair is meticulously styled as is his slight beard. The woman explains in Mandarin that I'm here to see him, and Detective Chang glances at me. He nods to her and opens his door wider, motioning for me to come in. After thanking the woman, he closes the door behind me, and I'm stuck in a place I'm not sure I should be with a man I don't know and don't trust. A man who's asking questions in a language I haven't spoken in months. Do I want a drink? What's my name? How can he help? Would I like to sit down?

My Mandarin is good, but I'm not sure it's good enough to say what I'm supposed to say, so I clear my throat and ask, "Do you speak English?"

He sits in his chair, elbows on his desk. "I do." His accent disappears completely, and he studies my face. "How can I help you?"

I take a deep breath to dissolve the nausea that could be from not eating, from no sleep, or from fear, since I'm not sure what the words that come out of my mouth will start. "I have something you may or may not want."

"Okay, why don't you have a seat?" He waves his hand toward the plump leather chair across the desk from him.

I ease into it, my legs cold and wobbly. "I was told to come to Taiwan and find you and only you. I'm really hoping you'll understand why." The sooner he understands, the sooner I can get home to Marcus and live the life we should've been living all along.

Detective Chang gives me a half-smile. "It's my job to understand, so I hope so, too. Let's start with your name."

Which one? Zhang, Mei Li? Peggy Bromley? Mei Li Miller? Mei Li Mitchell? I clench my fists in my lap and settle on the name I've known about and had the longest. Hiding hasn't gotten me anywhere but away from Marcus. "Zhang, Mei Li. And I have something to give you that I hope makes more sense to you than it does to me."

Detective Chang leans forward in his chair. "Okay, you've got my attention." He smiles, his eyes flicking from me to my bag as I pull out the box of tampons. He raises his eyebrow until I open the box, dig to the bottom, and haul out the diamond necklace, bracelet, and one earring.

Detective Chang sits straighter. "That's a lot of diamonds…and an interesting place to keep them."

"I hope you know what to do with them because they've brought me nothing but trouble."

"What kind of trouble?"

"The kind that ruins lives."

"Where are you from? And who told you to come see me?"

Chaz didn't give me a script, so I go with the truth. "Originally, I'm from here, but I've been in San Francisco since I was eight. And more recently, everywhere. Because of these diamonds." I set them on the desk, and they glitter in the sun shining through the window. "My cousin told me to bring these to you. His name's Zhang, Chen Wei but he goes by Chaz. And I don't know if I can trust him." I don't know if I can trust Detective Chang, either, but I want to. I want to hand him all the fragments of truth that make up my life and let him put them back together because I'm done trying.

He stands and walks around his desk to open a filing cabinet drawer. He pulls out a plastic bag and holds it open for me to drop the jewelry in.

"Do you know Chaz?" I ask and press my lips together while I wait for his answer.

He stares at the bag of diamonds before sealing it and sets it on his desk. Then he moves his chair in front of mine, facing me. If he knows Chaz, he must know Nick. And if he knows Nick, he might know that my family was in America illegally and—

I glance at the closed door and stand, but Detective Chang reaches out, resting his hand on my arm.

"My apologies," he says. "I didn't mean to startle you. You are perfectly safe here. Please."

Hesitantly, I sit back down.

"Zhang, Mei Li. As in Zhang, Tai Sun's daughter?" he asks.

I wonder if I should admit it or not since the answer is really no. I close my eyes so he can't see the confusion but snap them open again because only Marcus can read my thoughts in my eyes. Detective Chang isn't Marcus. I'm so, so far from Marcus.

Detective Chang is watching me, so I nod. "Yes, but he's not my real father."

"Okay. So, sounds like we have a lot to dissect and discuss." He settles back into his chair and crosses his legs. Striped orange and white socks peek out from under his pant leg, a bright spot in this dark moment. "Why don't we start with the diamonds. Where did you get them?"

"Are you familiar with a man named Nick Chao?" I swallow the thick disgust that rises when I speak his name.

"The Nick Chao also originally from Taiwan but currently in or around San Francisco?"

Or Indiana. I nod. "Do you know him?"

"I'm very aware of who he is. Also very aware that Tai

Sun and his father were business associates among other things."

I breathe through the words like they might strangle me. "If you know who he is and who his father is, then you must know what he does, and I'm hoping you can do something about it."

"I've been working with the FBI to find Nick Chao and lock him up. But there hasn't been enough evidence. He's good at what he does, but we're better, and we'll find him." Detective Chang nods.

"Evidence?" My voice shakes. "I was there. I saw everything he's doing. I was the anonymous tip that pointed police in the right direction. Nick attacked me, but I got away. I was wearing these diamonds. And he's been hunting me ever since." My mouth is dry like my memory is running away from that moment. "What I don't know, and what Chaz wouldn't tell me, is why. He said there are influential people who wouldn't like the diamonds getting into the wrong hands. I'm hoping your hands are the wrong ones."

Detective Chang's eyes are soft as he leans back in his chair, hands at the back of his head. "I'm sorry for what you've gone through, Mei Li. The good news is, you've done the right thing, and my hands are definitely the wrong ones for Mr. Chao. Honestly, it's going to take a few days to process everything and get you answers. Do you have a place to stay in the meantime?"

"I was planning on going to my aunt's house in Kending."

"Until I know more, I'd like you to stay closer. It's safer."

Safer. I haven't been safe in…ever. Especially not since I moved to America. Why start now?

Detective Chang studies my reluctance. "I'll work as fast as I can, I assure you. But part of my job is to keep you safe, and the hotel across the street is great—you can lie low. Catch up on sleep while you wait to hear from me."

"What are you going to do?"

"My job. Which is to figure out how all these pieces fit together." He rubs the stubble on his face. "And for now, until I have all the pieces, I need you to refrain from contacting anyone. I don't want to turn on a giant spotlight for Nick Chao to find you. Okay?"

Is he talking to my body in the room with him now or my heart that's back in Indiana with Marcus? Only five days—a week at most—I remind myself and say, "Okay."

CHAPTER 37

One week later

I roll over and grimace when the remote jabs my ribs. I freeze, then slump back into the couch again, remembering where I am. And that Mei's not here at Johnny's with me. It's been a week and a half since I saw her last. Ten days, working on eleven. No word from her to tell me she's okay. Or tell me where she went, maybe? If she plans on ever coming back once she "fixes" everything?

It's just me, Johnny, and his roommates. I'm the stranger here, but it's a billion times better than being the stranger at The Clubhouse with New Mom. Actually, no—I'd have to have an original mom to have a new one, and we know how that went. So just...Kenna. Kenna who's nice. Kenna who makes Dad smile like I haven't seen him smile, ever. Kenna who loves Jesus and is honest and straightforward and who I think I'd even like if Dad wasn't all over her. If I hadn't walked in on them on the couch. The same couch, in the same compromising situation I once was with Mei. Wish Meemaw was the one to walk in on that private moment instead of me.

Think I'd like Kenna if having her around didn't remind me that I'm a guest at The Clubhouse now, a third wheel. I'd probably like her if having a girl around didn't remind me every second of every day that I'm Ray Miller 2.0: no girl and will hate women for the rest of my life because they ruin everything. Dad only made it single for eighteen years. I'll crush his record.

I snatch the remote and turn on the TV, desperate for noise to drown my thoughts, but the Food Network is featuring Chinese cuisine. Click. The Discovery Channel's uncovering the secrets of Asia. Click, click, click. HGTV is doing House Hunters International. In Taiwan. Of course they are.

I swear, shut off the TV, and toss the remote on the floor. Johnny's apartment is pretty quiet since it's four in the morning, and he and his roommates just went to bed a couple hours ago. It's only been two days since Dad dropped me off here. I thanked him and hugged him goodbye before closing the apartment door. In all the time I spent worrying about Dad being alone, it never crossed my mind I'd be the one flying solo in the end.

I dig my fingertips into my chest over my heart. I swear I'm bleeding internally. I woke up every ten minutes last night feeling like I was suffocating, but it was just me gasping for air that smells like moldy laundry and stale grilled cheese.

Thoughts and memories of Mei are crawling all over me, pinning me down and forcing me to remember the past nine months. When my phone finally says 6 AM, I stagger to my feet, adjust the brace on my leg, and fold up my couch bed. I hobble into the bathroom and brace myself against the counter. Looking at the mirror, I wanna rip it off the wall. Smash it. But Johnny saunters in, dressed for work.

"Hey, man." He stands beside me and adjusts his tie in the mirror. "Get any sleep last night?"

"Nah."

He glances at me out of the corner of his eye, buttoning his shirt sleeves. "Listen, maybe it's time to—"

"Nope." I shake my head, hoping he'll stop.

"Okay, okay. Fine, but I'm gonna help you through this, bro. Promise." Johnny looks at me with as much sincerity as he possesses. "It's all gonna be smooth. You work on getting that facial hair under control, I'll work on the rest of your life. Like getting you a job. I'll see if they'll hire you at the restaurant. That cool with you?"

I nod to satisfy him. Johnny slaps my back, and I teeter a little. He laughs, so I slap the back of his head.

"Alright, alright—sorry, man. Forgot you're crippled. For the first time in our lives, I could cream you. Wanna go for a run later?" He ducks and darts out of the bathroom when I try to hit him without losing my balance.

"Okay, but for reals," he says, popping his head around the doorjamb. "Couple people coming over this afternoon. I'm trying to get off early, but if they get here before me, answer the door, man. Let them in. Act civilized. Catch you later. Eat whatever you can find."

But what I'll actually do is lay on the couch, stare at the ceiling, and slip back and forth between reality and memory. Torture myself with Mei thoughts and wonder where she went. Think about her note and what it meant or didn't mean. Why'd she have to be so vague?

I shower and brush my teeth but don't bother shaving before I assume my position on the couch, my leg itchy and hot and restless. A few hours later, someone knocks on the door and since Johnny isn't home, I push myself up and hobble over. I open the door and stare at the person on the other side, my hand gripping the doorknob.

Her eyes widen and travel down my body, then return to my face, confused. "Marcus?"

I've given a girl everything I have—emptied myself for her. So when my eyes meet this girl's, it takes me a few long seconds to register who she is. But once I do, everything stills. "Tavah?" My voice sounds like I'm happy to see her, but my jacked up heart retreats farther inside my hollow body, unable to offer emotions.

"It's…been a minute." Her eyebrows go up, then down. She's confused. Not sure if it's from seeing me or seeing me like this. "Prom seems like forever ago."

My heart burrows deeper. "Sorry. Yeah, wow. You surprised me." She hasn't taken her eyes off mine, and my insides are squirming. "It seems like a lifetime ago."

"Yeah." A smile finally spreads across her face.

A giggling group of girls comes up the stairs behind her, and Tavah turns toward them. "You'll never believe who's here, guys!"

The girls stop and stare. I recognize them from high school but have no clue what their names are, so I smile and offer a half-wave. "Uh…come on in. Johnny'll be here in a bit." I edge the door open wider, looking down as the girls walk in.

I try to recover and drag my eyes to Tavah's whose are just waiting. But for what? Acknowledgement? Actual words? I can't even breathe normally these days, so thoughts to words? Not likely.

"What are you doing here?" she asks, her smile shining right on me. "And what happened?" She points to my brace.

With superhuman effort, I haul my voice up from its depths of despair. "Uh, I live here. Now. As of two days ago.

But just for now. Just until next semester starts. Hopefully. Looking for a place. I...had surgery."

Tavah tilts her head. "I thought you were at Stanford."

The statement punches me—lays my mind out cold. But before I can pick up my brain and slap it back to life, the front door opens again, and a wave of relief that Johnny's home crashes over me.

But it's not Johnny. And he didn't warn me that Lin was included in the "people coming over".

She flings the door shut and turns around, and when her eyes sweep across me, they crash land on my face. The impact jolts me so hard I bolt for the bathroom, limping and hobbling until I slam the door and ease onto the closed toilet. I lean forward, breathing in and out, and the swell of nausea subsides. I have to get away from girls who aren't my wife but are too much a part of her. Away from silence that leads to memories. I want the memories, just not with Tavah and a bunch of girls watching me. Not with Lin and all the questions she'll ask that are so much bigger than the ones I want to ask her. Like if she knows where Mei is.

———

I'm three blocks from The Clubhouse. My leg is throbbing, my armpits are screaming from the crutches, and I'm breathing like an eighty-year-old lifetime smoker. Or maybe it's anxiety from being back in Chinatown. I thought being here would freak me out way less than being at Johnny's, surrounded by girls who aren't Mei. I was wrong. I'm being violently reminded why I moved to Johnny's a few days ago.

Dad had called in the middle of my meltdown, and I'd answered. He'd called to catch up and invite me to Sunday dinner, but I told him I wanted to drop by tonight instead.

His voice had gone from shock to excitement. I'd gotten out of Johnny's apartment as fast as I could, telling the gawking girls hanging out in the kitchen that I had an appointment as I'd hobbled past them, Lin on my heels trying to talk to me until I shut the door in her face.

I stop my desperate pilgrimage to The Clubhouse when I round the corner and see Zhang's. But it's not Zhang's anymore; it's a breakfast place I hadn't noticed in my post-Indiana, post-Mei, painkiller haze.

I stand on the sidewalk, watching people walk through the door. The croissant sculptures in the window display don't even know they've shoved a part of my life completely out of existence. I wanna limp through the door and yell at someone for not leaving one freaking piece of my life where it belongs, but a voice I wasn't ready to hear calls to me. I look around and meet a pair of familiar eyes and a smile that squeezes my heart.

"Marcus Miller, I have missed you so, boy." This woman looks like Guo and sounds like Guo, but it can't be Guo. It's a different old woman sitting in a wheelchair outside the shop where there used to be a bamboo chair.

"It seems we are very different than the last time we saw each other," Guo says, motioning toward my leg. She sets her forearms on the arms of the wheelchair like it's an old friend.

I can't find my voice; it took off at the sight of her. Finally, I manage to gather enough of it to form two audible words. "What happened?" I rasp and cautiously move forward to take her hands. "Guo?"

"Ugly Chao happened. Though he wasn't brave enough to do the job himself, of course, so he sent another ugly man to break my knees. He didn't get what he wanted and threw a fit about it." She holds my hand, letting out a long sigh. "But I think you must know what he wanted his ugly men to do because he tried the same on you, yes?" She searches my face, but I look away. "I am so sorry, boy." She blinks up at me but I'm frozen, information slamming against me. "Tell me everything. Why you are back. And where is Mei Li?"

What am I supposed to do? Sit and cry to Guo who's in a wheelchair because of Mei and me? Given the chance, I'd kill Nick for what he did to Guo, then kill him again for what he did to us. I shake my head. Look at the cement, my eyes following the spiderweb of cracks. "She's fixing her life. Without me. So I'm here. Starting a different one, I guess."

Guo studies her lap. "Do you know where she is?"

I shake my head. "No. Do you?"

Guo doesn't answer my question but asks another. "So she is alone somewhere?"

"Yep." Makes two of us.

"That's not good."

"Nope," I say, barely a whisper. "Guo, I...unless you know where she is, I don't wanna talk about her."

She smooths my hand but won't look at me. "I do not know where she is."

I want to go back to when I knew—all the way back. Rewind time and walk by this shop, talk to Guo about my day, and steal looks at Mei's window, hoping to catch a glimpse of her. I want to leave notes for her again and wait for the text telling me she got them and can't wait to see me after school. I want Guo to tease me and have functioning legs and all the answers like she used to. I could use a whole pot of her tea, laced with everything she's got that will take me away and make me forget.

"But I do know one thing," she says.

My head snaps to Guo, my spiraling thoughts suspended on their way down. "What?"

She taps the arm of her wheelchair. "She could never stay away from you."

My jaw clenches. "She's done a great job of it. For almost two weeks. No call, no text, nothing. A few vague words scribbled on an envelope saying she was out."

Guo nods, silence weaving between us when what I want is answers from someone about where Mei is and why. I know I said things. I know my words hurt her, but to leave? I've never once considered leaving her, no matter how frustrated or hurt I was.

I turn from Guo so she can't see the tears in my eyes. I get myself under control and turn back to her, but a woman inside the shop distracts me. For a second, I swear it's Mei, and my body jerks to a stop. But then the woman turns. Not Mei. Of course not. Mei's out there somewhere, far away from here and me. Somewhere Nick could find her.

I look away, and all I can see is Guo in her wheelchair and this once-familiar street that feels tilted and empty despite the crowds and cars. My old bedroom window, the invisible trail I wore in the sidewalk between Mei's apartment and mine, mentally and physically. The only thing I don't see is Mei, but something inside me builds. The woman in the shop wasn't her, but Mei's out there somewhere. She can't leave me with only a note that says nothing. I wanna ask her why. Talk to her. Apologize. Work things out or make her tell me we're over to my face.

"I'm so sorry, Guo." I'm sorry for failing, for disappointing her, for everything that happened to her because of us. For the choices we made and the running and the lying and the stupid diamonds—the reason we had to keep running. And Mei took them with her when she left, like she wanted a target on her back so she could run some more.

I swallow. We didn't get to talk about any of this before

she took off. And I still haven't told Dad what Nick was really after; there was too much happening, and my feelings were blocking the way for any real words to come out. But if I took him up on his offer to find Mei, he'd find the diamonds. If he found those, he could use them to lure Nick. Hopefully far, far away from Mei. If he finds Nick, the whole thing's over. Problem fixed, Mei and me together, no more running.

My heart picks up and I squeeze Guo's hand, grounding myself. Then I kiss the top of her head. "Gotta go. But I'll stop by again soon."

I turn and hobble across the street. An oncoming car screeches to a stop, and I limp faster toward The Clubhouse. Seeing Guo's willpower to keep going despite everything she's been through loads me with guilt and sadness but also gives me a shot of determination. Maybe she's right: maybe Mei really wouldn't stay away from me. Maybe there's another reason she left. I don't know. But what I do know for sure is that Dad finds missing people for a living and this time, I need it to be Mei.

CHAPTER 38

My eyes open and adjust to the haze of morning light floating into the room. I roll over and check the clock. 8:35 AM. There's been a series of mornings just like this. Is this morning number eleven? Twelve?

Yes. I count in my head. Twelve days. Almost two weeks on the other side of apart from Marcus. I should be home, not hiding in this hotel room. I promised myself and Marcus I'd be back by now, but things haven't been as quick as I'd hoped. First was the mix-up with my name. Or…actually… my entire existence. Turns out, there is no record of a Zhang, Mei Li born to my parents. Chang—as everyone calls him— had to dig deep to find out I was born Zhao, Xin Yao and my birth certificate only had Mama's name on it. They changed my name when we illegally came to the United States and forged a fake birth certificate for Zhang, Mei Li.

Then it was roadblock after roadblock as Chang tried to track down the owner of the diamonds. Everything came back unresolved, and every unresolved day is another day away from Marcus. I've been at this hotel waiting for answers and wishing I could call or text Marcus. Anything. But every day, I'm reminded of how life and death it is that I don't contact anyone, not only for my safety and to protect the investigation, but also for Marcus's. But I haven't been doing nothing for the past week. The same day Chang gave me my birth certificate, I got to work filling out the Taiwanese passport paperwork and visa. If I have to wait until it's safe to return to Marcus, I'm going to do something that will help me get back to him and stay with him for good.

It's been almost a week since I begged Chang to take me to the Ministry of Foreign Affairs to submit my paperwork. He'd been reluctant at first, but I was persistent. I told him if he didn't take me, I'd go on my own. After turning in my application, the agent told me it would take around ten days to process. I'm still waiting. But I will get my passport, and I will make it back to Marcus soon.

A knock rattles the door. I pull my sleep-heavy body from bed, dragging myself to the door, and peek through the peephole like Chang told me to do. Just in case it isn't him. It's always been him, though. Same time, every day.

He stands on the other side, breakfast in hand. When I open the door, he flashes me a smile. "Hey, sleepyhead."

"Hello again," I say, opening the door wider for him. "Come in."

He walks in, sets breakfast on the small table, and pushes his hand through his hair. It's not as neat as it usually is, like he didn't get around to doing it before work.

I close the door behind him and fold my arms over my pajama shirt to hide my bra-less chest. "Any news?"

He nods. "Yeah, actually. I stayed at the office all night."

"Really? That sounds promising…"

He shrugs, his eyes dropping to the floor before leveling with mine.

"What is it?" My hope slams against his hesitation.

He clears his throat. "The diamonds trace back to some highly influential people back in the States. People whose lives would be ruined if this connection comes to light. Nick's in the middle of it all and is desperate to get them back so the people he's working for don't dispose of him."

My chest tightens, and the best I can do is whisper, "How do you know all this?"

"Your father, or who you knew as your father, is in prison here in Kaohsiung."

My stomach bottoms out. "What…? He's here? Why didn't you tell me?"

Chang puts his hand on his chest. "I'm sorry. I should have. I needed to make sure of some things before I said anything. But yes, he's here. And he was willing to shed some light on the situation. He doesn't have much to lose at this point."

I drop into the nearest chair as anger pushes through all the layers inside me. He's not even my real father and he's ruined my life, not saved it or given me a better one. "Why did he agree to talk? That man wouldn't do anything good unless it benefitted him somehow. So what did you promise him?"

Chang sits in the chair across from me, elbows on his knees. "If what he told me is true, his sentence will be shortened."

I cover my trembling mouth with one hand and shake my head, pushing back tears that I will not cry for him.

"And…I told him I'd talk to you about going to see him. He has some things he wants to say. But that's your choice. I promised him nothing regarding you."

My thoughts are backed up against the inside of my head. "I have nothing to say to him."

Chang's eyes are soft and a little sad. He says, "That's not all, Mei Li. And I'm so sorry for all of this information and turmoil, but I have news about your cousin, Chaz."

"What did he do now?" Nothing Chang says will surprise me.

"He's dead." Chang's words drop between us, lifeless on the floor. Final. Surprising after all.

"What?" My question comes out in a whisper.

"He was murdered. Nick put a hit out on him, no doubt. There's not enough evidence to prove it was him, but we're working to find it. It will take more time." Chang shakes his head. "I'm so sorry."

The escaping tears are painful, laced with meaning. It's not true. There's no way. Chaz was always untouchable.

"Are you sure it was Chaz?"

Chang nods. "His body was identified."

"How did he die?" My voice trembles, and I wipe tears from my cheeks.

"He washed ashore in Jamaica. A bullet in his head."

Everything goes static. The room dims to a dull grey, like someone's trying to shut off the world and leave me trapped in it.

"Also..." Chang rotates a ring on his middle finger, watching it circle. "Because we suspect Nick of ordering Chaz's death, we have reason to believe he knows about you being here. And that he'll put a hit out on you, too, if he hasn't already."

I watch his face for clues about whether I should be scared, but his eyes are gentle, like a soft place I can land if the world falls out from under me. "What does that mean for me going home? What happens now?"

Chang stands, steps toward me. "It means...you're safe here. I feel confident we'll find Nick. I promised you I would help get you back to the States, and I will. We just need a little more time to make sure he never hurts you again."

Chaz is dead. I could be next. I'm not going home.

I glance down at my clenched hands and the heaviness of the information presses on me, holding me in this place. All I want to do is rewind every step that brought me here. I need to get back to Marcus. I need him to know why I'm here. But now nothing is as straightforward as it was supposed to be, and Chaz, the barrier between Nick and me, is gone. I can't go anywhere until Nick is locked up. But I don't have time to wait for that. I left my note to Marcus purposely vague so he wouldn't stop me from coming here, but he'll think I'm never coming back. There's no way I can call him, and even if I could, how would I explain my reasoning? How would I explain that his worst fear—me leaving—came true?

My throat tightens, and my heart pounds. Maybe I should call despite Chang's warning. But if I do, and Marcus finds out where I am, he'll be on the next plane here. And Nick could find him.

Chang shifts and a bag rustles. I jerk my attention to him, disoriented. "I, uhh, got what you asked for," he says, handing me a paper bag.

Blinking, I focus on it in my hands, and it sucks away all thoughts of calling Marcus. Avoiding Chang's eyes I say, "Thank you."

He nods. "Yeah. No problem. And before I go...I don't know what brought you here or what you're going through, but...I'm here to help in any way you need. I don't have to know the circumstances, how or who. Whatever the results of that," he says, nodding toward the bag and what's inside it, "I'm here for you, and I'll make sure you're safe and have whatever you need."

My heartbeat fills my ears while tears fill my eyes, but I blink them away. "Thank you. Really."

"I'm sorry to leave you after all this news, but I have to get back to the station. I'll stop by on my way home, though. Anything else you need, let me know, okay?"

"Yeah. Sure." I give him a weak smile, and he disappears through the door.

My breath catches in my throat, and I stare into the emptiness that's now swirling with new fears and questions. But I have bigger questions that began days ago.

I stand, hands trembling, and brace myself on the back of the sofa before walking to the bathroom, paper bag crinkling in my hand—the only answer I can actually get right now.

Breathing like I just ran around the room a dozen times, I turn on the bathroom light and close the door behind me, trapping myself inside with my emotions. I pull a box from the bag and set them both on the counter. I stare at the pregnancy test, unsure how to approach it now that I'm alone with it.

After a few heavy seconds, I undo the box flaps, slide out the foil package, and tear it open.

Three minutes...

In San Francisco, we were used to earthquakes, but when they hit, ten seconds always felt like ten hours.

The package in my hands is an earthquake that could level my world, and three minutes is a lifetime.

I sit on the toilet.

Three minutes is months full of memories and places and *him*. Like the time we were eating at McDonalds, discussing the percentage of real beef in our burgers. "It's probably donkey," Marcus said. "And I'd know the difference since I grew up on a donkey farm."

I'd choked on my burger, and he'd had to slap me on the back.

He's the only person that can make me laugh like that. Not even Lin had that power. He's also the only person who can scare me speechless. Like the night in Vegas when he borrowed our role-playing neighbor's Batman costume and hid behind our bedroom door in the dark. When I came inside from getting the mail, he jumped out, hands on his hips, and I dropped to the floor, screaming and curling into a ball. He'd laughed so hard, he could barely lift me off the floor, and I'd hit him—hard—and then he'd kissed me. Hard.

When Marcus wasn't making me laugh or cry from fear, he'd been gentle and caring. Like the night I'd pouted before his first day of work in Indiana because I hated being away from him. That night as I'd slept, he'd taped notes all over our apartment, and the next day, I'd woken up and rolled onto a small pile of notes in his empty space beside me. I'd found them everywhere that day—in the cupboard, the shower, under the toilet lid.

I place the stick next to the sink and stare at my reflection in the mirror. I count under my breath, and when three minutes are up, I wait longer, still staring at myself because this might be the last time I see this version of me. The me who lived in another lifetime where Marcus woke me almost every morning with a kiss on the back of the neck and told me he loved me more that day than he had the day before. A lifetime where he came home from work, kicked off his shoes, and stripped off layers of clothing, walking around the apartment with his pants hanging low on his hips, my eyes obsessed.

The night I'd sat blindfolded on the kitchen counter while Marcus hand-fed me Jelly Belly's one at a time, making me guess the flavors.

"You should be here right now," I whisper to him like the words will drift all the way back to him. "I should never have left. I can't do this. We've never been this far apart before, and I shouldn't be doing this without you." Tears drip onto the counter and I swipe my face. I imagine him in the bathroom with me, and I give into the tears, my pain echoing off the walls as it rushes out of my broken insides. When the torrent is over, I'm shaky and empty, holding onto the counter until silence settles too heavily on me.

I pick up the stick, swallow, open my eyes…blink. Look again. My heart swells, and fear dissolves as I spread my hands over my stomach. Tears puddle in my eyes and happiness pushes away the pain, leaving love and determination to get back to Marcus and turn the two of us into three.

ACKNOWLEDGMENTS

For Monster Ivy Publishing and its magical captain, Amy Michelle Carpenter: "You will make dreams come true for two very grateful authors."

For our copy editors, Kristiana and John: "Your eyes, like a thesaurus, will make words sparkle."

For Natisha and Artevi: "Your creativity and genius will bring beauty to the world via a fabulous and most beloved book cover."

For Reba, Shellise, and Taegan: "Brutal honesty and endless support will give greater depth to our beautiful story"

For our families: "Your patience and understanding will illuminate dreams."

For our Heavenly guides and cheerleaders: "You don't need a fortune because you already know all, and two authors are eternally grateful to know and experience that."

For Cats, San Juan Island, The PCH, Motorcycles, and Valets: "Your presence shall be felt upon the page."

For gummy bears: "Your sacrifice is a sweet memory."

For our bookish Instagram friends: "Good karma will be yours for spreading goodness far and wide."

For Mary Gray: "Your formatting prowess will put chaos into creative order."

ABOUT THE AUTHORS

Emily Cox is a fast-walking big thinker who believes in aliens, has a mostly-titanium face, and a rhyming maiden and married name (Box-Cox). She lives in Utah in a house of all boys.

Nicole Allen is a live-theater lover, crime podcast junkie, and the highly disputed funniest person in her family. She believes in karma but is skeptical about dinosaurs.

CONNECT
with us

STAY CONNECTED BY
JOINING OUR MAILING
LIST AND RECEIVING
UPDATES!